BLEEDING
HEART

A novel

Lauren Bishop

Cover Design by Les Solot

CHAPTER ONE
NEIL

I see her again, her hair blowing as she rushes out the front door. She has a cup of coffee in one hand and she's fumbling for keys with the other. I've been waiting here for her, upsetting every driver behind me. Fuck them. I'm here to see her. I need to see her, I've been waiting all week and today could be the day she notices me. I hurry to jump out of the truck, yelling out "Morning!" as I approach her trash cans. She turns, one foot in the car, one out. *Her legs*. I missed what she said, but looked up just in time to see her smile and slide into her seat. *Man is it fucking hot*. I find myself breathing again once she drives away. I'm able to rummage quickly through her garbage to see what treasures I can find. My collection is getting quite impressive. I grab an empty perfume bottle and a stained blouse and stuff them into my jacket pocket. Hoping no one saw me, I empty her trash into my garbage truck.

I make sure she's my first stop every morning I take this route. I don't need any distractions on my way here. I like a clear mind to think about her. I have a long day ahead of me and looking at her face will help me make it through. After work is done for the day I usually come back around to get more looks and to learn more about her. Today I don't. I need to get home. Traffic doesn't care too much about my wants. I'm getting stuck at every light while her things are burning a hole in my pocket. *Music, that's what I need.* Jazz comes from the speakers calming me a bit. Tunnel vision as I drive and caress her blouse. Twenty more minutes.

ooo

Finally, I'm home. I head up the stairs to find that the front door is unlocked. I never leave it unlocked.

"Simone!" No answer. "Simone!" Nothing. I storm into her room to find it empty. Kitchen, empty. Bathroom, empty. *Where is the little bitch?*

The front door slams shut and there she is. Simone standing there with her eyes wide.

"Oh my God Neil- I, I mean sir, I'm so sorry I didn't know you would be back so soon. I was just out back drawing."

She's visibly shaking, which excites me. Her full lips in a pout, eyelashes fluttering quickly and that red mop of curly hair on her head. *Why is it so fucking hot?* I'm now standing over her, close enough to see every freckle on her smooth brown face.

"Simone did I say you could leave this house? Did you ask if you could go out back?" She doesn't make a sound. "I asked you a question."

"No sir. But it was just the backyard. I wasn't doing any-"

She stops speaking when I step closer and grab her wrist. I stare at her a little while longer, her chest heaves up and down, up and down. Small sweat beads line her nose and I see a bit rolling down her neck. I'd really like to wrap my hands around that pretty little neck, then I think of 'Her' and speak instead.

"Lucky for you I'm in a good mood today."

Her eyes that were cast down to the floor suddenly shoot up to my face in shock. I turn to head downstairs. I hear her scurry into her room before the door shuts. I'll deal with her later.

The stairs are creaking as I make my way to my favorite place. I've got to do something about that. At the bottom of the steps, I head towards the door to my right. The key turns smoothly under my fingers. The smell arouses me almost instantly. Once I get inside, I catch myself with my eyes closed, biting my lip. I remember the blouse in my pocket. I want to lift it to my nose and inhale deeply, but I remember it's been in the trash. Nothing a quick spray can't fix. I spray her blouse with her favorite perfume that I bought about two weeks ago. I know it's her favorite because she goes through this scent like water. I place the empty bottle I grabbed today atop the dresser I've set aside for her. It has an antique feel to it with curly black steel legs with matching knobs. I plop back in my chair, stare at her almond eyes staring back at me from her framed picture on the wall and think. She will be mine.

I've watched her for months now. She's been the star of secret photoshoots. I know what she eats in the morning and I know her favorite ice cream. The perks of being her garbage man. She shreds all of her mail though, leaving me clueless to any real information I could use. She won't be able to hide from me forever. Her future is with me.

I used to think Simone was the one. But she just doesn't listen. No matter what I do, she doesn't fucking listen. All she's done is make me crave more. But she's a special girl. In her looks anyway. I've never seen anyone like her. I had to have her. Light brown skin, freckles, green eyes with specks of gold. Her fiery curly hair bounces when she moves. And her lips. Those are my favorite. Nice and round and full like she just sucked on a lemon. But that's where her charm stops. I thought I would be able to mold her, with her being so young, but all I've done is have to punish her over and over. I know 'She' will be different. I can feel it when she looks at me, even though she doesn't ever really see me. That's going to change I'll make sure of it.

Before I know it I've been down here for over an hour. Fantasizing. All of this thinking has made me pretty hungry. I should go see what Simone is up to, have her cook me breakfast. Maybe pancakes.

I hear music coming from Simone's room. Some R&B bullshit. I know the door isn't locked, she isn't allowed, so I welcome myself in. She's lying down, writing in a notebook. I can't help but notice her lack of clothing. She must've just showered. She's in a white tank top, braless with white sheer panties. I'm suddenly no longer hungry. I feel myself warming. Simone turns around when she hears my heavy breathing and tries to hurry under the covers.

Too late.

CHAPTER TWO

SIMONE

Neil just left for work. It's Thursday so he'll be gone longer than usual. He's always late on Thursdays. I don't know why, I don't really care. I just know I have more time to myself. I don't get a lot of that around here. Unless I'm in trouble.

He wasn't always so mean. Things seemed great in the beginning. I had a new home, food to eat every night and clean clothes. He used to take me out all the time. That's until people started asking questions and I started to "disobey." It was a few months before my 16th birthday when I first met Neil, that was almost two years ago and the last year and a half have been really hard. I guess he couldn't keep up the nice guy act anymore. I know I should've left a long time ago but I have nowhere else to go. I have no family, no friends. I have no one to help me. I have no education. I'm stuck here.

ooo

It's a beautiful morning. The air is pretty still which is a pleasant surprise. The perfect time to sketch some frustrations out. I grab my canvas and charcoal and head out to the backyard. I have to use the front door because Neil has the back door sealed. One way in, One way out.

The lines come to me naturally. I'm drawing my mother. My work always comes back to my mom. She was so beautiful. Chocolate skin, jet black hair and a beauty mark right below her right nostril. I draw her with my curls. My way of thinking of us still being together. I was 11 when she died. Her and my Dad. It's been a long time but I can't forget them. I'm not living the life I know they would have wanted for me but these were the cards I've been dealt and life isn't always a fairytale for everybody.

The sun warms my skin as I hum to my own melody. The birds' songs calm me further. The grass feels soft on my legs. I imagine my Mom in a garden. Roses and lilies and sunflowers surround her. Pollen floats in the air. I remember she used to tell me it was good luck to make a wish and blow the fluff out into the world. If only that were true. A tear drops from my eye right below my mother's as if she's crying too. I set the drawing aside, take a deep breath and lay on my side with my knees bent in towards my chest. Just as I close my eyes I hear Neil's truck pull into the driveway. Then the sound of doors slamming. I leave the picture and charcoal behind and run inside. I see Neil standing in the middle of the living room. He spins around and I instantly get scared.

"Oh my God Neil- I, I mean sir, I'm so sorry I didn't know you would be back so soon. I was just out back drawing." He walks up to me and gives me the coldest stare.

His eyes are like ice. He's flexing his jaw and his nostrils are
flared. I can't hold his gaze. He asks me if I had permission
to go out, I tell him no and try to explain but he grabs my
wrist , hurting me, so now I'm sort of tuning him out because
I know what's next. I hear him say something about being in
a good mood. I look up in surprise and he's already started to
walk away. *What the hell?* I run into my room and close the
door. I can't believe I wasn't punished. That's a first. This
actually makes me more nervous. There's no way that was
just the end of it. I sit on the edge of my bed and cry quietly.
I'm so stupid. *What am I doing here*? I'll just take a shower
and attempt to clear my mind.

By the time I get back to my room I'm a little more
relaxed. I put on some music to make me feel better. I guess
it's time for my daily journal entry. I like to get out
everything that happens here. A form of therapy I guess. Neil
doesn't know I keep a journal. There's no way he would be
okay with it. I just tell him I'm writing poetry and songs and
what not. I have separate books filled with lyrics just in case
he ever wants to see.

I'm lying on my bed when there's a weird noise
behind me. I turn around and see Neil practically foaming at
the mouth. I try to hurry under the covers but I'm not quick
enough. He grabs me and flips me over hard. He grabs my
wrists and throws my notebook onto the floor. His hot sour
breath is on my neck, making me sick.

"Neil, please. No! I'm tired. Please."

He slaps me so hard that my face stings and tears roll down my cheeks. He rips my panties and puts his hand over my mouth to cover my screams. My teeth sink into his fingers. Big mistake. He hits me this time with a closed fist in my right eye. I give up trying to fight. There's no use. Just give him what he wants and he'll leave quicker.

I let my mind wander off into a dream. A much happier place. Not here.

CHAPTER THREE

SIMONE

9 Years

"Simone, wake up honey." I feel Mama lightly shaking me, my face burrowed under the covers.

"Just a few more minutes. Pleeease?" My voice scratches as I whine.

"You must have forgotten what today is." Mama says as if she's singing. "Don't you still want to go up to the cabin and sled, make s'mores and tell stories by the fire? I guess not. You just want to sleep all day. I'll make sure to tell your friends you couldn't make it this year."

I burst from under the covers, jumping, smiling. "We're going today?! How come nobody told me? I get to see Ashley, Audrina and Brittany?!" I'm so excited I'm practically squealing. I've barely had a second to breathe.

"Calm down, Mo." Mama says smiling at me. "Daddy and I were surprising you. Now hurry and get ready for breakfast. I'm making your favorite."

As she turns to leave I notice she's laid out my outfit for me. Dark blue jeans with rhinestones lining the front pockets, my favorite cream colored turtleneck sweater and chestnut riding boots. I grab my clothes and dart to the bathroom. I've never showered so fast before. When I step out of the shower I grab Mama's perfume spray and spritz some all over. I go back into my room and find my gold heart necklace I got for Christmas last year and fasten it around my neck. My small gold hoops pull everything together. There, now I'm ready.

ooo

The smell of breakfast invades the house as I make my way to the kitchen. I sit in my usual spot, the center chair at the breakfast table facing the big bay window. I can see the snow falling lightly, hitting tree branches and building their own snow mountains on the ground. Mama sets a full plate in front of me. Eggs, bacon and my favorite, pancakes with cut strawberries and strawberry syrup on top. I don't know how I'm going to eat it all but I'm sure going to try. "Well don't you look like a little lady. And you smell lovely. Just like me." Mama raises one eyebrow at me with a smirk forming on her lips. "You put your jewelry on all by yourself?"

"Mommm," I whine rolling my eyes, "I am almost 10 you know. I can do things on my own." I see her shake her head at me in the corner of my eye.

"Sure honey," she says.

"Where's Daddy?"

"Oh he had to run to the store. So it's just me and you for the next couple of hours until he gets back. Then we can get on the road." She pushes a red curl from in front of my eye and tucks it behind my ear. "After you eat I'm going to do something about this head of yours."

"Mom, just let my curls free. Please?"

"No way little lady. It's freezing out and we need to fit a hat on your head."

I smack my lips. "You never let me win." She ignores my comment and sits a glass of orange juice in front of me. She grabs her own plate and juice and takes a seat next to me. She starts singing to herself as she eats. She does that a lot. I smile at her as I stuff a bus load of pancakes in my mouth. She sees me and gives me a wink.

A little less than two hours later Daddy comes home and it's time to go. I run upstairs, right past pictures of all our smiling faces, and beeline for my room. My bags are already packed. I just have to grab Sophie, my favorite doll.

After Mama helped me put on all my snow gear, which I hated, I made it outside. Daddy was still packing things in the trunk. He leaned over and peeked his head around the truck, snow glistening off of his blonde hair. "Hey kid. You ready to hit the road?" Daddy always said driving to Minnesota was more fun than flying because we would have an adventure. It was a way to get two trips in one.

"Yes! It's gonna be so fun! I can't believe you tricked me." He just smiled and came around to the driver's seat. Mama was already in her seat, book in hand. She said it helped her relax.

"Daddy can we stop and get hot chocolate?"

"It's no way you're cold. I've got the heat all the way up, it's baking in here." He says pointing at the vents like it made it more true.

"No. I just like to see the marshmallows melt."

"Well we won't stop just yet. The first pit stop we make you can have all the hot chocolate you want."

I pout and Mama notices. "Mo we've got a long way to go so I have some of your favorite movies for you to watch, okay?"

"Okay."

Mama puts a disc in the radio and flips down the tv from overhead and "The Little Mermaid" comes on the screen. Mama told me this used to be one of her favorites too. I hug Sophie tight and watch Ariel in the sea.

ooo

I wake up and see a sign that says we are in Indiana. I don't remember falling asleep but now that I am awake I really have to go to the bathroom.

"Daddy how much longer before we stop? I have to go to the bathroom."

"Just hang tight until I see an exit." He pulls away from the toll lady and we drive about 10 more minutes until he gets off the highway. We end up at this little Christmas shop that has all kinds of cool things. There are big trees, snow globes, little elves and reindeer statues, all kinds of lights and there's even a small eatery with cards and books by the register.

"Excuse me ma'am but is there a bathroom we could use? My daughter really has to go." Mama says to the lady behind the counter that looks like Mrs. Claus.

"Oh sure dear. Go all the way to the back and turn right. You'll see it."

We get to the bathroom but it's only one stall so Mama waits for me outside. I make sure to put toilet paper all around the seat like Mama showed me. The toilet flushes really slowly and the water is freezing. I don't see any paper towel so I have to use toilet paper to dry my hands. I come out and Mama is still standing there waiting for me. We walk back towards the front and I see little ice skater figures skating in circles around a miniature Christmas tree. I go to touch it and notice a snow globe small enough to fit in the palm of my hand. I pick it up and shake it and sparkling flakes fly around. In the middle there's a small girl with her pink mittens outstretched over her head catching the glitter snow. I make sure to bring it back up front with me to ask Daddy if I can have it.

"Mama how much longer until we get to Spirit Mountain?" I ask, still shaking the snow globe.

"It'll be a while. We haven't been on the road that long. Maybe we can play a game in the car to pass some time."

"Ooh, I spy?!" I blurt out full of excitement. Mama nods yes and I turn away smiling. We make it back to the register and Daddy hands me a small styrofoam cup.

"Here's your hot chocolate. Sorry they didn't have marshmallows." He gives me a nudge on the shoulder. The hot chocolate warms my cold fingers instantly. I put it close to my lips, feeling the steam touch my nose.

"That's okay Daddy. I don't really need 'em. Hey look at this cool globe. Can I have it please?"

Before Daddy could answer Mrs. Claus turned to me and said, "You know that globe there is one of a kind. My husband made it with his own hands. Keep that with you and you'll have all the luck in the world." I spun the globe around in my hands, eyes glowing with awe. *A good luck snow globe?*

"How much for it?" Daddy asked the lady.

"Oh, don't worry about it," she said waving her hands. "She's the first one to want that old thing. Plus everything is on clearance for after the holidays. It's on the house." She gave me a big smile and shooed us out of the store.

Nine hours later and we're finally in Duluth, Daddy's hometown. He grew up alongside Spirit Mountain's terrains. He loves to tell stories about "the good ole days." How in the winter he used to snowboard and ride snowmobiles. And go mountain biking, camping and swimming in the summer. I've only ever been here during the winter. We used to come for Christmas every year until Grandma and Papa weren't around anymore. Papa had cancer and I think Grandma was just too sad without him. This is the third year without Papa and the second without Grandma.

Their house reminded you of the beach in summertime. Sandy brown wood so light it could almost be white. Sky blue shutters. A white wrap around porch and a white balcony overlooking the front yard. It was a lot different from the 4 bedroom, brick, 2 car garage home we lived in back in Okemos.

My best friend Audrina lived three doors down from my grandparents in a cute little burgundy house. Our Dads grew up together. They always go out to grab "brewskis", whatever that is, whenever we come to town. Mama pretty much stays in and hosts my sleepovers. When I'm not at Audrina's that is. When Daddy comes back, and if we aren't asleep, he'll light the fireplace and tell us scary stories while we eat the cookies we would've made with Grandma, but now with Mama. I put my face on the window and wait for us to get to the cabin.

ooọ

As we drive up the long circular driveway I see that the cabin Daddy rented this year is more like a resort. It has a logged exterior and tall windows on either side of the glass door. There are two wooden columns just at the top of the steps holding a balcony that wraps around the entire top floor. Snow covers the roof and all the surrounding trees. I feel like I'm looking at a postcard. It's beautiful.

Daddy barely stopped the car as I jumped out. My breath visible, the snow crunching under my feet, I dive into a snow pile and move my arms and legs. In, out. In, out. As I stand up, being careful not to ruin the snow angel I just made, a snow ball lands right on top of my head. Mama races to my side to help beat Daddy. I ducked low behind Mama to make my snowballs and fire away but he's too quick. He runs behind the truck. I go one way, Mama goes the other. He's facing me when Mama sneaks behind him and BOOM, a snowball hits his neck. He laughs and jumps as the snow finds its way down his coat collar. When he turns to her I run up and jump on his back.

"We beat you Daddy! We won," I say laughing. He spins me around, facing him now, he gives me a kiss on my red nose.

"You're getting too good at that. And too heavy," Daddy says as he puts me down. "You guys go inside. I'll bring everything in."

Walking into the house I feel like I'm in a castle, if castles were in the middle of a winter wonderland forest. The floors are hardwood, dark like the color of cherries.

I start to take my coat off, my boots, then my snow jumper. There's a coat rack to the left of the front door. I can't reach it so I just pile everything alongside the wall, stuffing my socks inside my boots. My toes sink into the plush white rug in the entryway. In front of me are steps leading down to the living room where there's two big chestnut leather couches and a fireplace in a stone setting. I can't wait to sit at the fireplace later, nice and toasty, listening to stories.

I go up the stairs that are to the right of the kitchen to find my room for the week. When I go in my room I'm facing double glass doors, frosted by the ice leading out onto the snow covered balcony. A wooden bunk bed sits on the right wall with an entertainment center on the left. Next to the bed, in front of the closet, there is a desk. Perfect for my coloring and pictures I like to draw. I climb the ladder to the top bunk, get under the comforter and quilted blanket and drift off into a nap.

ooo

I wake up and smell cookies. *Why is Mama making them without me?* I climb out of bed and notice an art set on top of the desk. I sit down and flip through the empty sketchbook, thinking of what I can create. There's a soft knock behind me. Daddy appears in the doorway.

"Hey Mo. Sleep good?" He asks. I nod and a yawn escapes my mouth. "Well if you want to go to Audrina's come and get ready. We're leaving in about 15 minutes." I stretch out real good and follow him downstairs. Mama's in the kitchen setting the cookies on a plate. She wraps them in that clear paper that sticks to everything. I can never get it right but she somehow does it perfect every time.

"Simone go put your coat and stuff on. We're going to

Heather's in a few."

"Are the cookies for Ms. Heather?" I ask realizing she didn't leave me out of our cookie making after all.

"Yes they are. But I'm sure Audrina will be the one eating them all." She says putting the plate down and heading towards the front door.

"Me too!" I yell out after her.

She comes back with my boots and coat. *Guess I don't have to wear the jumper.* Yes! I hate that thing. None of the other kids have to wear them. Mama says I'll thank her later for having to wear a monster of a snow suit. I doubt it.

It's dark outside, darker than it was this morning when I woke up. It's like I missed the whole day, it just passed us by on the highway, like all the snow filled trees. It doesn't take us long to make it to Audrina's. I see the familiar burgundy house, under a spotlight from the truck's headlights. Everything is just how I remembered it, except for the new wreath on the front door. It's green with frosted pine needles, gold bows and silver glitter. Little crystal balls that remind me of tiny icicles are glued all around it, making the wreath sparkle in the night sky. I can't help but look a couple of doors down to my right. It's still there, my grandparents' house. Still sandy, still with the same blue shutters. No lights are on. It doesn't look lived in. It looks lonely.

I didn't realize that Ms. Heather had opened the door for us. Mama tugs me in, the sudden warmth makes me shiver. Hellos, hugs and smiles fill the room. Mama and Ms. Heather head towards the kitchen while Daddy and Mr. Jackson (Jack for short) head towards the family room. Then there's me, still fumbling around trying to take off my boots. I nearly fall on my face when Audrina runs up and gives me a massive bear hug, saving my fall.

"What took you so long?! I've been waiting for you ALL day!" Audrina smile is from ear to ear.

"Sorry. I didn't even know I was coming. Did you?" I ask, finally yanking my boot off of my foot.

"Yeah. My Mom told me a couple of days ago. She said not to say nothing to you." Audrina's hand is on her hip. Her shirt loud with pink sparkly hearts. "Brittany and Ashley are coming over tomorrow. Then maybe we can go to the mountain and sled or something."

She leads the way to her room. The pink room. You might've thought pink was your favorite color until you met Audrina. Her room looked as if pepto bismol was spilled onto every surface. Fuzzy pink. Sparkly pink. Hot pink. Soft pink. Pink, pink, pink.

Spongebob Squarepants is on the TV. Her favorite. We sit on her bed, the canopy sprouting pink sheer fabric that falls to the floor. She kneels down behind me and begins to take out my ponytail. We always play beautician so I guess it's time for a new look. She pulls my head left and right, combing with a vengeance. When she's done I look in the mirror and see a very crooked part down the middle of my head and two big twists that could've been a little tighter. She really needs to work on her styling.

"Cute. I like it," I tell her while lifting my face at different angles, still looking in the mirror. "Your turn." Audrina's hair is always easy to do. It's chocolate brown and bone straight. It hangs to the middle of her back, cut bluntly in a straight line. As I'm braiding her hair into two fishtails she starts telling me about Ashley and Brittany and their boy craze.

"Brittany's always going on and on about some boy named Liam. About how he's just sooo cute," she seems pretty disgusted by the word cute. "It's so gross. She says he has pretty teeth. I mean who cares about teeth anyway?"

I agree it is gross. I didn't know they liked boys. Here I am, watching Spongebob in the pink room while Sophie waits for me back at the cabin, and they're giddy over boys. They are two years older than Audrina and me but still, boys? I suddenly feel much younger than I did this morning when Mama asked me about the jewelry.

"What about Ashley? Does she have a boyfriend?" I feel my lips twisting up as the word escapes my mouth.

"I don't think so. She just agrees with Brittany about Liam. Ugh, Simone, we're never getting boyfriends, "She exclaims, shaking her head, holding her hand out in a 'stay away' gesture.

I shake my head too. "Yeah, never."

We stay at Audrina's house for about two hours

before Mama and Daddy say it's time to leave. I'm not complaining one bit because after this long day I just want to sleep. We say our goodbyes, promising to see each other the next day and we head back to the cabin, drained, all three of us. I don't even bother with trying to get a spooky fire lit story, cookies or anything else. I simply crawl up the bunk bed ladder, Sophie in tow, and snuggle under the sheets. I don't even have to count sheep. I fall asleep almost instantly.

ooo

I clunk my feet forward. I wobble as I keep my balance with the ski poles. The wind whips across my face, smacking me hard. My hands, that are now three times their normal size because of my massive gloves, grip the poles tight. I take a deep breath, blowing into my scarf that is wrapped around my mouth and nose, and push down the hill. I almost want to close my eyes so I can imagine I'm flying. It sure feels like I am, gliding down through the snow.

"Hey, Mo!" I hear Brittany yell my name. I turn my head to the right and see her zooming down the hill in one of those water tubes. She's screaming from excitement and waves a gloved hand at me. Before I can say anything back I lose my footing and tumble the rest of the way down. The snow is hard and cold on my face. One of the ski poles gets lost somewhere. I push myself up and remove my feet from the skis. Brittany is running towards me, the tube left behind.

She falls to her knees and crawls over to me.

"Oh my God! Are you okay? Are you hurt?" She's checking my arms and legs for injuries even though they're covered by my jumper and coat. She grabs my face, squeezing my cheeks, making my lips pucker like a fish. "You're red!"

"Maybe because you're squeezing me," I say pushing her hand off of my face. "And it's cold. I'm fine." I stand up and turn around in a circle. "See." I wince a little feeling my ankle burning.

"Are you sure?"

"Yes, I'm sure."

"Well, forget skiing. Do you want to go tubing with me?" She asks, standing now, brushing snow off of her knees.

"No, not yet. I'm gonna go find my mom." Walking up this hill is a lot harder than gliding down it. It doesn't help that my ankle is now on fire.

Mama and Daddy are at the top of the hill talking with Mr. Jack and Ms. Heather. They're all holding cups, probably filled with coffee. Mama notices my limp and missing pole. "Hey, what happened? Are you alright?" Her brow wrinkles in concern.

"I just fell. I think I might've sprained my ankle or something."

"You need to sit down. Let me look at it." I slowly position myself on the ground with my right knee bent up.

Mama grabs my left foot and wiggles my boot off really carefully but it still hurts. The cold air is like daggers to my toes. My thin sock is not coming in handy right now. She lifts my pant leg and sees a purple ankle. She tells me to move my foot around to see if there are any broken bones. I flex my toes and move my ankle in a circular motion. Though it hurts Mama doesn't think it's broken. My snow-capades are cut short. Mama says she thinks it's best if I go back indoors and relax. She says I can invite my friends over later for a girls' night in.

000

The fireplace is crackling loudly and everyone is sitting on the floor on top of pillows, except for me. I'm on the couch with my foot propped up under an ice pack. We all have warm cider to go with our ginger bread cookies Mama made. The icing isn't the typical sweet kind. It's more of a cream cheese flavor that is just so good. I've had five pieces already.

"Geez Simone, leave some for the rest of us," Ashley whines while reaching for her fourth cookie.

"Oh Ashley, shutup. You've had just as many and it's a whole jar full in the kitchen." Audrina comes to my defense before I can even say anything to Ashley.

"What? You're gonna give some to Sophie too?" Brittany giggles at her sister's joke. Ashley smirks as if she's said something brilliant.

"Girls, cut it out. I didn't know we made fun of friends here," Daddy says. "Everyone needs to just be quiet so I can tell you the story about a haunted mansion in Connecticut." He goes to turn off the lights. We can only see shadows of each other's faces lit by the fire. Daddy comes to sit at the head of the circle. "So there was this woman who had 6 children, with four being dead-"

Audrina comes and sits next to me while Daddy is telling the story. "Forget what Ashley said. Sophie's cool. She's probably just mad that some dumb boy didn't say 'Hi' to her today." She rolls her eyes and laughs slumping down into the pillows.

God, I hope I never act silly like that over a boy.

CHAPTER FOUR
SIMONE

I'd give anything to go back to that winter day long ago in Duluth. Where my biggest troubles were a twisted ankle and a snotty friend. When I thought my parents telling me 'No' was the worst thing in the world. Seems like a fantasy, so long ago that it wasn't even real.

It's been days since I've been locked down in the basement. I don't really know how many days exactly. Sunlight doesn't make it down here. There's nothing but a small wet mattress in the corner to keep me company. It's damp and cold down here. Neil didn't even let me bring a blanket and I'm still only wearing a tank top and panties. My eye is swollen shut and it's constantly oozing. It even hurts to breathe.

After Neil raped me I thought I was in the clear for going outside but then he read my journal. I was curled in the corner of my bed when he turned to leave. On his way out he stepped on the notebook that he earlier tossed aside in a rage. The papers crunched under his big feet. He went to kick it out of his way but bent down and picked it up instead. I was frantically trying to come up with a diversion for him not to read it but he paid me no mind. He leaned against the wall, one foot crossed over the other, reading my thoughts. His eyes were moving so rapidly across the pages I wondered how he was even reading that fast. His face became increasingly red as each page turned. And as each page turned I began to shake a little more. I felt like my insides were so jittery that they would jump right out of my body. I became dizzy as I held my breath awaiting Neil's reaction.

I watched as he ran his hand through his sweaty, stringy hair. His other hand was balled up so tight his knuckles were practically transparent. "Sir..it's-it's nothing I swear. I was just- I was just, um-" I couldn't even think straight. My words were coming out a jumbled mess.

"Simone," Neil was almost whispering. "Haven't I been good to you? You want for nothing. I took you in! When you had nowhere else to go. It was me who was there Simone, me!" His voice was shaking. His eyes were glistening with what seemed to be tears. "You think I'm a monster, don't you?" He was bawling. "I love you Simone." Neil was then in my face with his thick hands around my neck. "Do you hear me?!" Spit dribbled from his mouth as he squeezed harder. I began kicking air and clawing at his fingers. "Oh, am I hurting you Simone? You ungrateful bitch." He slammed my head against the wall then threw me to the ground.

"Nobody can see this. I don't want you spreading lies. You can't do this to me." Neil was pacing in circles talking to himself more than to me. I was still lying on the floor when he started to rip my journal into shreds. He walked out of the room and I heard the click of the stove. Neil came stomping back in my room and forced me into the kitchen where I saw what was my journal engulfed in flames.

"This is what happens when you disobey me Simone. It's for your own good."

I craned my neck towards the back window. My eyes landed on my mother's picture still lying on the ground. Neil followed my gaze and looked back into my eyes.

"What's out there?" He asked me. But I didn't answer.

He left me standing in the middle of the kitchen. I leaned against the refrigerator, barely able to balance my own weight. Neil disappeared out of the front door and I saw him reappear in the backyard, standing over my Mom. He stared at the picture a while before he brought it back in jamming it into my face.

"What the fuck is this Simone? What did I tell about this?" He demanded me. But I still didn't answer "I'm sick of seeing her face!"

I stared down at my bare feet. Neil grabbed my chin making me look right into his evil eyes. He punched a hole right in the center of the canvas destroying my mother's beautiful face. He tore it from the inside out and tossed the frame aside.

I fell to the ground in tears crawling to her. My mom. He destroyed her. My body trembled and my lips quivered as snot gushed out of my nose. I struggled for air as I shook with tears.

"NOOO! MAMA! No, no, no, no, no." I hugged what used to be her smile.

Neil bent down and whispered into my ear, "I'm your only family now. And you're never leaving this house again."

He grabbed me by my hair and wrapped it tight around his wrist. He pulled me forward towards the back of the kitchen to the basement door. I tripped over my feet the entire way but he didn't slow down. I tensed up when we reached the cold basement floor. I thought he might have been taking me to his secret room. Instead he pulled me to the left, away from the locked door. He finally let my ponytail go and pushed me away from him as if I were the disgusting one.

We stood there in silence as he stared at me and I stared at the door at the top of the stairs. He was shifting his weight from each foot when he finally spoke.

"Make yourself at home."

CHAPTER FIVE

NEIL

Vanessa. I finally know her name. I find myself saying it under my breath over and over. *Vanessa. Va-nes-sa. Nessa. Nes-sa.* My mouth waters after each syllable. If I were to open my mouth I'd probably turn into a fountain of drool.

It was Thursday morning last week when I saw Vanessa having trouble starting her car. Of course I was there to help. I had been sitting there waiting for her to come outside. I just wanted to stare. Look at her smooth caramel legs being carried by the skinniest heels I've ever seen. I didn't plan on being a hero that day but I couldn't pass up on the opportunity. I would have probably never gotten that chance again. It was perfect timing. I needed Vanessa. I needed her to know me.

Her car battery was dead. Too bad I was in my garbage truck and not my pickup. Neither one of us had what we needed to give her a jump. I offered her a ride to work. Yes, in my nasty fucking garbage truck. And that's just how she looked at me. Like a nasty fucking garbage man. I begged Vanessa to let me help her. She kept saying 'No' but I wasn't letting her get away. I put on my best 'good citizen' voice and smiled the best I knew how. I told her she was my last stop so it wouldn't be any trouble. She finally agreed, only because 'She was running late and I seemed nice enough.'

She sat with her knees locked together, shoulders tense and her fists squeezing her bag. I tried to make small talk and that's just what it was. She gave me short and dry answers. But she was next to me, riding with me. I was happy with that for the moment.

She worked at some fancy art museum close to the university in East Lansing. There were a lot of important looking people walking in and out of the building. She looked embarrassed to be getting dropped off in a garbage truck. As she hopped out of the truck she waved a goodbye. Her hand flitted so fast into the air and back onto her purse I barely saw it. A 'Thank you' was uttered as she walked out onto the sidewalk, spraying perfume on herself along the way. She didn't even look back.

I waited there for 20 minutes. Waiting to see if she would come back. I searched all around the seat to see if she dropped something. I desperately wanted her to have forgot something, anything. But there was nothing and I was left with just the scent of her lingering perfume.

ooo

It's Thursday. My favorite day. It's been a week since I've seen Vanessa. A very long week. She's been all I could think about. She didn't seem too fond of me but I'm going to win her over. There's really no other option.

I actually take a shower this morning. I take my time to get dressed. Run a comb through my hair and viciously scrub my tongue with my old toothbrush. *Shit, I don't have any cologne. Neil you've fucked up again.* As much as I've noticed her perfume it never dawned on me that she would like a guy that had nice cologne too, until just now.

On my way to pick up my work truck I make a stop at the drugstore. I'm going down aisle after aisle when I see bottles of Axe body spray sitting with all of the deodorant. I don't know if this will impress her but it will just have to do.

There's this grandma of a lady holding up the line. She's got a basket full of random shit. I see candy, toilet paper, pantyhose, at least five gallons of milk. *Who the fuck needs all that milk?* Now she's pulling out a wad of coupons, setting one after the other onto the counter. She's moving in slow motion. No one seems to notice or care. *I'm never gonna get the fuck outta here!*

I can't help myself. "For Christ's sake lady, we don't have all day! Just pay for the shit and get the fuck out of everybody's way. Fuck the coupons!" Now I'm yelling at the clerk. "Is there anyone else in this store that can ring people up? Or are you the only moron working here?" It's like time has stopped. Every single person has stopped what they were doing and is now staring at me. Burning holes through my body. A couple of mouths are agape. I hear a few gasps.

"What the hell is his problem?"

"Somebody didn't get their coffee this morning."

"What a prick."

I hear them talking. I feel my chest filling with air and my face turning red. *Fuck this.* I stomp out of the store with the Axe still in my hand. I hear someone yell out, "Hey buddy! You get back here! Hey somebody get that man!" I'm already running towards my truck and I get the hell out of there.

As I'm driving I'm constantly checking the rearview mirror. My palms are sweaty and my hairline is dripping. I need to make sure no one is following me. *Just relax Neil. How important can a bottle of Axe body spray really be?* The average person probably wouldn't be worried, but I'm not the average person.

ooo

"Good morning Vanessa!" There's a genuine smile on my face and cheer in my voice. I almost scare myself with the unfamiliarity. Vanessa looks at me when she hears her name. Her eyes look like a warm brown pool that no one would mind getting lost in. Her skin looks sun glazed, playing peekaboo with me from under her black sheer blazer. She's wearing her hair in a ponytail today. It hangs to the middle of her back. A couple of wavy strands have fought their way out of her hair tie and fly in the light breeze. Her lips are a shiny pink, purplish color. Like berries. I think I love berries.

She looks a little surprised to see me. Not sure if it's a

good or bad surprised. "Good morning Ni-, Nigel was it?" She squints her eyes at me while she dangles her car keys on her index finger.

"Neil." *She forgot my fucking name?!* "It's Neil."

"I'm sorry, Neil." She laughs at me. "I said Nigel. I was close though right?" She's still laughing.

"Yeah, yeah you were. Um Vanessa-" I start to ask her out but she interrupts me.

"I'm kind of in a hurry. I'm always in a hurry, really." She's looking up at the sky while she talks to me. She moves her hand in circles and juts out her hip. "I don't mean to be rude but-"

"Then don't be." The words come out as a growl. I stare at her with an intensity that I didn't mean for her to see. She looks nervous now.

"Sorry there was a tickle in my throat. Something must be going around." I clear my throat for an added effect. "I just think you're beautiful and I would love to take you out sometime."

"Oh, I don't know if that's such a good idea."

"Well why not?"

"I mean, I don't really know you."

"That's why we should go out. So you can get to know me. So we can get to know each other."

"I'm kind of already seeing somebody."

My entire body pulses at the mention of someone else. I feel my lip twitch as I speak while trying to swallow my anger. "Are you guys serious?"

"No, but-"

"No buts. Do what you want to do."

"Yeah, but I don't think dating you is something I want to do. I mean you collect my garbage." I can tell she immediately regrets insulting me. She's blushing and fidgeting with her jacket.

"I'm sorry I didn't mean that." She's a liar.

"Yes you did." I'm shifting from one foot to the other.

"No, no I didn't. Seriously. I apologize. You know what, why don't you come by the museum later today and we'll talk there. Then I'll give you an answer. Okay?"

Her words were perfect but her eyes told a different story. They were pleading with me not to show up later. Good thing I don't listen.

"Sure. I'll be there."

ooo

When I get to the museum I notice that I'm definitely out of place. My old tattered jeans and lumberjack button down shirt stick out like a sore thumb amongst everyone else in their slacks and fancy shoes that click clack when they walk.

I'm not sure where to find Vanessa so I just wander around aimlessly hoping that no one talks to me. My fists are balled up in my front pant pockets. My eyes are moving a mile a minute. I pretend I'm looking at these "art" pieces, more like bullshit to me, but I'm really scanning the room for Vanessa. I look for her jet black hair. Those berry lips.

"Excuse me sir? Would you like an informational pamphlet on the artwork shown here today? It also has fun facts about the artists." I turn around when I hear the voice behind me. There's a girl standing there with big round eyes behind even bigger, more round glasses. She can probably see through my skull with those things. Her pea green sweater hangs off her rail thin frame. It swallows her and I wish she would disappear inside that ugly sweater. I figure she's read the disgust written on my face because she starts to slowly inch away from me. I take a step toward her and I notice her flinch at my movement. She begins to turn around when my voice stops her.

"Would you be able to tell me where I could find Vanessa?" My demeanor is cold but my voice is inviting.

She slightly frowns out of fake confusion. "Vanessa, who?"

I don't know her last name. This little stick is trying to make a fool out of me.

"Look, I think you know who I'm talking about. She works here. So cut the shit and tell me where she is." Before big eyes can respond, Vanessa finds me.

"Hi, you made it." Vanessa is wearing a big pearly white smile. "I see you've met Abigail. She's our new student intern." Abigail's mouth is slightly open forming an 'o' shape. She looks back and forth between the both of us.

"Yes I did. She's been telling me about some of the artwork here. She knows her stuff." My eyes never leave Abigail's.

She attempts a weak smile. She's caught and knows that I know she's full of shit. "Thank you sir. Um, I-I should go. You know, make sure no one else has any questions for me." She immediately turns on her heel and walks away very quickly.

I turn to Vanessa. "She's great."

"Yeah...she is." Vanessa is looking off, following Abigail's trail. "Uh, so..I'm actually surprised you showed up."

"Why would you be surprised? I told you I would be here."

"I just figured I offended you. You know, most people wouldn't still be interested."

"Well I am still interested. I'm not giving up that easy." I let out a fake chuckle and she buys it.

"I like that." Vanessa is nodding her head as she smiles up at me. "So Mr. Neil, do you ask out all the girls on your route? Or is it just me?"

"Just you, Vanessa. Only you."

"You've been keeping an eye out on me?" She nudges my arm as she laughs. I know she's only messing with me. *She is just messing with me, right?*

"You're sweating. Are you okay?" Vanessa looks at me with concern. "We have the air on. I can turn it up a little if you'd like."

I pull at my collar and wipe my forehead. My hand comes back shaking with sweat. "No, no. I'm fine."

"Are you sure? Because it's no problem to-"

I cut her off. "No, really, it's nothing. I'm just one of those people that are always hot, you know?"

Vanessa is looking at me funny, like she's not convinced. "Well I'm going to be here all day. I have to oversee the student exhibit. You can stay and hang out if you want."

"No, I should be going. But I'd love to cook you dinner. Just give me one shot, you might have a good time."

She stands there in silence for what seems like forever. She's biting the inside of her lip and looking away from me.

"You know what? What the hell, why not? When would you like to cook me dinner?"

My stomach feels like it fell out of my body. My heart stopped beating. I have the worst cotton mouth within seconds. *Say something Neil! You've got her. Fucking say something!*

"Earth to Neil." Vanessa giggles as she stares into my face. "I'm free Saturday. Pick me up at 5. I like to keep it early. Okay?"

I nod my head up and down like my life depended on it. My life does depend on it. "Yes, Saturday." I smile and try to shake off the bullshit that's got me acting like an idiot. "I'll see you Saturday."

All the noise in the world has stopped. Everything is gone except for Vanessa. I finally have her and she's never going to leave me. Ever.

CHAPTER SIX
SIMONE

It's been forever and I'm still in the basement. Still leaning against the wall for naps because I just can't lay on that disgusting mattress. I felt myself drifting when I heard a voice upstairs that wasn't Neil's. A female voice. There have never been visitors here so it snapped me out of my daze.

I struggled to make out what the voice was saying so I crawled up the rickety stairs. I was trying to be as quiet as possible when I leaned too hard and a step creaked loudly under my weight.

"What was that?" I heard the mystery woman say. I held my breath and froze every bone and muscle in my body like I was some weird gargoyle perched on top of a building. My eyes were shut tightly.

"Oh that's nothing. Probably just the wind." Neil's voice was nervous which is unusual for him.

"No I don't think so. It sounds like it came from in here." My ear was now pressed to the door.

"My daughter is downstairs working on a school project. I'll go and tell her to keep it down." I hear movement coming towards me.

"You have a daughter? How old is she?"

"She's uh, 17."

"Oh, I'd love to meet her." Mystery lady's voice is getting excited, and closer.

"NO!" Neil screams at her. "I mean she's pretty shy and I don't want to get her distracted. Maybe some other time." Neil must have led her out of the room because her voice is now very faint. She's said something about a date, maybe.

Neil's footsteps are right on top of me. I hurry back down the stairs, ignoring how loud I am and sit on the cold floor hugging my knees. The door opens and I see light. Fluorescent light but still, it's better than nothing. Frankly light from a thunderbolt splitting this house in half would get me excited.

"Simone," Neil is whispering. "Were you listening to my conversation upstairs?"

"I wasn't listening, sir. I just overheard a few words. I can barely even hear anything down here." My voice is whiny. I clear my throat and force a small smile.

"How dare you embarrass me like that in front of Vanessa?"

Who's Vanessa?

"I'm sorry. I didn't mean to. Please don't punish me. I didn't know. I really didn't. I don't even know what you guys were talking about."

"You don't fool me Simone. I know what you're doing."

"I'm not doing anything, Neil. How can I do anything

from down here?"

"Shutup! And now because of your little bullshit you just pulled you'll have to meet her."

"Why? Who is Vanessa?"

"She's you. Or who you should've been to me. But you're such a fucking cunt." I could tell his face was red even in the shadows of the cellar. "I swear Simone if you fuck this up for me I will fucking kill you."

He barely opened his mouth but his threat was spat at me with such force that I believed every word of it.

ooo

The next day Neil comes down in the basement. He's standing over me, the light from the top of the stairs makes him look dark and ominous. To my surprise he tells me it's time to go upstairs.

"You look disgusting. And you smell like shit." Neil pushes me up the stairs to hurry me along.

Once I make it to the kitchen I stare at the calendar stuck to the refrigerator. I blink my eyes over and over to adjust to the light. It's so bright that the back of my eyes pulse and my head is throbbing. I wipe my eyes with the ball of my hand, blinking even harder when I notice the date. I was in the basement for two weeks. Two weeks and two days.

Neil nudges me from behind making me lose my balance and I trip over my awkward feet falling into the doorway. I catch myself on the door frame and lean all of my weight onto it.

"Move it Simone! You need to take a bath." Neil waits for me to respond but the only thing on my mind is a real meal. My stomach growls and grumbles at the thought of all the food that surrounds me in the kitchen. For the past two weeks Neil had only given me oatmeal and toast. By the end of each day I was starving. I would inhale my next serving so fast you wouldn't even know it was ever there.

"Sir, please, can I eat?" I plead with him. My voice is low and my eyes are watery.

"You can eat after you look decent. My God Simone, what the fuck have you been doing down there?" *He can't be serious.*

Neil grabs my arm and guides me out of the kitchen, through the hall and into the bathroom. I stumble onto the toilet seat and rest my head on the window sill. He begins to run my bath water and checks the temperature with his fingertips. He grabs some lavender bubble bath and pours it throughout the tub. He dips his arm into the water and swishes it around in big circles. I see the suds starting to form and some sticks to Neil's arm as he pulls his hand out of the water and reaches toward me. I look at him in confusion, not even bothering to lift my head from the window. He grabs my hand, surprisingly gentle, and pulls me from the toilet.

He grabs me softly by the waist, holding me steady. His fingers slowly lift my tank top over my stomach. When he reaches my breasts I lift my arms straight into the air as he guides the shirt over my head. I immediately cover myself by crossing my arms across my chest.

Neil grabs my arms and puts them at my side. He runs his hand along my spine up to my neck. He grabs a fistful of my tangled hair and kisses me deep in the mouth, unbrushed teeth and all. He's looking me in the eye as he kisses me and I can't read his expression. As he pulls away from me he slides my panties down my hips. The once crispy white fabric falls to my feet. I kick my panties to the side, never letting my eyes leave Neil's.

This is a side of Neil that has been hiding from me for a long time. I missed this Neil. But I'm so confused as to why he's doing this now. I don't want to do or say the wrong thing that'll make him go away.

He looks at the bathtub signaling for me to get in. The warm water feels comforting to my skin as I sink down on my bottom. I dip my head back letting the water soak my hair. My hair drips down my back as Neil dips a washcloth into the water and begins to run it across my body. I shiver from his touch, the niceness so foreign to me now. We stare at each other in silence as he bathes me and I let him. He doesn't have to speak. He doesn't have to apologize. I know Neil is sorry.

CHAPTER SEVEN
SIMONE
15 Years

This is the third party I'll be going to this week and it's only Wednesday. I've been drinking vodka since about 5 o'clock. It's approaching 9 pm now. I'm staring at myself in the mirror trying my hardest to do something with my hair. But my head is spinning. I feel like I'm on a roller coaster going round and round.

"Simone what's taking so long? I'm ready to go." Amber walks over to me with her huge breasts spilling out of her cropped t-shirt. She wiggles them on my arm smiling at me with a drunken grin. "Let's get wild!"

"Get your tits off of me!" I laugh at her and playfully push her away.

She crosses her arms and leans on the bathroom wall. She's frowning at me as she pops her gum. "Do you need help or something? What are you even doing?"

"I don't know. I'm fucking wasted. Do it for me?" I hand her my brush and we go back into her adjoining dorm. I sit on the edge of her bed with my legs crisscrossed while she kneels on her knees behind me. Audrina flashes in my mind but I quickly push her away.

"How do you want it?" Amber's hip is jutted out with

her hand gripping her waist. There's Audrina's face again. *What the fuck?* I shake my head and clench my eyelids tight together. My fingers find their way to my temples. "You okay?"

"I'm fine. Just drunk." I giggle to sound convincing. "Just do whatever. Just make sure it's cute." I slap Amber's leg lightly to get her started. She's staring at me and she's still popping her gum. She rolls her eyes a little before she shrugs and begins to brush my hair. Amber's touch is soft and delicate. The bristles of the brush massage my scalp and makes me shiver. I imagine small butterflies tugging at the strands of my hair. My shoulders collapse and my head rolls back as I let out a moaning sound.

Amber's laugh brings me back to reality. "You really are drunk."

I don't respond. I just relax and let her have her way with my unruly curls. Amber taps the top of my head to let me know she's done. I stumble and the room swirls around as I stand up from the bed. I feel Amber's hand grab my arm before I can fall over. I try to shake out of my drunkenness and I shimmy from my head down to my feet, which doesn't really help at all.

When I get to the mirror above Amber's desk I'm surprised at my reflection. She actually did a good job. There's a french twist wrapping from the front of my head to the back and another twist snaking around from the side. The two twists meet into a big curly ponytail.

"So guess what I got for us?" Amber's face is lit up with excitement and she's bouncing on the bed.

"What?" I ask her, still looking at myself in the mirror.

"Blue dolphins." She's digging in her purse as she tells me. A small plastic bag appears in her hand with small pills inside.

"Ecstasy?" My voice cracks and goes up an octave. "I've never done that before."

"It's fun Si-Si." I cringe at the nickname. I hate when she calls me that but I never tell her. I don't want to hurt her feelings.

"I promise you'll love it." Amber sings her promise to try to convince me.

"I don't know Amber." I don't even believe myself.

"Just take one. If you don't like it, no big deal, you won't have to do it again. And what's there to be worried about? You'll be with me all night." Being with Amber all night isn't all that reassuring. I mean I've only known her for about a month. But it's so hard for me to say no to those big blue pleading eyes.

"Fine. Just one." I hold out my hand and she drops the tiny pill in my palm. I grab a small pop from the mini refrigerator. The crisp sound of fresh Coca-Cola pops in the air as I open the can. Before I swallow the pill Amber stops me.

"Wait, not yet. Let's roll a few joints before we take

'em. We're gonna need 'em." Amber goes in her sock drawer and pulls out a small bag of weed. Her slender fingers work fast and efficient. She's done this a thousand times. She wets the paper with her tongue and seals the joint together. She takes out another bud and tosses me the bag to roll the rest as she starts on her second one.

Amber sets aside the three joints and hops off of the bed. She glides over to her shoes and picks out red open toe spiked heels. As she buckles them she notices my old worn down tennis shoes I wear every day.

"What size shoe do you wear? I'm sure I have some better ones for you to put on." Instead of waiting for my response she quickly tosses me a pair of nude strappy platforms. I put the shoes on and they're a little snug on my toes but I squeeze them in anyway. My heel is sticking out a little at the back of the sandal so I crunch my toes inward to make more room to slide my foot down even more.

"I guess these will work. Thanks Amber." I hope I get drunk enough to ignore the sting in my feet.

"Don't worry about it. I never wear those anyway. You can keep them if you want." Amber then pops the ecstasy in her mouth and grabs my Coke from the table and takes a big gulp. She hands me the pop next and watches me until I swallow my own.

"Now what?" I ask.

"Now we can go party." She stuffs her phone into her back pocket and we're out the door.

ooo

Any other day walking down Grand River wouldn't be a task at all. The street goes on forever, but when you're stoned or drunk it's like an adventure. Whenever you're bored and have nothing to do, just walk up and down Grand River and you're bound to stumble upon some fun. But tonight my feet are screaming so loudly that I'm sure everyone around me can hear them. *God, when is this shit gonna kick in?*

I remember I have a small bottle of vodka in my bag. As I rummage around in my excuse for a purse it rolls into my hand. There it appears, in all its glory, glistening and swishing around inside the bottle just waiting for me to drink up. I finish it in two gulps and wipe my lips with the back of my hand.

The more we walk the more my feet turn into Jell-O. My skin tingles and I can feel every taste bud on my tongue. The breeze in the air feels more amazing than I could ever remember before. I hug myself and my skin is so smooth! I never knew how much I loved my skin. I breathe in the air deeply and run my fingers up and down my arms. I have a big goofy smile on my face. You can probably see every tooth in my mouth and I don't care.

"I see you like it, huh?" Amber's voice snaps me out of my trance. She's smiling stupidly, just like me.

"Oh my God! Amber, I love it! It's amazing. Do you

have any more with you?" I notice that I'm shouting at her, not in a rude way, but in a 'I'm so happy right now I can't contain my excitement' kind of way.

"You won't need anymore, trust me. Just wait, we're almost at Corey's house. We'll smoke and stuff when we get there. He won't care, everybody there will be fucked up." Amber's hair floats as she moves. Her eyes shine under the street lamps.

I see that she's no longer chewing her gum either. She's just rolling it around in her mouth. That girl can hold onto a piece of gum longer than I even thought was possible. Whenever I had a piece too long it deteriorated into a gooey mess that I couldn't stand but hers was always like brand new. She's good at everything she does, like Audrina was. She's the first person to be nice to me since Audrina. She has dark hair and dark features just like her, except for her big blue eyes. I think that's why I was drawn to her, she reminded me of a good time in my life. Although I can't picture Audrina drinking and doing drugs. I sometimes wonder how everybody in my previous life is like now. If my face pops into their mind like they do mine. But the more I think of them the more sad I get and the more fucked up I feel. It's very bittersweet.

Amber holds my hand as we head up the walkway. The house is humongous with big white Greek letters posted above the front door. There are different colored lights flashing through the windows and streamers falling out of trees, bushes, from everywhere. I feel the music vibrating throughout my body before we even make it inside. There are tons of people on the lawn, all drinking, laughing and dancing. There's even a table in the driveway where some are playing beer pong.

A messy haired guy yells out to Amber asking her to join the beer pong tournament. She waves him off with a smile and pulls me inside the big house. She wastes no time lighting a joint. She puffs a couple of times and passes it to me. I inhale and hold the smoke in my lungs before I exhale a big white cloud. I didn't realize how high I was getting off the E until now. The weed is bringing me down a hair. But I don't want the good feeling to leave me so I give her back the joint and start to dance.

"Hey, I'm gonna go look for Corey. I'll be back." Amber has to yell over the bass but it's still so loud I have to read her lips to understand what she's said.

As Amber saunters away I look around the room and notice how crowded it is. You have to strategically figure out a maze to get around all the people. Amber's head disappears and I'm left alone.

My head spins as I dance and the music fills my entire body. I'm in my own world. My eyes are closed, my hands touch myself and my body oozes out sweat. I feel light as air, as fluffy as a thick cloud high in the sky. I forget that I don't know anyone at the party but Amber, who ditched me. I'm having fun just like this.

Suddenly I feel two big hands, that are not my own, grab my waist. I feel an unknown body grind against my ass. I tense up and try to turn around but the hands are too strong. They move my hips for me in a circular motion. The stranger's thumbs massage my lower back. Their thumbs make tiny, deep, strong circles loosening me up. *Just relax Simone. It's a party. Everybody's dancing. Stop thinking. Have fun. Let go.* I smile to myself and lean against a strong chest. We continue to move like the waves and I feel their hands creeping up my stomach then they cup my breasts. I finally push away and turn to find the most beautiful guy I've ever seen.

His skin was the color of butterscotch with hair like ebony that sparkled even in the dark. There was sweat glistening off of his neck and his muscles were very apparent under his t-shirt. His bushy eyebrows framed his brown eyes perfectly. He was breathing heavy out of his mouth and I couldn't help but stare at his full lips. Lips that were up until now hiding perfectly pearly white teeth.

"What's wrong? Why'd you stop dancing?" Those strong hands wipe the sweat from his brow.

"Um, I-" I get nervous and words won't come out. Luckily, I'm saved by Amber. She appears at my side with Corey in tow.

"Calvin, you met my cousin," Amber's voice is overly perky.

"Your cousin?" Calvin raises his eyebrows and

Amber nods her head. "Well Amber's cousin, thanks for the dance." He licks his lips and begins to walk away.

"My name is Simone," I blurt out to him but I'm not sure if he hears me.

"Real smooth Si-Si." Amber giggles and turns to Corey. They start to whisper to each other. They swallow each other's tongues. I roll my eyes and walk away.

There's so much going on. I make my way through the crowd and see skirts pushed up, tongues intertwining, hands groping, hips thrusting. In a corner there's a circle of friends smoking and nodding slowly to the beat. The kitchen is like a bar and the floor is sticky from spilled liquor. I take myself on a tour while I listen to my heartbeat pulse through my ears.

I head back through the crowd towards the front door. I turn towards the staircase to my left and see another couple sucking each other's faces off. The girl is sitting in between the guy's legs with her own pair spread open showcasing her lack of underwear. I push past them, sure to lean against the railing so we don't touch. At the top landing there are too many doors to choose from so I choose the one to the far right.

I don't bother to knock before I open the door. The light instantly makes me squint and shield my eyes. They adjust quickly when I see a girl bent over the bed and some guy behind her, thrusting himself in and out of her. My mouth drops open and I'm stuck in the doorway. The guy looks up and asks me to join. I stand there like an idiot saying nothing. Not moving.

"Hello?!" He yells at me. "What the fuck? Get the fuck out of here!" He never stops moving his hips and the girl never even looks up. My feet suddenly work again and I turn around slamming the door shut behind me.

I quickly push past the people on the steps again and head out of the front door. Before both feet make it to the porch I run face first into Calvin's chest. *Shit!*

"You in a hurry?" Calvin's hands touch my shoulders and he holds me back from his chest.

"I'm so sorry! I didn't see you. I didn't mean-"

Calvin cuts off my rambling. "Hey, it's cool Simone." He bends down and looks me in my eyes as his hands still rest on my shoulders. *He said Simone.* My mouth spreads into a big toothy smile.

"You know how to play beer pong?"

"Um, no. I've never played before." I twiddle my fingers together as I shrug. Calvin's eyes doubled their normal size.

"What?! Never?"

I shake my head 'No.'

"Well come on. It's easy." He grabs my hand and drags me over to the table where everyone is yelling.

I play pretty shitty. I lose the game for us but Calvin doesn't seem to mind. I think we're both too drunk to care.

We end up sitting on a curb smoking and talking. I

thought the dolphins would've worn off by now but I'm just as high as I was walking down Grand River. I giggle at everything Calvin says and I can't keep my hands to myself. I'm basically in his lap when Amber walks up to us. She's giving me a suspicious look but smiling at the same time.

"Hey Si-Si I'm staying with Corey tonight. Just hang out by one of the back doors. Somebody should walk in or out so you can get in. Here's my dorm key though." She tosses me a small key ring but it falls short of my palm and lands in the dirt. I leave the keys on the ground and look up at her with big dough eyes.

"What? I-I can't go by myself." My voice is just above a whisper. My eyes dart around the night sky in a panic.

"Simone, what are you talking about? Yes you can. Have Calvin walk you back or something." Amber dismissively waves her hand in the air.

"I don't know him Amber. You can't leave me." I plead to her but she isn't fazed.

"Well, you seemed to know him good a few minutes ago. Look, I'm staying here tonight so are you going to my room or not?"

"Well where is your dorm Simone," Calvin interjects. "I'll walk you back. Is your roommate there? You know, so you won't be by yourself."

"I don't have a dorm. I don't go here."

"Oh. What school do you go to?"

"I don't-"

Amber jumps in, "She's visiting me for the weekend." I can tell she's starting to get annoyed. She walks closer to me and whispers so only I can hear her. "Simone what the fuck? What is the big fucking deal? Do you really want to ruin my chance with Corey tonight?" I shake my head no. "Well stop being such a baby and go to my room, shit. Where the hell else are you gonna go anyway? I'll call somebody to make sure the door gets opened for you. Okay?" She says 'Okay' with an edge to her voice. She's not really asking me to do this, she's telling me.

"Yeah, okay Amber." I look down at my red swollen feet and watch hers walk away. Amber is right. Where else would I go? Before I was staying with her I was in a group home.

Calvin interrupts my pity party. "Hey you wanna come back to my place tonight? You can sleep with me and feel safe." He gives me a sly grin.

"No thanks. I don't think I'll be doing too much sleeping tonight." I pick up the keys and begin to wobble away.

"You can't just go by yourself. It's dark."

I ignore Calvin and continue to walk with a purpose. I hear Calvin yell out my name as I bend down and take the heels off of my throbbing feet. Dirt and pebbles dig into my soles but it feels good. I look back as I'm now a block away and Calvin is gone.

Ten minutes into my journey I realize that it's pretty chilly out. I rub my arms with my ice block hands trying to create warmth but to no avail. *Just a few more blocks Mo. You can make it.* As my legs shiver I hear the sound of a car behind me. I turn around and see a pick-up truck creeping along. I pick up my pace and so does the truck. *Oh my God. Please go away. Leave me alone. Don't look back Simone. Just keep walking.*

The truck pulls up right beside me and the window rolls down. An old man, like my Dad would be old not old, old, calls out to me.

"What are you doing out so late by yourself?"

I ignore him and keep walking. My arms and legs propel me forward fast and strong, like I'm a power walker.

"Do you want a ride? It's nice and warm in here."

"No thanks mister. I'll manage just fine." Just then I trip over a rock, my own feet, or the empty air, I don't really know. My knee scrapes the concrete and I see the man getting out of his truck.

"Let me help you. Are you okay? Why aren't you wearing your shoes?" I look at the man's face but I can't see much. He's wearing a baseball cap that sits low on his eyes. He has stubble on his face that I'm sure is as prickly as a cactus and strong hands reaching for me.

"I said I'm okay." I hop up before he has a chance to touch me and continue to walk ahead.

The man yells out behind me. "You know, you

shouldn't turn down help when it's offered to you."

I turn around and he's shifting from one foot to the other as his hand pushes the brim of his hat up to his hairline. I'm not sure if he's trying to get a better look at me or if he wants me to get a better look at him.

I shiver as I look into his icy blue eyes, or maybe it's because it's cold. He grins at me in a way that I'm not sure how to explain. The man starts to walk back towards his truck. I should probably get going now but my feet are glued to the pavement. He hops in his truck and drives away while he looks at me in his rear view mirror.

CHAPTER EIGHT

VANESSA

Against my better judgment I've agreed to a second date with Neil, the trash guy. I must be going through an early mid-life crisis or something because I don't even know why I agreed to the first one. Well, I do know. Aundrea convinced me that I needed to be nicer to people. That I need to be more open and outgoing. Things haven't been going too well with Christian, my latest conquest. So, I figured I'd try out her advice and see if going for a different kind of man than I have in the past will make a difference. I'm not sure these good samaritan pants are a good fit for me. Neil's definitely a weirdo, but I'll give it another shot.

We're supposed to go to Malin's, an upscale seafood restaurant. I'm not a big seafood connoisseur but I should be able to find something on the menu that I'll semi like. Hopefully Mr. Garbage Man will have something other than a lumberjack shirt to wear. Riding around in a garbage truck was enough embarrassment for me.

I want to keep it simple tonight. Neil seems overly ecstatic about me as it is and I don't want to add fuel to the fire. I sift through my closet and pick out a pretty white dress with a huge flower print and an empire waist. My rose colored flats will go perfectly with it. I think I'll wear a ponytail too, to be less seductive.

My phone dings and a message from Neil pops on my screen, '*I'm leaving out now. I'll be at Malin's shortly.*'

Shit. I have to hurry and get ready. I haven't even taken a shower yet. I rush to the bathroom and take a little bird bath to freshen up. Luckily my dress is already pressed so I slip it on and sweep my hair into a quick ponytail. I dab a little pale pink lip gloss on my bottom lip and rub my lips together to even it out. As I reach for my favorite Jimmy Choo perfume I change my mind and go with a grapefruit scented body spray, you know switch it up.

I nearly slide on the wood floor as I hurry out of the front door. Once I get to my car I realize I've forgotten my keys inside, which I always do. As I'm walking back up the steps my phone dings again. '*I'm here. Where are you?*' I type back, '*Sorry I'm running a little behind. I'll be there.*'

I don't have time to try to figure out where I left my keys so I grab the spare set resting in the gold flaked bowl sitting on the small table by the front door. I make sure I lock the door behind me and make my way downtown.

ooo

When I arrive at Malin's there's a crowd of people standing in the entryway. I half hope Neil hasn't made a reservation and is in the crowd waiting to be seated so I don't look like a complete asshole for being late. I don't see his face so I squeeze through everyone and make it to the hostess stand.

"Excuse me ma'am? Is there a reservation for a Neil, party of two?"

The lady looks down at a small tablet. Her blonde hair falls in her face and she doesn't bother to move the strands from out of her eyes. She has a piercing near her collarbone and bright red nails. She looks up at me and I look at her dark plum lips and she says to me in a surprisingly chipper voice, "Yes miss. He's already here. Follow me, I'll take you to your seat. You have a lovely view of downtown from where you'll be sitting."

I follow her through the restaurant. With all the twists and turns we're doing I would be surprised if I even remembered how to get out of here. I see Neil as I approach the table. His leg is bouncing up and down and he's roughly rubbing his chin. He notices me walking over and he immediately runs the same hand that was rubbing his chin through his hair. He straightens his back and he clears his throat.

"Here you are. Your server will be right with you." The hostess pulls my chair out for me and places a menu down on the table. She walks away and her blonde hair floats behind her.

I turn to Neil and see sweat beads on his face. *What the hell is with this guy and his sweat?*

"I'm sorry I'm late Neil. There was terrible traffic. It

was an accident on the way here."

"Well where were you coming from? Because the roads were just fine on my way in." He clears his throat again.

"Um, I was leaving the museum."

"What time? Because I was in that area before I came here." His face is turning red.

"I mean I made a few stops when I left work. Look, can we just enjoy being here? I made it so that's all that matters."

Neil blinks his eyes much longer than I've ever seen anyone do and takes a deep breath. "You're right," he says. "I was just getting anxious. I didn't think you were going to show up."

I give him a small smile and direct my attention to the drink menu. I think I'll need several with how this is going. I keep my head down to avoid having to look at Neil's serious, always tense face. I'm still staring down at the menu when the waiter comes over.

"Hello, my name is Henry. I'll be your server tonight. Can I start you off with something to drink miss?" He's a young man, no older than 22. He has smooth skin with a crooked smile.

I look over at Neil and realize he's already ordered a drink and has a soup in front of him. *Geez, I wasn't that late. He could've waited.*

"I'll have a blueberry martini please, with an extra

shot of vodka."

"Okay, I'll be right back with that for you."

Before he can turn his heel I stop him, "Wait, I think we're ready to order as well." I don't bother to check with Neil.

"What are we having tonight?" Henry's slick hair sparkles under the light.

"I'll take the salmon with asparagus and potatoes please." Henry isn't writing anything down.

"And you sir?" Henry turns to Neil and beams at him.

Neil orders some weird squid thing. I suppose it fits him. Henry walks away and I'm left alone with squid boy again.

"So, have you been here before?" I ask trying to fill the silence.

"Yeah, I've been here plenty of times. I used to come here often, but not much lately."

"Why not?"

"Well, I haven't had anyone to come with." He looks me straight in my eyes and holds my gaze for a while before returning to his soup.

"What about your daughter? She doesn't like to go out for daddy, daughter time?" I'm poking fun at him but he seems to have missed the joke.

"My daughter has had a rough time lately. When my wife, her mother passed I guess I could've been there for her a little more but I was having a hard time myself. It's been quite some time but she's still adjusting. I'm not particularly her favorite person right now, especially with her being a teen now. She's always so moody."

He looks at his glass the entire time he's talking. I can tell he's nervous. He probably hasn't talked about this much before. Maybe I should take it easy on him.

"Neil I'm so sorry. I had no idea."

"How could you have?" *He's got a point.* "It's okay. I've come to terms with it, really."

Neil is just a single dad trying to figure it all out. I'm sure he hasn't been with anyone since his wife. I guess he's not so weird, just out of practice.

Henry comes over with our food. He's balancing everything on his arms like an acrobat. My plate glides off of his arm onto the space in front of me and Neil's slides in front of him. Henry places the sauces next to our dishes and asks if we need anything else.

"What the fuck is this?" Neil's voice is dripping with disgust. His face is fire red and his fists are balled tight. Henry is shocked and his eyes bulge from his head. He stammers, which doesn't help him at all. "I asked for this to be fried with melted butter. That's not what the fuck is in front of me."

"My apologies sir. I must've misheard-"

"So do you purposely not write down orders to fuck with the patrons?" His fingers grip his knife so tight that I'm scared it's going to pop out of his hold and go soaring in the air.

"No, not at all. It was an honest mistake. I'll bring you a new order, sir, on the house."

Neil's breathing slows down a bit, back to normal. He loosens his grip on the silverware and clears his throat. His hand runs through his hair and he turns back toward me as Henry disappears.

"So, how's your salmon? It's usually delicious." Neil is smiling and his voice is chipper as if he didn't just rip our waiter a new one.

What the hell have I gotten myself into?

ooo

"You are so dramatic, Vanessa! It was not that bad." Aundrea sips her coffee nonchalantly, not believing a word I've said. Her chocolate hair is curly today, with golden highlights. Her eyes always seem to have a smile behind them. She's like the good angel on your shoulder. You can talk to her about anything and she always has great advice.

"I'm telling you, this guy has a screw loose. I'm not making excuses like usual, I swear."

"Maybe he was just in a bad mood before he got there. Maybe his daughter pissed him off or something, you never know. You said he was fine the first time you guys went out right?"

"Yeah, I guess. I mean, he was weird but-"

"But nothing. You always try to find a way out. I'm

not letting you this time." Aundrea unconsciously goes to tuck her hair behind her ear. "Just one more date. If he gets a third strike then fine, throw 'em away." She shrugs her shoulders.

"Why are you so 'Team Neil'? You don't even know him. What's wrong with Christian? He's great." My voice cracks and I drink my coffee to try to disguise it.

Christian is this hotshot architect I met about six months ago at an unveiling of his new building in downtown Chicago. I just so happened to be in town studying art at their different museums there. I overheard someone talking about the event that night and I decided to stop in and see what all the buzz was about. The building was beautiful and Christian was even better. He had a glow about him like he just came from some grand tropical vacation. His brown eyes and perfect smile captivated me. He had one dimple on his right cheek and the perfect amount of stubble on his exquisitely sculptured face. He swept me into his grasp that night.

"No, he's got money." Aundrea's eyebrows raise and she tilts her head slightly to the side, like a dog that's heard a whistle.

I laugh at her, "And? What's wrong with that? Money never hurt anyone?"

"Whatever you say." She looks at me in a way that makes me feel bad. She always has a way of making me cave in.

"Fine. I'll play your little love doctor game one more

time, but that's it." Aundrea seems pleased with my answer. But I'm not sure if I'll actually do it.

◦◦◦

'Vanessa??'

'Hello?'

I ignore Neil's text messages. I don't feel like dealing with his circus right now. I need a fresh breath of normal, so I call Christian. He doesn't answer. *Typical.*

I have the day off, which is much needed, but I also don't know what to do with myself when I'm away from the museum. I usually shop and find something social to do downtown but I'm not really in the mood. And last I was in my closet it was bursting from every nook and cranny with tag sporting clothes. I think I'll give the mall a break.

It's 1 o'clock in the afternoon and I pour myself a glass of wine. Wine is good at any time. I curl up in the corner of my new comfy sectional with my fuzzy white blanket and turn the tv to Lifetime. Whenever you're having a lazy day Lifetime movies and wine are your best friends.

Just as the crazed surrogate mother pushes the real mom down a flight of stairs my phone dings.

'Sorry babe I've been in meetings all day. I'll call you as soon as they're over.'

A text from Christian.

I text him back. *'Can you just come over when you leave the office? I'll make dinner :)'*

I stare at the 'Delivered' memo for a few minutes before I click my screen off. *Whatever.* He'll get back to me when he can.

I'm halfway through my third movie when I start to doze off. I've gone through two bottles of wine and I haven't moved from this couch in hours. I stretch my body and reach for the sky. A huge yawn escapes my dry mouth. I scoot off of the couch and toss my blanket aside.

The sun is starting to go down, shining orange and pink beams into the house. As beautiful as it is, it's blinding me. I use my hand as a shield and a cool breeze catches my armpit. I was sweating a little under my blanket and I remember I haven't showered all day.

My feet sink into the plush carpet as I walk down the hallway leading to my bedroom. I toss a fresh pair of lace panties onto my bed so I can just slip them on after my shower. I glide through my neatly organized walk in closet into the master bathroom. The cold tile immediately sends chills up my body. I turn the shower knob completely to the left, scalding hot, just how I like it.

The hot water beads cascade over every curve and pierce every pore of my body. My usual tan skin is turning red. I just stand under the downpour with my eyes closed for at least five minutes before I lather my loofa with shower gel. The big puff of suds are nice and fluffy and cover me like I'm made of snow. I let the scent open my nostrils and the smell of pomegranate fills me up.

Just as I turn around to rinse the remainder of the soap away and drench my hair, I hear a funny noise. There's a clicking sound that seems far away, but also pretty close. It sounds like a lock being turned. But it's so brief I just brush it away. I'm sure I'm just hearing things.

I wrap myself with my robe as I step out of the shower. The shower door clicks shut behind me and I nearly jump out of my skin. My hand is over my chest and my heart is racing. *Why am I being so paranoid? I had a little too much wine.* I look in the mirror and my cheeks are flushed and my eyes look tired. *Maybe I just need to go to sleep.*

I drag myself out of the bathroom, through the closet, into my bedroom and sink into my big king sized bed. I need to find something to watch me fall asleep. Funny commentary on celebrity outfits comes through the speakers. *Ooh "Fashion Police."* It's a rerun but I leave it anyway. The ladies' cackling on the tv lull me into a deep benadryl-like slumber.

ooo

I left my blinds open last night. The sun is peeking through the window, willing my eyelids to open. I scoot down deeper into the covers and roll over to my nightstand. I check my phone, that I forgot to charge all night, and I have two missed calls and a text message from Christian.

'I was going to stop by for that dinner. But I'll just catch you another time.' 10pm. He texted me at 10 pm. I roll

my eyes and toss my phone next to my pillow.

Wait! The sun is out! Shit, shit, shit.

I glance at my phone screen and see that it's going on 9:30 am. I'm so late for work. I usually wake up at 7 to make it there by 8.

I quickly brush my teeth and throw my hair into a bun. I grab the first outfit I see, jeans and a thin sweater, and I dash for the kitchen. I grab a banana and a small water bottle. This will just have to be my breakfast.

When I step out onto the front porch there's a crunch under my feet. I look down and there's a single red rose resting on my '*Welcome*' mat. There's no note or anything. I pick up the flower and wonder how it got here. I don't have one rose bush in my garden.

The petals flap in the breeze and I close my eyes as the scent fills my nostrils. Then it comes to me. *Christian.*

CHAPTER NINE
NEIL

"This is how you treat your father? Get the fuck over here. Now!"

The boy doesn't move and the man's hands begin to unbuckle his belt. It slides smoothly out of the loops. It's done this a million times. His steel toe boots stomp across the room. His rough hand squeezes the boy's arm and throws him to the floor.

The leather belt whips across the boy's backside while the man's booted foot holds him down.

"This is what you deserve."

ooo

My eyes burst open and my body is covered in sweat. My heart is racing and my breathing is erratic. These dreams are normal for me but they've become a lot more frequent lately. I don't know how to get rid of them. I'm fucking sick of them.

I peel off my wet shirt and wipe my face with the towel I keep on the nightstand. I look at the clock and it reads 4:17 am. I might as well stay up now and get ready for work.

I peek in Simone's room on my way to the bathroom.

She's sleeping with one leg under the covers and one on top of them. I have to fight the urge to go in and pull the covers away from her body. Her beautiful body. I shut my eyes and rub my temples. I can't let her distract me right now, she's done enough of that.

She's been sucking me into her web ever since she's been out of the basement. I don't like it. My mind has been all over the place and I can't concentrate.

She's done the laundry without being told. Cooked breakfast, lunch and dinner. I haven't heard a word about that bitch mother of hers. She's been doing everything right, which is wrong. It's wrong for Simone. She never does anything right. I can't help but feel like she's up to something.

Worrying about whatever the hell Simone is doing fucked up my date with Vanessa. I couldn't be on my best behavior. But I don't remember being outrageous. She hasn't answered my calls or texts. It's been a week. I have to figure out a way to make her see she's overreacting and making a mistake she doesn't want to make.

I use this new body wash Simone told me is better than the Irish spring soap bar I normally use. Dior something. I don't know how the hell she knows about it but it actually smells good. My skin feels softer after every shower. I'm starting not to recognize my own self.

I don't stay in the shower long. I need time to shave. New skin, new face, maybe a haircut. Looks have to matter to someone like Vanessa.

I hear dishes clattering in the kitchen. The smell of bacon and coffee is in the air. I walk into the kitchen in unbuttoned jeans, work boots and an open flannel. Simone is standing at the sink, facing the window. She's just staring out at the backyard. I see a plate of cheese eggs, toast and bacon sitting on top of the stove. Steam is coming from the food, floating in the air. She hears me grab the plate and turns around.

"Good morning sir. I made you breakfast." Her voice still sounds scratchy from sleep.

"I see that." I bite a corner of the toast and she stares at me. "What?"

"Um, do you think I can get a new sketchbook and a couple of canvases?" Simone twiddles her fingers as she talks to me. She's looking down at her bare feet.

I scoop a forkful of eggs into my mouth and gulp down my coffee. "We'll see. I gotta go. Have some food ready when I get back." Even though Simone has been sneaky lately and I don't know her plans I guess I can get her some art shit. Give her something to do, keep her happy and out of my hair.

It's a little earlier than when I normally leave but I have business to handle. Driving to Vanessa's is going out of the way to get my work truck but I don't care. It's still semi dark when I get to her street. Mostly everyone's porch lights are on, but not hers. I drive a couple of houses down to park but not before noticing her car isn't in the driveway.

I casually walk up to her home like it's an everyday thing, like I live here myself. There aren't any lights on. But then again why would there be? It's 6 am and she doesn't get up until 7. I walk around to the back yard that's fenced in. I jump the fence and follow the stepping stones that lead to the patio. I press my face to the glass door and cup my hands around my eyes. Everything looks normal. *So where the fuck is she? Why isn't her car here? Maybe it's in the garage. But she never uses the garage.* Then I move down the path some to the kitchen window and see a few dishes left in the sink and I know she's gone.

"Excuse me? What are you doing back there?" An older woman in a silk robe and short white hair is leaning out of her bedroom window. I've never seen her before. This whole block is usually sleep at this hour. Her hand holds the front of her robe closed and she's squinting her eyes. I ignore her but she's persistent. "Hello?" She seems like the police calling type. "Hey I'm calling the cops!" *What did I say? Cunt.*

"Hi miss. I'm just Vanessa's gardener. She's usually home to let me in the shed at this time. She hasn't answered her phone so I was just taking a look, that's all."

"Her gardener?"

"Yeah, Tom." I smile big and wide and she seems to loosen up.

"Oh, well sorry Tom, but she's been gone the past couple of days. I can tell her you stopped by when she comes home."

"No need miss. I'll just leave her a message. You have a good day now." I walk over to the fence and take a big leap. I feel the old lady's eyes burning a hole through my back as I walk down the driveway.

Where the fuck would she be for a couple of days?

ooo

I'm done with work and I reek of old gym socks. It's weirdly hot as hell today for April. I've been sweating all over. But I'll stick to what I said and get Simone her supplies.

I walk up and down the aisles of this arts and crafts store for a few minutes before I find what I'm looking for. There are too many sketch book choices. I don't know which one she wants. Simone is usually with me when I get this stuff but no more gallivanting around for her so here I am, clueless.

I don't see one employee in this store besides the half asleep cashier. *I don't know anything about this shit.* I suddenly feel overwhelmed and I feel myself getting angry. I pick up a Strathmore book and flip through the pages to see how they feel.

Holy shit! I've got it!

Simone and Vanessa are both into this artsy fartsy stuff. That's my way back in. It's no way she can turn away a young budding artist. She manages an art museum for Christ's sake. I'll just bring Simone with me to the museum for "research" purposes and I'm bound to bump into her.

When I get back home I'm so excited that I burst into Simone's room. She's taking a nap and she wakes up immediately to my loud voice.

"Simone get up! We gotta go. Don't you wanna go somewhere nice? A museum?" I sound like a little kid giving Santa his Christmas list.

"What?" Simone yawns and rubs her eyes.

"An art museum. Don't you want to go?"

"Yeah, sure. I guess."

"Okay, get up. Get dressed. We have to go before they close." I pull at her arms willing her to get out of bed.

"Now? I'm sleepy."

"Close your eyes in the car. I have a surprise for you. We have to go. It's almost 5 o'clock."

She nearly falls on her face getting out of the bed. *She's so damn clumsy.* Before she can fully stand up I'm already throwing a t-shirt and jean shorts at her. She catches the shorts right before they hit her face. She leaves the room and heads towards the bathroom.

"No, we don't have time for a shower. Put the clothes on now."

Simone stares at me and opens her mouth as if to say something and shuts it as soon as I raise my eyebrow. "Now."

She turns her back to me and removes her sweatpants and beater right in the hallway. She puts her clothes on really fast so I don't get to look at her too long.

I don't move when she squeezes past me to throw her clothes into her hamper. Her ass grazes against my leg and my fingers get a brief feel. *So soft.* She doesn't say anything.

I follow her bouncing red curls out the door as I stare at her bouncing ass.

CHAPTER TEN

SIMONE

Neil and I pull in front of the university's museum downtown. I've been here plenty of times. I actually met Amber outside of this building. I was sitting on a bench drawing flowers forming on bushes and petals dancing in the sky.

She thought I was a student at the school and she just knew I was acing all of my art classes. I didn't say much, I just let her believe whatever she wanted. I saw Amber almost every time I took a visit to the museum. She had a class about a block away. Or some guy she was dealing with lived a block away. I can't remember.

The more she saw me the more she would talk to me and she seemed friendly enough so we became bench buddies. She noticed my raggedy clothes and I ended up telling her the truth. I was living in a group home and didn't have much. That's when she invited me to stay at her dorm with her. I thought I finally had a good break for a change. That I had a friend. That feeling didn't last very long.

When we get inside there's a lot of new pieces here I haven't seen before. I'm actually surprised Neil wanted to come. He's never been interested in art as far as I knew. He always yelled at me for wasting time with "bullshit." He's walking around all excited. Pointing to things and asking me questions. It's weird. But he has been on this nice kick lately.

I wander away to the student exhibit. There are paintings, 3D installations, portraits and even original clothing. A piece that works with paper manipulation catches my eye. It looks like black construction paper on a white board. The paper takes on many different shapes and it's following a pattern. There are four different squares with four different designs. It's beautiful. I trace my finger along the zigzag line.

"Sorry. You can't touch the artwork." I turn around and see a beautiful woman.

I immediately jerk my finger away. "I'm so very sorry. I-I didn't know." Instinctively I look to the floor. The woman's high heel shoes appear right in my eyesight, next to my converse.

"It is beautiful though, isn't it?" I look up and nod even though she's not looking at me. She has hair as dark as coal and it shines as bright as the sun. Her skin is the color of nice sweet caramel. I can tell her nails are freshly manicured. The pale pink polish sparkles. I notice my own chipped orange nails and stick them in my pockets.

"So what brings you in today? You know anyone from the exhibit? " The lady smiles at me. I've never seen her before. She must be a new employee.

"Oh, no. I'm just here with a friend."

As if on cue, in walks Neil. He puts on a happy voice but I can tell he's annoyed.

"Vanessa! What a surprise. And you've met my daughter."

So this is the famous Vanessa. This is why he brought me here.

Vanessa looks surprised. Maybe a little upset too. "Your daughter?" She looks at me and then back to Neil. "What are you guys doing here?" She smiles but her voice tells a different story.

"I'm taking your advice. Having a little daddy, daughter time. Simone here is an artist herself. I thought she'd like this."

Why the hell is he calling me his daughter?

It looks like Vanessa rolls her eyes at Neil before turning back to me. "You're an artist?"

I glance at Neil before I answer. He gives me his "don't fuck with me" face.

"I guess. I draw portraits sometimes. But I'm more into landscapes." I look at Neil as I talk to Vanessa.

"Well I would love to see your work. Maybe you can be in this museum too."

"You can come by anytime." Neil interjects. He doesn't like when the attention isn't on him. "You know, to look at her things and give her advice or whatever."

Obviously Neil is trying to impress Vanessa and get

her to like him. Just like he did with me. He doesn't care
about my work. I don't know if Vanessa is buying what he's
selling but he sure wants her to. I've never seen him this
sweaty and nervous before.

I walk around and look at different pieces while he
and Vanessa talk. I pretend I'm not paying them any attention
but I am. He's all fidgety and smiling all over the place. It's
hilarious. I'm not sure what his angle is and what he's up to
but I'll play along for now. This could be entertainment for
me. It's not like I get a lot of that. He also can stay off of my
back if he's occupied with someone else.

I go back over to them. Neil is trying to get her to go
out somewhere with him. She doesn't seem interested but it's
Neil she's talking to, he doesn't notice or care.

"So, Vanessa...you and my dad are dating?" I see Neil
look at me in my peripheral vision but I don't turn my gaze
away from Vanessa's perfectly shaped face.

"Um, not exactly. I mean we've gone on two dates but
I wouldn't call us a couple." She nervously laughs and
touches her hair. Neil doesn't like her answer. His chest is all
puffed up and I cut him off before he gets a word out.

"You're not interested in a third date? I mean look at
him? Why not, you know what I mean?"

She blushes. "I-"

"It would be nice having another woman in the house.
We could have girl talk." I don't know where I'm finding
these words but they sound good coming out of my mouth.

And it's nice seeing Neil squirm for once, with all the shit he's done to me. I'm sure I'll pay for this later but right now I like it. "Come on. It'll be a family date. I never have anyone to share my art with. It'll be fun." I give her a big flashy smile and twirl a red curl in my finger. I've seen this work for Amber plenty of times.

She hesitates. I grab Neil's arm and give it a big squeeze. "My dad would love it. We're not leaving until you say yes." I smile again. I look up at Neil and give him a wink. If she agrees it's no way he can be mad at me.

It seems like an eternity before she finally says, "How could I say no to you? You're adorable. Sure I'll come by."

ooo

Neil is pissed. I swear I can see actual smoke coming from his ears the whole ride home. His knuckles are snow white as he grips the steering wheel. His turns are sharp and his stops are crazy hard.

"This is why I can't take you anywhere Simone! Why the fuck did you embarrass me like that? Be a little nice to you and look what you do. You shit all over it, every time."

"Neil-" he looks at me with murder in his eyes. "Sir, I don't see what I did wrong. I went with whatever you told her. I got her to agree to go out with you. I did a good thing."

"I don't need your fucking help."

"Sir please, I wasn't trying to disobey you. I promise. She likes you. I can tell." *And I'm really Paris Hilton on her way to her mansion.* I hope this Vanessa really shows up. If she doesn't I really just dug my own grave. And for what? A laugh? *God I can be really stupid sometimes.*

ooo

Neil puts me straight to work as soon as I walk through the front door. Clean this, fix that, put that away. I should've changed my name to Cinderella a while ago.

We don't have that much time before Vanessa gets here and he wants the house spotless. He was much more casual when he met me. Maybe he's trying to go the extra mile because she does seem pretty fancy. She's probably got high standards. The kind I could've had if I had a different life. If my parents were still here.

Now that I think about it she's probably the reason Neil has been so nice lately. Maybe they talk about me and he feels bad for always being mean. I wouldn't care at all if he had a relationship with her. I know what happens between us isn't right. I'm not that dense. I like when he's affectionate and good to me, but those days are far in between. I would love it a lot more to be rid of Neil altogether. The way I see it, Vanessa is the answer.

CHAPTER ELEVEN
VANESSA

I was not expecting to see Neil today, let alone his daughter. I also was not expecting to agree to spend another evening with him at his home. But his daughter seems like a really sweet kid. If she comes from him how bad can he really be? Aundrea may have a point. I could try to give this guy a fair chance.

I have been getting along with Christian lately. I've been spending a lot of time at his place and him leaving me a rose as an "I'm sorry" was really sweet. But we're not dating exclusively to my understanding so what can it hurt to explore my options?

Abigail sneaks over to me and taps my shoulder. "Just letting you know I'm leaving for the day." Her golden hair is in a high bun. She's wearing a red sweater today, a nice change from her favorite green one. Her fingers are covered in different sized rings.

"Okay. Thanks for letting me know. I'll see you tomorrow."

I begin to turn away but Abigail lightly grabs my arm. "Um, Vanessa?"

"Yes?"

Abigail has a worried look on her face. She pushes her glasses up the bridge of her nose.

"Never mind. Have a good night." She turns on her heel and walks so quickly out of sight that her sweater flaps its wings behind her.

ooo

I almost want to stop home after this long day and just shower and sleep. But I made a promise so I'll stick to it. If I don't show up at Neil's tonight who knows, he may pop up at my job again. So I'll go and get this over with.

I hear a lot of different noises inside before I knock on the door. Feet shuffling, furniture moving, a vacuum. I knock really hard so that someone will hear me. I see the curtain flutter at the corner of my eye and then hear the sound of the lock turning. The vacuum stops and the front door swings open.

"Hope you like Chinese!" Neil is beaming in the doorway. He's changed since he left the museum. He's wearing dark wash jeans and a navy pullover sweater. A pleasant surprise.

It smells really nice too. Like cherry blossoms and fresh candles. I step inside and see Simone rolling the vacuum down the hall into a closet.

"Yeah, sure. I love Chinese." I set my purse down on the couch and we all three walk into the kitchen. There's a buffet lined up on the counter and three wine glasses sitting on the table. *He lets his 16 year old daughter drink?* "Where are the plates?" I ask Neil.

"I'll make our plates. You just have a seat."

Simone follows him to the cabinet that holds their dishes and he turns to her and says, "You too. Go sit down." She hesitates before she turns around and sits next to me. Neil piles our plates with almond chicken, white rice with gravy, egg rolls and vegetable fried rice. He pours a dark red wine into all three glasses and sits down. He smiles and rubs his hands together.

"Simone would you like to say grace?" Neil's eyes are bright and so is his smile.

Simone looks taken aback by his request. "What?" She looks at me. I just smile and shrug my shoulders.

"Grace. Bless the food so we can eat." Neil reaches out both of his hands for each of us to hold. He doesn't wait for Simone to begin speaking before he closes his eyes and bows his head.

The silence seems like forever before I finally hear Simone say, "Dear Lord, please bless this food we are about to eat. Let it nourish our bodies and keep us healthy. Amen."

"Amen." Neil and I speak in unison.

The food is really good but I have to hold my breath every time I take a sip of wine. I normally stay away from red wine. It's so bitter and I like my wines sweet. I don't want to offend Neil though so I just pretend it's delicious.

"So, Simone what school do you go to?" The room

went quiet. No more clattering of forks and sips of drinks. Their eyes were locked on each other's. Simone began sputtering out words but couldn't make a sentence.

"Um, well. I-I uh.." She giggles. Then Neil speaks up.

"She attends Okemos High."

I scrunch my eyebrows. "Okay. Well, do you like it there?"

"Um, I guess it's okay. I don't have many friends so it can be kinda boring."

"Having a lot of friends isn't so important. You're there to focus on your studies."

"That's what I always tell her," Neil says.

"You know, I always say your family are your best friends. Hanging out with siblings and cousins is so much more fun."

Simone then looks really sad and says, "Well I don't have any family. It's just us."

In that moment my heart aches for Simone. This young girl doesn't have a woman figure in her life. She has no family or friends. It's just her and her dad. I have no idea how lonely that can be. So when she invites me over for movie night in a few days I have to say yes.

I leave feeling better than I did on the way there. I'm glad I could come and keep those two company. My stomach is nice and full and my brain is nice and relaxed when I finally reach my long lost bed.

ooo

I get to work the next day in a great mood. It's my half day. The perks of being the manager here. The student exhibit is ending in a few days. I'll have to find something else for Abigail to do for the rest of the semester. Maybe I can set up some type of workshop that she can oversee. I send her a text to come meet me in my office.

Abigail walks in wide eyed but still looks sleepy at the same time. Her frizzy golden curls fall to her shoulders. She has on a baby blue pin striped shirt, khakis and her favorite pea green sweater.

"Hey Abigail. How are you this morning?"

"I'm okay. A little tired but I'll make it." She yawns as she takes a seat at my desk.

"Fun party last night?"

"No. I was studying. Finals are coming up."

"That's right, they are. Well speaking of the year winding down I have a cool idea. What do you think about overseeing an art workshop here after the student exhibit is over? I was thinking we could split the days up into age groups. Like one day we can have arts and crafts for elementary kids, painting for middle schoolers, 3D installations for high schoolers and that kind of thing."

Abigail pushes her glasses up before she answers me.

"That sounds fun. Yeah I would love to do that."

"Okay, great. I'll work out the details and get a schedule to you."

Abigail just smiles and fidgets in her seat. She's really quite pretty when you look past her wardrobe. She gets up to leave but then I stop her with a question.

"You said you graduated from Okemos high school, right?"

"Yeah. Why?" Her hand still grips the doorknob.

"Did you know a girl named Simone? She would've been a few classes after you. Pretty light brown skin, freckles, red hair?"

"No, not from high school. But there was this girl Simone with that description that used to go here, I think. She hung around my old roommate all the time. "

That's odd.

"Okay. Well, we can't be talking about the same girl. No big deal. I'll let you know when the schedule is done."

All I see is a puff of gold hair leave my office.

A few hours later I head home. I love leaving early. There's no traffic. The sun is high in the sky and I have all day to do whatever I want. I decide it's a good day for gardening. I haven't touched any of my flowers since the snow melted a month ago.

When I get inside I head straight for my closet. I put on some old "Mom" jeans, a pale yellow polo and pumpkin seed shoes. I grab a white sun visor and head out back to the shed.

I come out with my gloves in my back pocket. I have seeds in my right hand and my trowel in my left. I'll have to stop by the store to get more plants. Something exotic.

I have an iPod dock and speakers set up in the patio area. With wood flooring, columns and panels overhead, it's the perfect relaxation place at night. At night is where you can enjoy the lights I have intertwined through all the panels.

I plug my iPod in and turn to Lana del Rey. Her voice gets me nice and calm. I'm on my hands and knees digging away and humming along to Lana's soft crooning voice.

I used to help my mom in her garden all the time. There were flowers on top of flowers and plant after plant. There wasn't any grass, just dirt and stones. You felt like you were at some far away spa oasis. The only downside were all the bees. They swarmed all around the house during summer time. So I decided to take a more sensible approach to bringing beauty to my home. My grass is always cut and lined perfectly. I have two spiral topiary trees greeting you at my front door. Flowers line the walkway in the front and back of the house. The bench swing in the backyard is under a blue moon wisteria canopy. It's my little paradise.

A car pulls into the driveway next door. Nancy, my neighbor, steps out of the car. Her bright red toe nails dance in the sunlight. Her white hair looks freshly curled. She's obviously spent her day getting pampered.

"Hi Nancy! Beautiful day, huh?" I wave to her as I walk over to the fence separating us.

"It sure is." She takes a look at my attire. I have dirt on my knees and shoes. "Are you doing some gardening?"

"Yeah. I figured I should be productive somewhat today." I laugh and place my hand on my hip.

"Well your gardener was actually here yesterday morning. You weren't here so I told him I'd give you the message."

"My gardener?"

"Yeah. He was a middle aged fellow. Kind of tall and a bare face."

I just stare at her confused.

"He said his name was Tom."

"I don't know a Tom. I don't even have a gardener. I do it myself. Are you sure he was looking for me?"

"He said Vanessa. I saw him in your backyard and that's when I asked him what was going on. He seemed kind of odd."

"I have no idea what that could've been about. But thanks for letting me know."

Nancy smiles and waves a goodbye as her kitten heels carry her into her house. I'm left standing at the fence confused and worried.

Who is Tom? And why was he in my backyard?

CHAPTER TWELVE
SIMONE

Tonight is movie night. Surprisingly, Neil is letting me pick what we will watch. I think a comedy will be the best choice. Laughing always helps to loosen people up. I remember watching "Houseguest" years ago with my parents. My mom loved it. I thought it was funny too. Neil doesn't have the movie so he's out on the hunt for it. This whole Vanessa thing is amazing. Neil is in the best mood I have ever seen. I even heard him singing in the shower! I had to peek in the bathroom to make sure it was him.

When I woke up this morning Neil already had breakfast made, something that hasn't happened in over a year. He made french toast with scrambled eggs and oatmeal. I didn't even know he could make french toast. It was perfect with cut strawberries on top. Like my mom would've made it.

Everything is still cleaned and neat from the other day. I don't have much to do besides wait for them both to get here. It's such a nice day. Birds were chirping early this morning. The sun is shining. There isn't a cloud in the sky. It's days like this that I wish I could be normal and actually enjoy the weather. Enjoy the beauty outside. Have someone to go swimming with, or fly a kite, fishing, anything. The green grass is calling for me to come out, to keep it company.

But I have to ignore it. I've been doing good and I don't want another lockdown.

As I lay on the bed with my eyes closed, my mind keeps going back to the basement. The dampness of the air, the cold traveling from my toes up to my scalp, that damn mattress. No, I definitely don't want to spend any more weeks down there.

When I wasn't down there alone in the dark, Neil would be near in his secret room. He never spoke to me on his way in or out. He always seemed in such a rush on his way down the steps. It was like a stampede. But on his way upstairs it was as if he didn't have a care in the world. He walked slow and smooth and his tense body would be relaxed. I have no idea what's in there and that scares me. Knowing Neil, I can't imagine it to be something pleasant. Then again he seems calm when he leaves the room so maybe it is good. I want to know as much as I don't want to know.

I hear the front door slam shut. Big feet trample the floor and fly down the basement steps. Neil is going to his secret room. I tiptoe out of my room and walk down the hallway and turn left into the kitchen. On the kitchen counter is the movie "Houseguest." *He actually found it.* Before I can make it all the way to the basement door I hear another door shut. I peek downstairs and see light coming from up under Neil's secret door. I was too slow. I don't want to linger too long just in case he opens the door unexpectedly.

I decide to go back into my room and I take the movie with me. Sinbad's head is poking out of a mailbox and his face is smiling right at me. I hear Mama's big hearty laugh and Daddy's little chuckle. I really miss them.

I'm not sure how much time has passed but after a while Neil comes into my room. He hangs in the doorway for a bit then says, "Get ready." He goes into the bathroom and shuts the door.

I look down at my destroyed jeans, on purpose of course, and blue jean shirt. *I thought I was ready.* I didn't know movie night had to be so formal. I technically don't even own anything nice. Everything is casual.

I change my jeans to ones without holes in them and put my unruly curls up into a bun. I slick my edges down with olive oil edge control. My brush lays my hair down wavy and perfectly. I take my hoops out and switch them to diamond stud earrings. I don't think they're real diamonds though. They're from Neil.

With my hair pulled back I can see the tiny scar along my hairline given to me by Amber. I wince as I remember the pain done to me by my once friend and "cousin." The emotional pain much more long lasting than anything physical.

"Simone! What the fuck are you doing?! I take the wrap for us and this is what you do?" Amber looks from me to Corey with daggers in her eyes.

"Amber, we're not even doing anything. I swear." I

move from Corey's lap and reach to give Amber a hug. She snatches her arm from my grasp. "I was just really worried about you. We were just talking. I wouldn't do that to you."

"Liar. You don't give a shit about me. You've been using me. Don't think I don't see through your bullshit Si-Si. You left me to get arrested so I'd be out of the picture. You want to be me!"

"I do not and did not. I freaked, I'm sorry. But you know why the police can't find me. You're my best friend." Amber's eyes seem to soften a bit but she still has a scowl on her face. Her shoulders are stiff and her fists are balled at her sides. "I mean you weren't even really arrested." Wrong thing to say.

"Fuck you Simone! Get the fuck out of here and don't ever come near me or Corey again."

"I don't want Corey. I swear to God Amber it's nothing like how you think. Corey tell her." I look at Corey for support but I don't get any.

"Amber I don't know what her problem is. She just kept pushing herself on me. I tried to stop her but she wouldn't quit. I just gave up. I'm sorry." This little piece of shit.

"He's lying! Amb-" Before I can finish my sentence Amber lunges at me. She punches my cheek and grabs a fistful of my hair. She pushes me hard to the ground but before I hit the floor my head hits the corner of the coffee table. She sits on top of me and rains punches on my head. I

don't fight back. There's blood seeping from my head
staining the wood floor. She finally gets up and spits in my
face.

"Bitch. I'm going home and don't even think about
coming." Amber leaves and Corey runs after her.

I stare at my reflection, not even knowing who is
looking back at me. Simone, Mo, Si-Si? I turn away and call
out to Neil, "I'm ready."

ooo

Surprisingly, neither Neil nor Vanessa have seen
"Houseguest" before. I can't help but to laugh and tell them
"Watch this part," before every funny line as if they aren't
already watching. Neil gives me a couple of evil looks so I
have to try to be quiet. Vanessa doesn't seem to mind though.

She's wearing peach colored pants that are rolled up
at the ankles. She has on a crisp white shirt and a dainty gold
necklace. Her hair is in loose curls that fall in her face. She
even brought food. Homemade nachos loaded with cheese,
sour cream, beans, chicken, guacamole and jalapenos. I've
never had chicken in my nachos before and man is it good.

"Do you make these all the time? They're so good!"
My mouth is full with chips and cheese. I cover my mouth as
I talk. I don't want food flying everywhere. I take a big gulp
of coke.

"Thank you. Yes, I make all kinds of food. When I
was younger I used to help out at my Dad's Mexican

restaurant. Some authentic dishes and some more Americanized ones too. Maybe next time we can have chimichangas or tamale."

"Yes, please. I love Mexican food. Any food really." I smile as I stuff another chip into my mouth.

"I'm more of an Italian food kind of guy. Can you make that stuff?" Neil chimes in.

"Of course I can. I mean, what's so hard about pasta? Anybody can cook that." Vanessa laughs and I can tell she's joking. Neil isn't too fond of jokes.

Neil doesn't respond. He justs turn his attention back to the movie, just in time to see Sinbad's "best friend" shove his ice cream cone into his boss's face. I burst out laughing and my elbow knocks my glass to the floor. Coke spills everywhere. I jump up really fast and dart to the kitchen to grab some paper towel. I frantically clean up the mess and I can feel Neil's eyes on my back. I mutter "I'm sorry. It was a mistake." Vanessa touches my arm and I swear I jump out of my skin. I can feel that my eyes are open big and wide. She looks at me with a strange look. Sympathy?

"It was a mistake, really." I still haven't looked at Neil.

"I'm sure it's okay." *No it's not.* "It's just pop. No one is hurt." *I will be.* "Here, I'll help you." Vanessa grabs the wet paper towel from my hand and tosses it into the kitchen trash. She comes back with more and wipes the rest of the floor dry. "See, just like new." She helps me back onto the couch and we watch the rest of the movie without me making another peep.

As soon as Vanessa walks out the front door I hurry to my room. If only I could close the door without making things worse. To my surprise Neil doesn't come after me. I hear him gather the dishes and the sound of the kitchen sink soon follows. I tiptoe down the hall and peek my head into the kitchen doorway. His back is to me. He reaches into his back pocket and pulls out a key. He walks towards the basement door with Vanessa's nacho dish still in his hand. The steps creak as he walks down the stairs. He leaves the basement door slightly cracked behind him so I'm able to peek through without making any noise.

I hear the sound of a key and lock turning. He pushes open the secret door and flicks the light on. I'm only able to catch a glimpse of old looking furniture before he closes the door behind him.

CHAPTER THIRTEEN
NEIL

I can't get Vanessa out of my head. Good thoughts. Bad thoughts. I don't know what to think anymore. She came over for movie night the other day. I was so excited to see her. I didn't even care that Simone picked out some shitty movie for us to watch. But I did care that she was taking all of the spotlight. She had to sit next to Vanessa. She had to laugh the loudest. She had to let you know that she's seen the movie before. And Vanessa was eating it all up. She barely said two words to me. She was there to spend time with me, not Simone! *Right?*

I haven't called her. I'm waiting for her to make the first move. I know she will this time. She has to. If not, Thursday is right around the corner. There won't be any Simone. She can't ignore me then. I could bring her a gift, maybe more roses. She never even thanked me for the other one I left for her now that I think about it. *Maybe she didn't know it was from me. But why wouldn't she know?*

I'm sitting on the couch, staring at the blank tv screen when Simone walks in.

"Sir?" She's twiddling her thumbs together.

"Hey, go get me a beer." For once she doesn't

hesitate. She walks into the kitchen, grabs me a cold beer and looks at me with those big eyes. I nod my head letting her know it's okay to speak.

"Can I sit on the front porch? It's really nice out and I can use some fresh air."

"You could use some fresh air?" I raise my eyebrow and twist my lip. "What do you need fresh air for?"

"I mean I've been inside ever since the museum. It's getting claustrophobic in here."

"Claustrophobic? Nice word. Where the hell are you hearing words like that?" I set my beer down on the coffee table and lean down onto my knees.

"Neil I'm not an idiot." She rolls her eyes.

"Oh, you're not?" I sarcastically laugh at her.

"I just want to sit on the porch. What's so bad about that? You were just starting to be nice again." Her voice is whiny and it makes my skin crawl. My fists instinctively ball up and I have to take a deep breath before I speak.

"Will you ever not be ungrateful? I do everything for you. You don't have to do shit but sit around all day. If it weren't for me you'd be living on the streets looking for a buck. Just starting to be nice again?" I laugh again. "Don't even fucking try it. I can get rid of you in a second."

"No you can't. I'll tell everything Neil. You'd be in big trouble." She places her hands on her hips in a confident stance. But her eyes are worried.

I stand up and get right in her face. Towering over

her. "Are you threatening me Simone? Don't forget I can make you disappear you little cunt."

"Then how would you keep Vanessa? She'd be wondering where I've gone. What are you going to tell your precious Vanessa?" Her lips are trembling. I can tell she's nervous. *So why the fuck is she testing me?* I could knock her fucking head off right now and nobody would care. She has nobody. Nobody but me. Fuck Simone.

"Go to your room *Mo.*" She hates when I call her that. She told me when she first got here that her parents used to call her Mo. She was so emotional telling me about them. Her eyes were never dry. Nose always running. I had to pretend like I cared. I needed her, she was beautiful. She is beautiful. And she's right. What would I tell Vanessa if she's gone? My head is pulsing. *Fuck!*

She makes me crazy. Her red curls tumble down her back. Her freckles look like a map. A map to destruction. She looks up at me with those golden green devil eyes.

"I don't want to see your face for the rest of the day." My voice is low and dry.

I wait until she goes in her room before I fall back into the couch. I hold my head in my hands. I'm in a fucking mess.

ooo

My days have been running together. I don't know if I'm coming or going. I'm more fidgety than normal. My sleeping is erratic. I'm more hostile than usual, which is a big feat. I have a void that is eating away at me. Only Vanessa can fill it. Not Simone, but Vanessa. Every time I think of her or say her name my tongue swells up. My temperature rises. My whole body tingles.

I hate Simone more every day. She doesn't make me feel the way Vanessa does. No one ever has. All the searching and all the failures have led me to her. I knew it would happen eventually. It had to. A win is bound to happen after so many laughable losses. And Simone was definitely a laughable loss.

Simone seemed so innocent and helpless when she first caught my attention. I used to see her walking around during the day with a sketchbook in her hand and a pencil sticking out of her pocket. I would watch her. She would go to different parks and draw. She would go to different spots on the college campus and just sit for hours. The occasional sleeve would go up to her cheek and wipe what I assumed were tears. Her clothes were ratty and old looking. Her shoes had seen better days. But I saw through all of that. I saw her. Or so I thought.

The more she hung around the campus though, the more she blossomed into my "it girl." I noticed some dark haired, blue eyed girl she started hanging around with. With Blue Eyes around Simone's clothes got better. Her big round tits stood out more. Even her hair looked curlier and brighter.

I never saw her actually going to any classes. I

thought maybe her classes were while I was at work. She had to be a student at the university right? Wrong. Her ass was so round and her lips were so full, just ready to be wrapped around my cock. How was I to know she was only 15? I have to admit when I found out that little information I wasn't mad at all. I was excited. Nice and ripe. Ready to mold and be exactly who I wanted her to be. I was the knight and shining armor who saved her. But obviously Simone doesn't think so. She's nothing but a little bitch.

I should've known something was wrong with her. If not, somebody else would have snatched her up already. Why was the most beautiful piece of ass I'd ever seen homeless and on the street? But I couldn't help myself. I still get hard thinking about her, when I can separate her body and face from who she really is.

She acts like she's never done anything wrong. Like I'm the big bad wolf. Like I should feel sorry for her because she's an orphan. She should be happy she's an orphan. That led her to me. But she doesn't appreciate me. My gut tells me Vanessa will.

Vanessa is different. She's easy on the eyes. She's smart. She's sophisticated. She's everything I've ever wanted but didn't think I would ever get. Why would a woman like her want a guy like me? She has a job. Doesn't need me for money. She has a house. Doesn't need me for shelter. I waited so long to speak to her and let myself known because I couldn't think of a way I could persuade her onto my team.

But she came willingly. She's giving me a chance and I'm going to make sure she loves me the way I love her.

ooo

"Dad is Ma coming home today?" I haven't seen Ma in weeks. She told me she was going to work but Dad has never been at work this long.

"Your Ma ain't coming back." Dad is sitting on the plaid sofa with his favorite tank top and boxers on. There are four beer bottles by his feet. He's halfway done with the one in his hand.

"But she said she was coming back after work. What's takin' her so long?" My voice squeaks and Dad hates that. He throws his beer at me. It smashes into the wall, just missing my head. The wall bleeds beer and bubbles.

"Boy didn't I just tell you your Mama ain't coming back. Your Mama is nothing but a whore, that's what she is. She ain't got no job. She's gone."

"But...but she said-"

"I don't care what she told you! She don't want you! And she sure as hell don't want me so forget about her." Dad's fat face wobbles as he yells at me. Spit flies from his mouth. He's as red as the tomatoes I eat on my burgers.

Tears sting my cheeks and Dad gets up and smacks them right off.

"What the hell I tell you about crying boy?! What did I tell you?"

My head bangs on the wall each time he shakes my shoulders. I cry more.

Dad throws me on the floor and gives me a good kick. "Stupid kid."

ooo

I wake up kicking the sheets away from my body. My lungs are empty and I look around for help and Vanessa is lying right next to me. Her slender fingers touch my clean shaven cheek. She smiles at me.

"It's okay Neil. It was just a dream." Her voice seems muffled. Like I have cotton shoved down my ears.

I blink hard two times and she disappears.

"Vanessa!" I throw the sheets everywhere. I lift the mattress with one arm. Under the bed, in the closet. She's not in here. I sit on the edge of the now naked bed and run my hands through my hair. *She was just here! Where did she go?* I stomp the floor in frustration.

"BEEP BEEP BEEP BEEP!"

I jump up ready to fight whatever, whoever has taken Vanessa. I look around and it's just me in the room.

"BEEP BEEP BEEP BEEP!"

Then what the hell is that noise?

As I get closer to my nightstand I realize it's just my alarm clock. I was ready to fight my alarm clock.

I unclench my fists and wipe the sweat from my face. I look down and my whole body is covered in sweat. I run to

the shower and wash myself so quickly that the water barely
has time to warm up.

I crack the bathroom door a little while I shave. As
the steam leaves the room I notice I don't smell breakfast.
There's always breakfast. What the fuck is Simone doing?

I throw on my jeans and t-shirt, giving Simone more
time to get her shit together. I take my time putting on my
socks and even comb my hair. Still, no smell of breakfast.

The kitchen is deserted. The lights are off. *That's
fucking it!* I storm past the refrigerator headed toward
Simone's room when I notice the calendar. Thursday. Today
is Thursday!

I suddenly could care less about Simone and her not
taking care of her duties. She doesn't matter right now. I've
been so distracted that I didn't even realize today is my day. I
don't even care that Vanessa hasn't reached out to me yet
because she'll see me today.

My feet unconsciously skip out of the house and I
have a big stupid grin on my face. If I wasn't me I would
want to knock me right down, call me a fairy. I'd be disgusted
with myself. I physically wipe the smile from my lips and
climb into my truck. My palms are sweaty as I try to grip the
wheel. My hands are slipping and I have to wipe them on my
jeans to help me out.

I couldn't have gotten to Vanessa's quicker. The drive
seemed like an eternity. I'm looking forward to seeing her
rush out of her front door. Zipping to her car with a focused

expression. I can't wait to see her suckable lips and shiny hair. Too bad I don't see any. She's not home, again.

Vanessa's car is not in the driveway. There are no lights on anywhere in or outside her house. I punch the steering wheel and the horn blows. I take a few minutes to calm my breathing before I get out of the garbage truck. My brain is all red with anger and I need to get it back to mellow.

The truck's door slams and I lean against it racking my brain on what the fuck is going on. *Why the fuck is she not here?*

I decide to get to work. I'm dumping things in the trash when I hear a door creaking open. It's the old bat next door to Vanessa's. I keep my head low and try to hide under the brim of my cap.

She's staring at me. Watching every move I make. I can't tell if she can actually see my face, if she recognizes me. She's holding her robe with one hand and the other is over her eyes like a visor.

The door closes and I peek to see where she went. The bitch is looking out her front window, holding the curtain slightly to the side. Looks like she's going to be a problem.

ooo

After work I find myself sitting in my truck outside of Vanessa's museum. My hands have a slight tremble. I look back and forth from my phone to my car door to the museum.

I don't know what I should do. I look in the rearview mirror and I look sick. My skin is pasty and my eyes are rimmed red as if I'd been crying. *Have I been crying?*

I'm filled with too many emotions for a man. I'm pissed Vanessa was who knows where doing who knows what. I'm confused as to why I haven't talked to her or seen her. I'm sad because I miss her. My heart is swelling and with each beat it feels like it will explode.

My finger hovers over her name in my call log. I don't blink and my eyes start to sting. I feel sweat forming on my nose and hairline. I just stare at her name.

My hand shakes much harder than before. It vibrates through my body. Then I realize it's my phone. It's ringing. Vanessa's name is plastered across the screen in big bold letters. I immediately duck down in my seat. I try to squeeze in the space between the steering wheel and my seat. *She knows I'm out here. She's going to confront me. The old bitch ratted me out.* I almost miss her call as I'm trying to hide. Out of breath, I finally answer.

"Vanessa? What a surprise." I peek over the dashboard, knowing I'll see her standing right there. But I don't. It's just me.

"Hey Neil. How are you?" She sounds normal. Not like someone who just discovered the guy who has been following her around.

"I, um, I'm okay." I say 'okay' as if I'm asking a question. "What's going on?"

"Nothing much. I'm calling because Saturday we're starting our art workshop program and I thought it would be something Simone would be interested in. So it would be every Saturday, Monday and Wednesday throughout the summer. Since she's high school age her time slot would be 4 to 6."

You mean to tell me she called me about motherfuckin' Simone?! I close my eyes and pinch the skin in between my eyebrows.

"Hello? Neil, what do you think?"

I take a second to calm my voice. I have to concentrate really hard not to clench my teeth and grunt the words out. "I think it's a great idea. She'll love that."

"Yeah. And it would be good to have some training before she starts college."

"Are you teaching this class?"

"No. Abigail will. I'll help out sometimes if we get slow enough."

I can't help but feel plotted against. This is Simone's doing. I know it is.

I slowly crawl from my hiding spot back into my seat. My back is on fire from being crouched down even in that short time. I look around the car from all angles. There is no one around. I see no faces looking from the museum's windows. I'm still alone.

Vanessa brings me back from my mini investigation, "So you'll bring her by Saturday?"

"You bet. We'll be here, I mean there." I slap my palm to my forehead. "Does she need to bring anything?"

"Just herself. Well, I've got to run." I see movement to my right. A woman is exiting the museum's front door. She's wearing an eggshell skirt that moves when she walks. Heels click on the pavement. There's a sea of black hair covering her face. She flips her hair back and I see she's holding a phone to her ear. It's Vanessa. "I'll see you then." She hangs up and I watch her place her phone inside her purse.

I've left my body. I'm looking at myself from outside of my truck. She gets closer and closer to where I'm parked and I can't move. My body is frozen.

She stops mid-stride and stares into space. She quickly turns around and walks back toward the building. She must've forgotten something inside.

My heart starts beating again and I fumble with the keys. I finally get them in the ignition and I back up. My truck is hidden behind a huge bush. There's a tree alongside the bush which casts a shadow on the windshield. There's no way she'll notice me when she comes back out.

It doesn't take long before I see her smooth legs walking around the building. She turns right on the sidewalk and walks about four or five cars up before she presses the remote key to her red wine Buick.

She takes forever to pull off, but when she does I creep behind her. I stay a good distance away. I even let a few cars cut in front of me. My eye stays locked onto her car. I have to make sure I don't trail too far behind and lose her. We make a few stops. She goes into a Home Depot and comes out with some flower shit and paint after what seems like forever. Then she stops at a grocery store. Being cooped up all day in my car normally would piss me off. But I'm on a mission to find out where little miss Vanessa has been hiding.

I'm disappointed. Vanessa goes home and I'm stuck parking around the corner. I spy from across the street, in the bushes of the corner house. Vanessa starts to take her bags in the house and on her second trip Old Bitch pulls into her driveway next door.

Her flabby ass slides out of the seat and she lifts her sunglasses from her eyes, letting them rest in her hair. They begin to talk and the old bitch is pointing to Vanessa's backyard to where the garbage truck was this morning. There's a lot of head shaking and hand movements. I can see the wrinkles on Old Bitch's fingers from here.

I duck down lower when they part and each goes into their home. I wait a good 10 minutes and then I'm right at the Old Bitch's front door. I look over my shoulders a couple of times as I knock.

"Who is it?" Heels click on the floor. I move to the side of the porch so she can't see me out of the peephole. "Hello?"

I never respond but the door swings open anyway. *What an idiot.* I push my way inside and slam the door behind me.

The floor is a marble of cream, gold and brown. The crystal chandelier overhead lights up the whole room. *Time to change that.* I turn around and find the light switch and the room is now dark. I lock the door and face my new friend.

"Wha- Who are you? Get out of my house!" She walks backwards with her wrinkled claws shielding her face and chest. She loses her footing and falls onto her staircase.

I bend down to her level and I'm looking eye to eye with her. I remove my hat so she can see me. I want her to know it's me. I smile, but it's not friendly.

"You!" She screams and lifts her leg as if to kick me. I catch her foot and slam it down. My left hand smashes her knee while my right hand squeezes her throat.

Old Bitch is hysterical. Her eyes bulge from her head. She kicks her one free leg. She tries to push my face away, even scratches me but I don't budge.

'That's right boy. Just like I showed you.' My Dad's rough voice cheers me on.

She's gasping for air and I enjoy seeing the life leave her. Suddenly her thumbs dig into my eyeballs. She pushes down so hard I have to be blind now. My grip loosens and she takes that opportunity to kick me in the balls and run upstairs.

'Well, shit. Don't fuck up now. Go get her!'

I have to hold the railing while I push myself up the stairs after her. I hear a door slam to my right. I wiggle the handle and it's locked.

I kick a few times and shove my shoulder into the door before it finally gives in. I catch her in time to see a phone in her hand. I snatch it and smash it against the wall.

"What do you want? I'll give it to you, just leave." Her eyes dart across the room and focus back on me. She's looking for an escape, too bad there is none.

"What have you been telling Vanessa?" My voice is dark and raspy. My skin is on fire and I can't think past my rage.

"What? I-I haven't told her anything! I swear. Please just leave." She's backed into the corner of the room with her arms placed on the walls to hold herself up.

Liar.

I take a couple of big steps towards her and raise my fist. Before my arm swings down Old Bitch lunges at me making me lose my balance. She jumps on my back kicking and screaming like a damn animal. I throw her to the ground and give her a good boot. That shuts her up.

'Just like your old man. I knew you had it in you.'

"You fucking bitch. You think I was going to let you ruin things for me?!" Another boot.

My Dad is cheering in my head. He finishes a beer and slams it in excitement. I've never seen him so happy.

Old Bitch is face down on the floor and she's not moving but I see that she's still breathing. I take a fistful of her white hair and lift her face. Her eyes are closed and her mouth is wide open. Blood covers her face. I scoop her up into my arms and carry her to her stair banister. I don't even bother giving it a second thought before I throw her over. Her body hits the chandelier and she falls with a loud thud. Crystals fall from the ceiling and land all around her.

I dash down the stairs and tiptoe up to her and see blank eyes. Her arms and legs are splayed around her at weird angles. Her hair is all over the place. There's blood leaking from the back of her head. It's pooling out turning her hair dark and sticky. The heels on the bottom of her shoes are broken. *Not so pristine anymore now are we?*

It's a beautiful sight before me. Dad pats my shoulder for a job well done. My heart swells with happiness and pride. A smile creeps up to my lips and spreads across my face. I've finally made my Dad proud.

I'm satisfied and it's time to go. Her purse sits on a small table next to what looks like a bathroom. Her wallet is cream with threaded patterns. It's lined with diamonds. Inside is $1,000 cash and a shit ton of credit cards. I stuff the cash in my back pocket and I walk out her front door with no remorse. She deserved everything she got.

CHAPTER FOURTEEN
SIMONE
15 years

I wake up on the hotel floor tangled in crisp white sheets. I'm wearing a t-shirt with the back cut out, that's barely long enough to cover my bare ass. I see a crumpled mess of hair to my right. Amber's hair. Her back is bare. I lift the sheets and see she's completely naked.

I see a couple of people scattered about. There's Sydney, Jessica, Corey and Jason. Amber's friends.

I'm the only one awake.

Jessica is lying next to Corey on the couch. Her arm rests on the waistband of his boxer briefs. Sydney is balled up in a big cushioned chair in the corner. And Jason is next to the couch, his back holding him up with his head resting on the arm. The queen sized bed is completely empty.

There are empty liquor bottles all over the place. Weed roaches in ashtrays and juice bottles. There are pizza boxes and empty chip bags overflowing from the itty bitty trash can. I don't remember much from last night because we were high off Xanax and weed.

I think there was a game of truth or dare and some card games I knew nothing about. I don't think I drank anything. I was too out of it from the pills. Yesterday was my first time trying Xanax. I'm definitely feeling the effects right now. My memory is shit.

What I do know is that Amber and Corey were glued together, so why he's lying with Jessica and I'm lying with Amber, I have no idea.

I see Jason do a 'wake up' stretch so I hurry and look for my pants. I find them on the bathroom floor crumbled into a ball. Black leggings. Jason walks in the bathroom just as I shimmy into my leggings. He doesn't even seem to notice me. He goes right to the toilet and begins to pee, right in front of me.

"Seriously?" My eyebrows furrow and my lip upturns towards my nostril.

Jason turns around, still aiming for the toilet bowl. He smirks at me. "Wanna give me a hand?"

I scoff at him. "You wish."

"I didn't have to wish last night." His smile grows larger. He shakes and leaves the bathroom without washing his hands.

"Asshole." No way did Jason and I do anything. I mean, I don't remember but there's literally no way. He's tall and gumpy. His t-shirts are always a few inches too short and his eyes are too close together.

I follow him out of the bathroom and see no one else has woken up yet. I look at the scene in front of me and feel slightly embarrassed that I don't know what led to being in a hotel room with five other people, an obvious party aftermath and questioning hook ups.

Jason stretches out on the bed and turns the tv on. He crosses his legs and stuffs his hand down his pants. He looks right at home and obviously isn't bothered like I am.

He catches me staring at him. "What's your problem?"

I blink away his question and join Amber on the floor. Her eyes are smudged black all around like a raccoon. She has her left hand up to her mouth like she might've been blowing it for warmth throughout the night. I shake her but she doesn't wake up. I shake her harder and she just grunts and turns over.

"Amber wake up." I whisper in her ear and shake her more. "We *have* to go, now." I'm talking through my teeth. She doesn't move so I get up and look for her clothes.

Jason has the tv so loud that everyone wakes up except for Amber. I see Jessica hug Corey before she peels herself off of him. His hand grazes her thigh when she moves. He catches me looking and grins. He sits up and reaches for the pizza box on the table and devours a slice.

"Amber!" I yell this time, tired of her playing opossum.

"Jesus Christ Simone! Leave me alone." She doesn't even bother to open her eyes.

"But I'm ready to go."

"Then go. No one's stopping you." Amber waves her

arm at me in a shooing motion. She buries her face into the crook of her arm and pulls the sheets over her head.

"But what about you?"

"I'm fine. Go."

I look around and no one seems to be paying us any attention. They've managed to put their clothes on from last night and they're all eating old pizza.

I look at Amber one last time before I slip on my sandals and head out the door.

When I get outside I notice the street signs. The hotel is at least 15 minutes away from campus, which would be a pretty long walk. Lucky me, it's a nice day.

Before I get out of the parking lot I hear a voice yelling behind me.

"Hey, Red!"

I turn around and see an older white guy jogging up to me. As he gets closer I recognize him as the man that saw me walking back to Amber's dorm from Corey's party a few weeks ago. *What is he doing here?*

"Hey, where you headed? You walking?" He reaches me and is slightly out of breath.

"Are you following me? Why are you here?" My arms are folded and I take a step back.

He laughs and fiddles with his hat. There are those icy blue eyes. "No. Just a coincidence I guess. I saw you walking out as I was checking out."

I don't remember seeing anyone in the lobby.

"Guess you didn't see me. What are you doing here by yourself?"

"I'm not by myself."

"You look like you're by yourself to me." The man stuffs his hands in his back pockets.

"Well I'm not. My friends are upstairs."

"So, what? You're just getting some fresh air or something?"

"I-" I can't think of a good reason without telling the truth. I look down at my feet.

"That ride still stands. What do you say?" The man shifts from foot to foot and he smiles when he looks into my eyes.

"I-I don't know."

"I don't bite. I promise." He holds his hands up in surrender. "I'm just trying to do the right thing. I see a nice young lady like yourself in need of help and I'm just trying to be a helping hand. It's just a ride. It won't kill you."

My mind answers a big fat 'No' but my mouth says, "Okay, sure."

I follow him around the side of the building to his black pickup truck. He gets in and I just stand at the passenger door holding the handle.

"Well come on. Get in."

I sit as close to the door as possible.

"So where are we headed?"

"Um, you can just take me anywhere on campus. I'll

find my way from there."

"It's no problem if I just take you home or to your dorm or wherever."

"The campus is fine, thanks."

His lip seems to twitch but he doesn't say anything. We ride in silence.

Once we make it to campus he drops me off in front of the library. I nearly jump out of the car.

"Thanks mister." I shut the door behind me and quickly walk away.

He rolls his window down and shouts after me, "The name's Neil, Red."

ooo

"Finally! I've been waiting forever," I say to Amber as she walks up to her dorm's entrance.

It's been a few hours since I left the hotel. I couldn't really do much at the library since I'm not a student and don't have a student ID. I sat by the river that cuts behind the library for a while. The ducks waddled about and looked at me for food.

I thought I was there longer than I really was. I don't have any means to keep up with the time besides asking people and I try to avoid talking to people as much as possible. I came to Amber's dorm an hour and a half too early. I figured she would've been back.

"It wasn't that long Si-Si." Amber rolls her eyes at

me. The dark makeup around her eyes now looks like an ashen gray instead of pitch black. And she managed to pull her crazy hair to the top of her head in a messy bun. Even with these changes she still looks as disheveled as she did when she was on the hotel floor.

"Well it was long enough."

We walk into the building and I head towards the elevators but Amber keeps straight ahead down the hallway. When I notice she's not next to me I run around the corner to catch up to her.

"Where are you going?"

"To The Den. My stomach is totally empty." Amber's belly growls on cue.

The Den is this cool spot on the first floor of most of the dorms. It's like a mini Starbucks and 7 Eleven all in one. It stays open longer than the cafeterias and is more convenient than even going to the cafeteria all together. It's a quick pit stop before, in between and after classes.

Amber orders mozzarella sticks and a slice of pizza. My stomach rumbles and she notices.

"You want something?"

"No, that's okay."

"It's cool. I'm using easy bucks anyway."

Easy bucks is basically money given to you by the university to spend on campus and some places off campus. The higher your meal plan the more easy bucks you get. Amber has the highest meal plan there is, so to her it's just free money.

"I'll have a slice of cheese pizza and a coke."

"She'll have a slice of cheese pizza and a coke." Amber repeats my order to the girl behind the counter.

When we get our food we sit at the corner booth hidden away. Her first two mozzarella sticks are gone in seconds. She picks up my coke and takes a very long sip.

"So Amber, you and Corey…" I hesitate to continue.

"Yeah?"

"Um, You guys are still a thing right?"

"Duh Si-Si. I mean we're not a couple if that's what you mean. But we're pretty much exclusive. He knows better than to hook up with some other girl. Why?"

"Well I saw him and Jessica together this morning."

"Yeah, they're friends. So what?"

"No, not like friends. They were sleeping next to each other. They hugged and touched and stuff."

"They hug each other all the time. I'm sure you didn't see what you think you saw. You don't know, you're only 15."

Amber dips her last mozzarella stick in marinara sauce. She gobbles the thing down without giving me a glance. What I've said hasn't phased her at all. You would've thought I told her that grass is green.

"I know what I saw Amber. I'm trying to help you out. Jessica isn't really your friend."

"So you're telling me that the girl who has been my

best friend since summer orientation freshmen year isn't really my friend and is scamming on my guy?" She laughs. "You're funny Si-Si."

"You're still a freshman. Amber listen-"

"Simone, drop it. She's my friend and she wouldn't do that. Stop being a troublemaker. Besides, you should be less worried about Jessica and Corey, and more worried about Calvin."

"What about Calvin?"

"You know what about. He keeps asking about you. Go out with him."

"I can't go out with him." I whisper even though there's no one near us. I feel my cheeks turn pink.

"Why not?" She gets up and throws out our trash. We make our way out of The Den back down the hallway to the elevators.

"Because I'm only 15. He's like 20, 21. He won't want me."

"Who said he had to know you're 15? God Si-Si. You're my 18 year old cousin. Remember that."

We get to her room. Her roommate Abigail is sitting at her desk with her face buried in a book.

"Just talk about fun stuff. Not school or your parents and stuff," Amber says. "It's depressing."

Amber flops down onto her bed and crosses her ankles.

Abigail looks over. "Gosh Amber. What happened to

you?"

"Fun happened to me Abigail. You should try it sometime."

"I do have fun. I just don't have to get drunk to do it."

"Study group is not fun." Amber laughs at Abigail. "You should come out with me and I'll show you a real good time. After you do something about that hair and those clothes though."

"What's wrong with my clothes?" Abigail's cheeks turn a rosy pink.

"Well you're in college dressed like my grandma. You need to loosen up."

"Leave me alone Amber." Abigail's voice is just above a whisper. She turns back to her book and her massive frizz covers her face.

"You people are way too sensitive for me." She gets up and heads to the bathroom. "Si-Si, wanna go out later? We can try to get into one of the bars on Grand River."

"Don't you have a final tomorrow? Maybe you should study."

Most kids my age would probably be jealous that I don't go to school. But I would love to be in a classroom, with people my own age and just being a normal kid. Something I took for granted.

Sometimes when I'm alone in Amber and Abigail's room I read their textbooks and notes, well Abigail's notes. I don't think Amber even takes any. I don't understand everything but it helps my brain not turn to mush.

"Abby here has done enough studying for the both of us." Abigail ignores her.

She's now standing in front of me, squeezing my hands as she bounces up and down. "Come on Si. School's almost over and I want to have some fun. Please?"

I sigh. "Fine. We can go out."

"Yes! I'm gonna go to Chelsea's room and see if she has a cute dress for me to wear." Amber saunters out of the room barefoot with a washed face and a spark of energy.

Abigail waits a few seconds after Amber has left to speak.

"Why do you hang out with her?"

"What? What do you mean? She's my friend."

"Amber is no one's friend. You seem like a good girl. She's a horrible influence."

I feel protective over Amber. Not since my parents died has anyone given a crap about me. Amber cares. Yeah, she can be a bit snappy sometimes but she's just outspoken.

"She is not! Amber and I are family and she has my back. Amber never says anything bad about you. You should think before you bad mouth her."

"Oh yeah? Well I happen to know a little thing or two about Amber. Do you? You've only been around for what? A minute? Why do you think she's around you all the time now and not her friends from first semester?"

"What's that supposed to mean?"

I tense up and I know my face is turning a deep red. Abigail is usually so quiet and to herself. I don't understand why she's saying these things.

"Nothing. Just forget I brought it up. I didn't mean to get into your business. I just thought that maybe you were...different."

When I first met Abigail she was sitting in the same spot, at her desk pushed up against the wall next to the window. Her hair was pulled back into a low bun and her glasses were at the tip of her nose just like a librarian. She wore faded blue jeans and a green cardigan.

She just gave me a closed mouth 'I'm just being polite' smile as a greeting. Amber never bothered to introduce us or give an explanation as to why I was staying in their small dorm. Abigail never asked either.

I pretended like I needed help in my writing and first year math class. Whenever it was just me and Abigail in the room I would pass Amber's books off as my own so that Abigail could tutor me. It didn't last long. She said she wanted to focus on her own work.

She was more than smart though. She was very artistic and creative. When she wasn't studying she was painting and making decorations for her side of the room. She often came with new sculptures to place in her territory that she said she made herself.

I never told her I was an artist too. Amber said I didn't want to blow my cover. She said if we got too close she would find out about my past and she wouldn't understand. So we ended up on a 'hi and bye' basis.

Amber barges back into the room.

"Okay, so Chelsea didn't have shit. We'll just go to the mall Si."

ooo

When we get to the mall we split up. It makes our "shopping" experience much easier. I've become a little expert at lifting clothes and shoes. Not having any money helped with that. I've had to take everything from tampons to deodorant. I never used to take clothes because I didn't care but being around Amber means I have to look good. Amber just steals for fun I guess. Her parents send her money every month but I don't know what she spends it on besides food and booze.

Amber let me borrow one of her oversized bags and by the time I leave it will be stuffed to the brim with new stuff. Forever 21 is my first stop. It's pretty much a one stop shop.

I grab a ton of tops and bottoms stacked so high I barely can see where I'm going. When I get to the fitting room the girl working tells me the limit is six items at a time. Easy. I pick any six and hang the rest outside my room door.

It takes a minute to get the sensors off but it's okay because it seems like I'm really trying things on. The trick is to pull the fabric away from the sensor and yank down really hard and it'll just pop off. This method leaves very small holes in the clothes but it's an easy fix. I've been knowing how to sew for years.

I swap out the things I don't want with the things I do. The fitting room girl is none the wiser. I keep five of the things I picked out. Leggings, a coral lace crop top, a white long sleeved prairie girl mini dress, jean shorts and a skin tight v-neck bodycon dress.

I put the loose sensors on top of the floor length mirror. The employees won't see them until the end of the day and it would be no way for them to know who did it. I walk out with a handful of stuff to pretend I've found my choices. I have tunnel vision as I head for the exit. I put the unwanted clothes on the closest rack near the exit and walk out without looking back.

By the time we meet back up at the bus stop I've gone to Forever 21, Bath and Body works, Victoria's Secret and Express. Amber is holding two stuffed bags. I don't know how she got away with that. We wait until we get back to her dorm before we pull everything out to show off our new finds.

Amber has a ton of cute stuff. She has all kind of accessories and short skimpy outfits. She loves to show off her body.

"So how are we going to get into a bar Amber?"

"I'm going to call some of my friends and see if anybody I know will be working the door. If they are then we're in." Amber holds up a navy dress that looks deep and royal next to her milky skin. It's long sleeved with sheer panels down the sides. "What do you think about this?"

"I like it."

"Cool. What are you going to wear?"

I hold up the v-neck dress I got today. It's a very soft pale blue. It almost looks white. "This one. But I don't know what shoes to wear."

"You can borrow my silver open toed heels. They'd look really good with that."

I cringe at the thought of borrowing any more of Amber's shoes. My feet took days to feel normal again after the party at Corey's house. But in my normal fashion I oblige.

"Okay, thanks."

Amber just smiles at me and flips her dark hair over her shoulder. I see Audrina's face and my heart aches a little. My mind wanders off to the last time I saw her.

ooo

"Mama can you take me and Audrina to get some ice cream before she leaves?"

Audrina came to town for the weekend for my birthday. Today is her last day here. We've had the best time.

"No sweetie. Audrina has a plane to catch soon and we don't want to be late. There's ice cream in the freezer if you want some."

Ice cream out of the freezer isn't the same as getting a blizzard from Dairy Queen.

"We'll just hang out outside." I leave Mama at the kitchen table and call down the basement stairs for Audrina.

"Drina! Come on, we're going outside!"

I hear her feet stomping up the carpeted stairs and she gets to the top with her hands over her head.

"How fast was I?"

"Seven seconds. I'm still the champion!"

We've been in competition all week. Who can get up the stairs the fastest, who can brush their teeth the fastest, who can eat their vegetables the fastest.

"Aww man." Audrina smacks her pink glossy lips. "How do you keep winning?"

"I don't know. I'm just good."

We walk through the white patio doors. The smell of flowers and fresh air hit my face. There's a small breeze and I notice the leaves and flower petals dancing in the wind.

I have a treehouse in the far left corner of the yard. It's so cool that it would make some grown-ups jealous. You barely even notice the tree with my house attached to it. It's big and brown with white trim. There's a two flight staircase to reach the front door. Mama put small hanging flowers down the railing and potted flowers around the base of the house.

There's a gold mail opening on the front door that reads "Simone." A small pink envelope sticks out of the *opening. I grab it and go into my treehouse. Audrina follows right behind.*

We go to the middle of the floor where there's a big fluffy orange rug. I open the note that was left in the door. There's a necklace inside. It's half of a heart, pink and sparkly with the word 'Forever' *on it. A note written in big curly letters tells me,* "I'm so glad I was here to celebrate your birthday with you. I had so much fun like we always do. I can't wait for Christmas! Best friends forever -Drina."

I look at Audrina and she's holding up the other half of the heart that reads 'Best Friends.' *Audrina's smiling and her big white teeth shine brighter than a box of diamonds. I give her a big hug and put on my new favorite necklace.*

ooo

"Simone, are you alright?" Amber's voice snaps me back into reality.

I shake Audrina from my brain and reassure Amber that everything is okay.

"I'm fine. I was just thinking."

"About what? You just had a blank stare on your face. I said your name like three times before you heard me."

"I can get really into my daydreams sometimes." I laugh. "It was nothing."

She gives me a weird look like she doesn't believe me. But she doesn't push it.

"We should totally straighten your hair tonight. Ooh

and do your makeup!"

"Makeup? Are you sure? And I don't even remember the last time my hair was straightened."

"Oh I just know it would be so pretty. Live a little Si-Si. Get sexy."

I don't know about sexy but I let Amber take control over my look. She always looks good so she must know what she's talking about.

I didn't think she would be able to get my hair super straight because our types of hair are completely different. But again, I look in the mirror and I love what she's done. She put a part down the middle and I'm looking at a long sheet of gorgeous red hair.

"Oh my God Amber! It's looks so good!"

I run my fingers through my hair and it's silky smooth. It feels so light and it cascades down to the middle of my back.

"How do you know how to do hair so good?"

"My mom is a stylist. I learned from her and I used to do all my friends' hair back in high school."

"You should get licensed." I turn to her and she's smiling. It's cool that she's happy doing nice things for me. Even if they're small.

"Maybe. Now let's get to your makeup. I learned from YouTube tutorials. I'm thinking smoky."

I listen to our back ground music as Amber paints my face. Techno music fills the room and we carefully bump to the beat. I look at her face and she has an intense look in her eyes. She's concentrated on every move she makes. She keeps biting her lower lip and her brow is slightly furrowed.

"Okay, all done." She stops and stares at me. On the surface she looks pleased. But there is a look behind her eyes that I can't quite read.

"You look great Simone." Amber's voice is soft and low. She's sitting on the bed with her legs bent and underneath her with her feet touching her butt. She looks down at her knees for a second and bounces off the bed.

I run to the mirror for what feels like the millionth time and I don't even recognize myself. I look so much older. And so good. The smoky eye makeup Amber did makes my eyes look greener than I've ever seen them. The soft subtle lipstick makes my red hair stand out.

"I look like my name should be something exotic. Like Esmeralda or something." I'm beaming. "I love it Amb! Now do yours so you can be...Franchesca!"

She rolls her eyes and says, "No thanks *Si-Si*. I'll always be Amber." She places her hand on her hip, raises her chin and flips her hair. She grabs her dress and goes into the bathroom. She looks back. "And you'll always just be Simone."

CHAPTER FIFTEEN

SIMONE
15 Years

Amber invited Chelsea to come out with us tonight. Chelsea called her older sister Brandi to come along too so that she could drive. We wouldn't be convincing as 21 year olds pulling up to a bar in a big ugly taxi van. At least not in this town. That was only for freshmen.

Brandi and Chelsea are sisters but you would never guess in one million years that they have the same parents. Chelsea is short and curvy with very pale skin. She has moles on her face and neck. Not gross moles, but pretty ones like the Mowry twins. Her hair is blonde, long and straight. Brandi on the other hand is tan with dark wavy hair. She's tall and thin with not a blemish in sight. Her lips are full and always in a pout.

Everyone seems so relaxed and sure we'll get in fine but I'm a nervous wreck.

"Are you guys sure we will be able to get in? I mean I'm nowhere near 21. It's no way this is gonna work?" I twist my fingers together and I know I look worried.

"You're close enough. And with your body no one

will question it." Brandi flips the mirror down over her head and reapplies her lipgloss.

"But Amber said her friend isn't working the door tonight!"

"So what? You're with me. If they ask for your ID show it to them. They won't care that you're only 18, because I'm not. And look at me. Trust me."

Amber whispers in my ear, "Simone you need to relax. You're going to fuck this up for all of us."

Chelsea and Brandi take a couple of shots of Patron right out of the bottle. Chelsea passes the bottle to Amber. She guzzles down some and dabs her lips with a napkin she took out of her purse.

It's my turn and the first sip burns my throat. I almost cough it back up but I don't want to look like an amateur in front of them. I squeeze my eyelids shut and drink some more. My whole body tingles and it feels like somebody turned the heat on.

Brandi tosses the liquor bottle in her trunk and we walk around to the bar's front door. The sign over head reads, "The Red Room." There is a roped off line of half-naked girls and guys that try to be cool. Brandi skips the line and we follow right behind her.

Brandi shows the guy her ID and squeezes his arm a little. She keeps smiling and talking to him as the shorter guy next to him searches her purse.

I start to get butterflies and I'm more jittery than

before.

"Amber, I don't even have an ID. What am I supposed to do?!" I talk through clenched teeth in her ear.

She slips me an ID of somebody named Zoe Bowman. She's 22 and from New Hampshire. She has dark brown hair, brown eyes and no freckles. We look nothing alike.

"I totally forgot to give you this earlier. Just smile and don't say anything."

"Where'd you get this?"

Amber doesn't answer me. She walks ahead to hand over her ID and her purse. When he looks at her ID he looks her over and it seems like he doesn't want to let her in. She whispers something in his ear and he nods his head for her to go on inside.

Now it's just me. I reluctantly give him the ID. I didn't bring a purse so I'm just waiting for his approval. I smile and look off into the crowd of people in the line. *God, please let me in this bar. I'd be so embarrassed to be turned away in front of all these people.* Obviously he buys that I'm Zoe or he doesn't care. He hands me back the ID and I walk past him with my heartbeat returning to my body.

Everyone's waiting for me just inside the doorway. Amber grabs my arm and pulls me alongside her. There are dimly lit red lights all throughout the building. There's a section of booths lining the back wall with red lit steps leading to the seats. A dance floor is in the middle of the room with red strobe lights shining on people's faces. The bar is to the right of the dance floor. There's a line at all angles waiting for drinks.

I notice just beyond the bar is a staircase. A couple of people head up the stairs.

"What's up there? Let's go see." I yell over the music, directing my question to any of the girls.

"It's like a second club. It's more mellow." Brandi leads the way to the staircase.

We walk up in a single file line holding each other's hands. There's three couches. One to the left as soon as you reach the top of the stairs, one on the back wall and another against huge windows overlooking the city. There's tables in front of each couch and a small bar to the right.

"Let's get some more drinks. I'm not even buzzed." Amber goes to the bar and leans over so her ass sticks out. I almost follow her but then I notice Calvin a few bodies away from her.

Calvin sees Amber and squeezes his way next to her. His hand makes its way to her lower back and he whispers something in her ear. Amber flips her hair back, as usual, and gives him a hug with her arms around his neck. She continues to talk to him with her hands on his shoulders. The only thing that breaks their contact is the bartender handing Amber her drink. They turn towards my direction. I hurry and look away. I don't want them to know I was watching. I find my way back to Brandi and Chelsea. They're sitting on the back couch with some guys and I join them.

Chelsea is flirting with this square jawed, muscle-y, handsome guy. He looks like he could be a model. She keeps batting her eyelashes and smiling really big. I wonder if he's even funny. Brandi doesn't seem too impressed with his friend. I'm sitting on the edge of the couch next to Brandi's admirer and I hear him trying his best to make conversation but she keeps shutting him down with one word answers. He obviously doesn't get the hint.

"Simone. Where the hell have you been hiding?"

I unconsciously jump at the sound of Calvin's voice. He's standing before me holding two glasses. His smile lights up the dark red room. I'm pretty sure if I stood close enough I would be able to see my reflection in his teeth.

"Come on, let's sit over here."

Without speaking I follow him to two empty seats by the window. It's automatic like a magnetic pull is between us.

"I got you a drink."

"What is it?" I take a sip and it's fruity but strong.

Calvin laughs and says, "Well it's a margarita. Amber told me you were already started on tequila."

"Oh yeah. It's just dark in here. I couldn't really see it." I try to cover myself. I don't want to seem inexperienced and young.

"Yeah, I'm sure that was all." Calvin smiles and agrees with me even though I know he knows I'm lying.

"So what have you been up to? I haven't seen you around."

"Nothing really. Just hanging out, working on my art I guess. I'm not that exciting."

"I doubt that." Calvin's eyes look right through me. They're smiling at me and I have a stomach full of butterflies.

"So you're still just visiting huh?" Calvin's drink is already gone and I'm not even halfway done.

"Yeah. I'm taking some time off from school."

"But it's only second semester of your first year, right? You need a break already?"

"Well I haven't started yet. I decided to start in the fall."

"You coming here?"

"Well, I'm not sure yet. I'm still deciding."

"If it was up to me you would stay here."

Calvin places his hand on my knee. My butterflies have intensified. I'm afraid to look him in the eye. I don't want him to know he has such an effect on me.

"Relax Simone. I'm harmless."

I look at his face. His brown eyes are kind and inviting. He smiles and shines those perfect teeth at me. I melt a little and my body loosens up. I hadn't even realized I was so tense.

"So, I didn't know you were into art. You should show me some of your work. Maybe I can hang some up around my place."

"Hang some up? Well how do you know if it will go with anything? You might not even like anything."

Calvin scoots in closer to me.

"Let me be the judge of that."

His hand touches my face and brushes my hair away from my cheek. My heart rate is through the roof.

"You look amazing," He whispers to me.

His lips brush up against my ear and I close my eyes when I feel the sensation he sends throughout my body.

"You wanna dance?"

Before I can answer, Calvin is standing and pulling my hand to follow him downstairs. We have to squeeze past people on the way down. He holds my hand the whole time.

The music is loud and energetic. I feel slightly tipsy so dancing comes easily. Our bodies flow together and we melt into each other. His hands explore me and my eyes explore him. It feels like it's just me and Calvin here, on our own private date.

In this moment I decide that I should forget my worries and fears and see what Calvin is all about. I just have to figure out how I'm going to hide my real self for long.

As my legs turn to noodles I leave the dance floor and find a few chairs nestled in a corner. I take a seat and Calvin sits right next to me. He scoots his chair closer and his leg touches my bare knee. A chill runs through me. It's amazing that he can make me feel the way he does without even speaking.

"What are you doing later tonight?" Calvin wipes sweat from his brow.

"I'm not sure. Amber will probably find some type of after party to go to. I'd rather go to sleep though."

"Come over my place. I'll take you back home in the morning."

I've never spent the night with a boy before, let alone a 21 year old man. I don't know how to act or what I should do once I'm there. But I don't want Calvin to lose interest in me after I've made up my mind that I'll try this out so I agree.

"Um, okay. I guess so."

"Really? I thought you'd say no."

"Why would you think that?"

"Because you're too good for me." Calvin's hand finds my fingers and give them a little squeeze.

Our gaze into each other's eyes is broken by Amber stomping her stilettoed feet in our faces. I look up at her and the Red Sea must have parted to let her through the crowd. She's standing there popping a piece of gum with her hands on her hips. I see a bunch of eyes on her. That's pretty normal for Amber. She always gets loads of attention.

"Simone where the fuck have you been? Aaron wants us to come back to his place for a party. There's gonna be all kinds of people there."

"Who is Aaron?" I no longer feel Calvin's touch on my fingers.

"The guy Chelsea met tonight. The model dude. He

says he has a brother." The excitement oozes from Amber's face. Another conquest.

"What about Corey?"

"You always have to have 21 questions don't you? It doesn't matter. We're hanging out with models tonight. Now come on."

I don't understand. Amber was the one saying I should pay attention to Calvin and go out with him. I'm trying to do that but she seems mad at me.

"But I had plans to go hang out with Calvin when we left here."

I look over at Calvin but he is no longer even paying attention. He face is in his phone and he's smiling at his screen.

Amber grabs my hand and pulls me from my seat. We take a few steps away and she whispers in my ear. Her voice is low but forceful.

"Si-Si I know you think you like Calvin but you'll probably like one of these guys better. I mean did you see Aaron? And he has a huge house. He told us. So I know this party will be the best. You have to come."

I look into Amber's eyes and it's like I'm looking into the ocean. I always get lost and she always convinces me to do whatever it is she wants. But something in me feels bad. I told Calvin I would go with him. I look over my shoulder and Calvin is still in the same spot we left him. His eyes are right on mine.

"But why do you need me to go? Chelsea and Brandi are going."

Amber rolls her eyes. "So what?!" Her voice sounds very irritated. "I want you there. You're my right hand man Si." She softens her voice. "Please?"

For the first time I don't go along with her plans.

"I'll go next time. I promise. But I really want to hang out with Calvin. I'll be back tomorrow."

I try to give Amber a hug but she pulls away from me. She doesn't give me a second look as she walks away and a dark sea of hair follows her.

ooo

I talk about Amber the entire ride to Calvin's place. I'm worried. I don't want her to be upset with me. She's my best friend and without her I have nowhere else to go, besides another group home and I can't do that again.

"She seemed really upset that I didn't go with them to the party. I think I hurt her feelings."

Calvin chuckles and says, "Hurt Amber's feelings? I doubt it."

"So why would she walk away from me when I was still trying to talk? You didn't see her face. She was sad."

"She'll get over it. You're family, she has to."

"I guess you're right."

I look out of the window and stare at the star lit sky. The stars are so bright that we barely need assistance from the street lights. I try to recognize some constellations Daddy used to show me but my mind is drawing blanks. So, I just make up my own. There's one for Mama, Daddy, Grandma, Papa, Audrina and even Ashley and Brittany. They're all close together. Mama leans on Daddy's shoulder. Grandma and Papa hold hands. Audrina, Ashley and Brittany are nearby sitting in the grass together. They're all looking at me with what I picture as smiles on their faces.

Calvin interrupts my daydream with a slam of his car door. I hadn't even realized we were here and already parked. To my surprise he comes around to my side and opens the door for me. He holds out his hand and guides me out of the car and into the parking lot.

The building is three stories high. There are white balconies lining the second and third floor. We get to the entry door and I see that the wood paneling of the building is a soft gray. Moths fly all around the light above our heads and some stick to the window. I unconsciously meld myself into Calvin's side to avoid one touching me.

Calvin's apartment is on the third floor. There are two flights in between each level. I would have loved to have taken an elevator but there are none so we climb the four flights of stairs. We reach the top and his door is the first one to the right. He uses a key card to unlock the door, like the kind you would use at a hotel.

Inside is nice and simple. Gray countertops and cabinets with silver handles. Black leather furniture. A glass coffee table with matching end tables. A 50 in flat screen tv is mounted on the living room wall. Gray curtains float on top of the white double balcony doors.

"You live here by yourself?" I help myself to a spot nestled in the corner of the couch.

"I have a roommate but he's never here so basically."

Calvin sits down and scoots next to me. He just stares with a smirk on his face. I suddenly feel self-conscious in my low cut dress. I look down and my cleavage is outrageous. I go to cover myself but he grabs my hands in his.

I don't know what to expect. My heart is beating out of my chest. He leans in closer to me so I lean in as well. He reaches past me and grabs the tv remote that was resting on the couch's arm.

Embarrassing.

The tv comes to life and within minutes and so does Calvin's snore. I sneak away and find his bedroom. I assume it's his because the other bedroom door was locked. His room pretty much looks like everything else in here. Black furniture with gray and white sheets.

I pull every drawer open until I find his white t-shirts. I peel my dress off and slip his big white tee on over my head. The fabric is cold and comfy. My feet feel amazing as they sink into the carpet. Wearing Amber's shoes is really a nightmare.

I don't bother to go back into the living room with Calvin. I stretch out and relax in his bed. The mattress hugs my body and the comforter is extremely soft. I don't know how he ever gets out of this bed.

The liquor in my system soothes me and sends me to sleep.

ooo

The sunlight shining brightly through the bedroom window wakes me up. It's blinding. I almost roll over and snuggle deeper into the sheets but then I remember I'm in Calvin's bed. My limbs scramble to find the floor. I tiptoe out of the room and peek down the hall. The bathroom is empty. The other bedroom door is still closed, probably still locked.

I make my way into the living room and find it empty. The tv is still on, whispering sounds from the speakers. I'm alone.

The refrigerator is fully stocked with a whole bunch of junk. I might as well make myself something to eat while I'm here. He has two boxes of apple toaster strudels so that's what I'll eat. I'm sure he won't miss two strudels.

After I eat my sweet breakfast I know it's time to go. I change back into my dress and reluctantly stuff my feet into Amber's heels. They hurt before I even stand up. I brush my hair down with my hands because there isn't a comb anywhere in this place.

This is going to be so embarrassing to take the bus dressed like I am at this time of day. But I wobble down the never ending stairway, out of the building door and down a long winding road. The road leads me to the front of the complex. There's a circular driveway and two benches. I sit on the bench closest to the bus sign.

I'm the only one out here. There's a breeze that makes me hug myself. The bus pulls up after what I guess has been 15 minutes of me sitting here. I get on and then I remember I didn't bring my bus pass or any money with me. *How the fuck didn't this dawn on me before now?*

"I forgot my pass. Can I still ride?" I'm scared to look the driver in the eyes.

Her voice is hoarse and scratchy. "Nobody rides for free darling. Either pay or get off my bus."

"I got it," A voice behind me calls out. A blonde curly headed boy comes to the front of the bus and swipes his bus card on the scanner. He smiles and starts to walk back towards his seat.

"Thank you so much. You didn't have to do that."

"Don't mention it. You look like you've had a hard enough day." He goes back to his iPod and doesn't give me another thought.

I've had a hard enough day?

I sit in the seat right behind the bus driver. I have a perfect view of the mirror and I see my face for the first time today. I look horrible. My finger comb didn't do much and my makeup from last night is smeared on my face. I didn't even think to wash my face. I completely forgot. I ride the rest of the way with my arms crossed and my face pressed into the window. We finally arrive at my stop and I run off the bus with my hands covering my face.

I'm let off on Grand River just outside of campus. Amber's dorm is a good ways away from here but I don't have any money for my transfer. I take a deep breath and walk across the street and through campus with my head down. I know people are giving me crazy looks. A disheveled girl in a club dress and stilettos walking through a college campus in the middle of the afternoon. I don't know anyone besides Amber's friends so thankfully I don't have to worry about anybody recognizing me.

My feet send shock waves through my body with each step I take. They're red and puffy. I wince with each stride and I'm amazed that I don't see blood filling the shoes and spilling onto the pavement. I would take them off but that would mean I'd have to stop walking. If I'm not moving it'll take me longer to get to my destination and the longer it takes me the more people see me.

After what feels like hours I'm just within inches of South Westmore Hall. The building looms over me and I've never been more happy to look up at its 12 stories.

Hopefully Amber skipped class today so she can let me in her room. I desperately need to lay down. I knock on her door and it opens almost immediately, but it's not Amber who answers the door.

Abigail yanks me inside and pushes me towards her bed.

"My goodness Simone! You look terrible. What happened to you? Are you okay?"

Abigail sits beside me and holds my hand.

"I'm fine. I just stayed out last night and didn't have any extra clothes. I forgot my bus pass too so I've been walking."

"You walked here from where? I thought you were with Amber."

"I was. Then I wasn't. I was with this guy but I don't know what happened to him, actually. He wasn't home when I woke up."

"So where is Amber? She hasn't been back."

"I don't know. I'm sure she's with Chelsea. Why do you care anyway?"

I hadn't forgotten the way Abigail talked about Amber yesterday. She doesn't have to fake concern.

"I may have my opinions about Amber but she's still a person and she's still my roommate. I would care if she was in trouble. You too."

As Abigail is talking I rip off Satan's shoes and my feet couldn't thank me enough.

"Yeah, sure." I roll my eyes and rub the balls of my feet. My shoulders slack and my whole body starts to shut down.

"You sure you're alright?"

"Yeah." My toes stretch and I lean back to fall into Abigail's bed.

Abigail stops me and holds my arm. "Um, you really should get cleaned up first."

Instead of taking a shower I get up and jump into Amber's bed. She didn't bother to make it up so I'm not messing up anything. As soon as my head touches the pillow I hear the room door open. Amber saunters into the room. She's wearing cut off shorts and a long sleeved crop top. Her hair is in a ponytail and dark sunglasses cover her face.

"What the hell are you doing?" Amber's voice is directed at me. "You look homeless. Get out of my bed."

"Sorry. I just really needed to rest my feet. It's been a long morning."

"Yeah, well you should've showered and washed that muck off of your face first."

"Don't be mean Amber." Abigail chimes in.

"You stay out of it Abby. She has no manners."

I stand in the middle of the room like an idiot. I don't know what to say.

Amber throws her purse onto her bed and I notice that it's brand new. It's the color of blush with gold accents. It looks like leather, real leather.

"Where'd you get that?" The more I pay attention to her I see that everything she has on is brand new. I've never seen any of it before.

"Wouldn't you like to know *Simone?* If you would just listen to me and follow my lead you would know the finer side of life too."

She sits down and whips out her phone. She smiles at the screen and I know I am dismissed. I look over at Abigail and her face is buried in a book. I'm left standing in the middle of the room with frizzy hair and muck on my face.

CHAPTER SIXTEEN
SIMONE

It felt amazing not getting up at the crack of dawn and slaving over a stove for Neil. He can be such an asshole sometimes. I didn't set my alarm clock and ignored his tantrum of slamming things. He acts like he can't put a piece of bread in the toaster himself.

I have all day to find something to do with myself and nothing comes to mind. I'm too nervous to begin another journal. I'm too nervous to sit outside again. It seems likes I can never do anything right. Chaos, sadness and disappointment seems to stick to me like a disease.

My good memories stopped the day Mama and Daddy never came home. Anything I thought would be good for me after that has blown up in my face. That's really why I'm still here with Neil. Yeah I have nowhere else to go, but I also don't care to have anywhere else to go anymore. It never turns out good anyway.

As the hours pass I watch episode after episode of this "Housewives" reality show. They're ridiculous and they fight over nothing constantly. It's pretty entertaining. I can live vicariously through them. They drive around in their fancy cars, live in their fancy houses and go on fairytale vacations.

The show has to be paying for all this because I don't think any of them has a real job.

I've been sitting on the couch so long I'm becoming a part of the couch. My legs sink into the cushions. My arm is now the armrest. My eyes get heavier by the second. I haven't moved all day. I'm tired from being immobile.

I'm not sure how long I've been out when Neil comes through the door. I jump out of my couch skin and panic races to my heart. He doesn't want me watching reality tv. He says it's a bad influence on me.

"I swear I was watching a cooking show. I must've hit a button on the remote while I was sleep." I explain myself immediately but he doesn't even pay attention.

Neil walks right past me. His feet are only protected by socks. He's carrying his work boots in his hand. The normally wheat colored boots now have splashes of another color, a deep dark red, maybe black. They drip on the floor. A trail of dark blobs forms next to each of his steps. He goes straight for the basement door and stomps down the stairs. He doesn't even close the door behind him like usual.

I follow him. He's now in his secret room and I look at him from a few steps down the stairway. He stands in the doorway for a few seconds. He looks around and takes a deep breath. He shifts from one foot to the other, driving me crazy. Then he just throws the shoes in a rage across the room. There's a loud boom and he slams the door behind him without ever turning around.

Neil stays locked away for a few hours. I have time to look closer at the droplets and they're definitely red. It has to be blood. If he sees this on the floor he'll know I've seen it and he'll freak out so I clean it up.

Maybe the blood came from a dead animal or something. He does collect a lot of garbage from tons of people.

I pretend to be preoccupied with the tv when Neil comes back upstairs. He still doesn't acknowledge me. He goes straight to the bathroom, strips down and jumps in the shower.

He leaves the door open so I tiptoe up to the doorway. His pants are on the floor next to the sink. The bottom of his pants have dark spots just like his shoes. I feel around his pockets and feel a key.

The water shuts off and I run back to the living room, leaving the key behind. A few seconds later his bedroom door closes. I go back to the bathroom to find it empty of him and his clothes. I need to lure him out of his room.

I softly knock on his door.

"Sir? Are you hungry? Let's go get something to eat."

He doesn't answer. I knock again.

"Hello? You know you want to go get a drink. Come on."

The door swings open. Neil stands before me, big and tall. He has on a white t-shirt and gray sweatpants. I peek around him and I don't see his soiled jeans. He moves in front of my line of vision. He steps forward, making me step back, and shuts his bedroom door behind him.

"We're not going anywhere. You can order some pizza."

"You look like you had a rough day. You sure you don't want to eat out and get a drink?"

"What the fuck did I just say Simone?! Don't get on my nerves or I won't let you order shit."

"Fine. I'll order pizza."

Neil doesn't move from in front of his door as if he's waiting for me to leave. We stare at each other for a moment before I turn and head for the kitchen.

If he's not drunk I don't know how I'll be able to sneak into his room unnoticed.

As I sift through the kitchen drawer full of takeout menus I find a Benadryl box mixed in with all the mess. *That's it!* I'll crush two pills up and mix it in with the pop I know Neil will have with his pizza.

"Hey Neil, sir," I yell out to him. "What kind of pizza do you want? If we get a large we can get wings and a 2 Liter too for $15."

"Get whatever."

He doesn't really mean "whatever." He means a meat lover's pizza. It's what he always gets and I hate it. Forget about getting it half and half. I always have to peel everything off and eat it as a sausage juice cheese pizza. And even though I know what he wants I still have to ask. If I don't he'll go crazy about me not respecting him.

After I make the delivery call I find Neil sitting in the living room staring at the tv. He doesn't seem engaged at all. He looks like he is caught in a trance. I sit down next to him and my hand touching his shoulder makes him jump. He looks at me like he hasn't seen me in weeks. I smile and his confused expression slowly fades away.

"The food will be here in 20 minutes."

He nods and goes back to the tv.

"You sure you okay?" I ask him.

Neil's lip twitches and his jaw tenses up.

"I'm fantastic Simone. Don't ask me again." He's now looking at me. His cold gaze freezes me. His voice sounds like anything but fantastic.

Something happened today and my answer is in that room.

ooo

Neil is out like a light. Just as I expected he wanted a tall glass of Coca-Cola. I crushed two pink benadryl pills and stirred them in with his drink. Thankfully coke is dark so he didn't notice anything. He's passed out on the couch and snoring loud enough to wake up the whole neighborhood. Hopefully he stays like this for a while.

I'm in his room and I can't find the jeans he had on earlier. They're not in his hamper, on the floor or in the closet. I even check under the mattress, nothing. I stand in the middle of the room and think. *If I were Neil where would I hide blood stained jeans?*

One of the drawers to his dresser is open just a crack. I open it more and see nothing inside besides white t-shirts. I pull the drawer completely out, the wheels off the tracks. And there they are. The jeans were stuffed behind the drawer. I search the pockets and they're empty. *Shit.* I put everything back the way it was and sit on the bed. I know the key is in this room somewhere.

I carefully look through every drawer here and find nothing. There isn't much in Neil's room besides his bed, dresser, nightstand, his closet and hamper. I've searched each one. The key is nowhere to be found.

I fall back onto the bed in frustration. Something hard sticks my head from the pillow. I don't see anything under the pillow besides the bed sheet. I wiggle my fingers inside the pillowcase and finally, cold hard metal warming to my touch.

I slide the key into my back pocket. Neil is still snoring so no need to check on him. Packed away is my old house key from my family home in Okemos. I've held on to it all these years. In the beginning I was in denial about my parents. I thought I would be able to use my house key again. Like every day of my life. That day never came. It's the only thing I have that connects me to them. No more Sophie, no more of my magical snow globe, special jewelry, nothing.

My key is just as I've left it, on a small key ring with old scratched up hair beads. It's underneath one of my shoes in my closet. It's my little secret from Neil.

I put my key in the place of Neil's in his pillowcase. Hopefully it will work as a decoy and he doesn't actually try to use it before I have a chance to switch the keys back. Neil's key is safe in my hiding spot. Tomorrow I'll get the truth.

ooo

Neil is gone. He hasn't seemed suspicious. He hasn't gone back to the secret room either which means he hasn't noticed that he has the wrong key. I'm so relieved. I couldn't sleep. Just knowing he was sleeping with the wrong key had me on edge all night.

Even though Neil has never come back to the house because he's forgotten something, I wait a few hours before I make any moves, just in case. The stairs squeak and squeal under my weight. I'm alone but I'm terrified. I can feel Neil's presence letting me know that I'm doing wrong, that I'm trespassing and invading his privacy. I ignore his presence and force myself to stand in front of the secret door. The key slides in the lock with ease. It turns comfortably and the lock clicks. I hold the knob for a few seconds before I finally open the door and go inside.

The room is fully furnished with Victorian-looking furniture. Shelves cover the back wall. Each one holds something different and none of it makes sense. Old dead flowers, broken cups, women's shoes, a casserole dish.

There's a makeshift closet in the corner. It's more of just a clothes rack and it's filled with women's clothing. I see the boots. They're thrown carelessly on the floor. One is next to the rack, one is on the other wall to my left. The stains are now fully dry. The toes are dark and underneath looks like paint peeling off. Red paint.

On the left wall is a dresser slash vanity with curly Q legs. It has a matching chair fit for a queen. Perfume bottles are perfectly lined up on top of the vanity. Some are full and some are empty. I take a seat and staring me in my face is Vanessa. Her face sits in a gold frame surrounded by other Vanessa faces. There are words all over the wall. It's a mural. A creepy one.

I feel a hard object touch my feet. It's up against the wall tucked into the back legs of the vanity. A camera. A very nice camera. I turn it on and skim through the photos. Every single one is of Vanessa. Every single photo was taken secretly too. Vanessa getting in her car. Vanessa going into her house. Vanessa leaving her house. Vanessa taking out the trash. Vanessa at her kitchen table, from outside of the house. Vanessa tending to her garden. Some are zoomed in really close to her face. Neil must have some extra lenses around here somewhere.

I start to open the drawers and they're filled with pictures. Most are of Vanessa but I see a few of other people. An older lady with white hair and pale skin has her own photoshoot. She's talking to Vanessa in some and some are of her alone leaving and going into her house. A lot of pictures with her are destroyed. They're crumpled, drawn on and scratched up. The last one I see of her has the word 'BITCH' written across her face in red marker and a big 'X' across her body.

I see myself. There are pictures of me with Amber. Us going to parties, walking around campus, at the museum. There are even pictures of me with Calvin. His face isn't visible in any of them. He's either scratched on or his face is completely torn out of the picture. But I know it's him. I wouldn't forget our moments.

And then I see a car wreck in a news clipping that's mixed in with everything. It looks exactly like the one Calvin was in. It is the one Calvin was in. There are happy faces drawn all over the damn car. *Did he have something to do with this?*

I suddenly feel light-headed. I can barely breathe. Neil is much crazier than I ever thought. I know he's abusive and angry all the time. But he's a stalker too. And what else?

I now know the blood on his pants and shoes were from no animal. They're from a human. He hurt someone worse than he's ever hurt me.

If Neil has pictures of me and now I'm here maybe he has the same plans for Vanessa. At first I was excited that she took focus off of me but I don't want her to end up like me. I don't want her or her friends to get hurt. I have to warn her to stay away before Neil gets to her first.

CHAPTER SEVENTEEN

VANESSA

Today is the big day. It's the first day of the art workshop I've set up. I want to see how Abigail will do as the class instructor so I'll just be observing her today. I've had Abigail spread the word via flyers around town and social media posts. So far we have had about 10 students sign up for the high school portion. Hopefully more show up today and we can have a full classroom.

The younger age groups are a lot larger. Ages 7-10 have 20 students and ages 11-13 have about 22, 23 kids. I'll definitely have to help Abigail out by teaching one of the younger classes on my own. I don't want her to get overwhelmed.

The class today will be student introductions, verbally and artistically. I thought it would be fun to have them draw a piece that they felt described them and their aesthetic. Abigail is in Showroom A, which will be our high school classroom, setting everything up.

Abigail came up with the idea of gift bags. Small sketch pads, charcoal, paint brushes and small booklets on famous artists are what they'll be taking home. I love the idea and I hope the students will too.

I join Abigail in Showroom A and we wait for everyone to arrive. Slowly people start to trickle in. There are three big round tables, two at the forefront and one slightly behind in the middle. The middle table fills up first. Not surprising. The last person to walk in is Simone. I wasn't expecting to see her. I haven't talked to Neil since I let him know about the class. I give her a smile and a wave. She barely looks at me.

"Hello everyone, welcome. My name is Abigail and I will be your instructor for the next few weeks." Abigail turns to me. "And this is Vanessa, the head director. She will be assisting periodically. Let's start by going around the room and everyone can introduce themselves."

A young man in a striped tee and dingy jeans stands.

"Hey, my name's Vince. I'm 17. I'm from Georgia. I'm here in Michigan this summer to visit my grandparents."

A girl with deep brown slanted eyes and fluffy hair stands next.

"I'm Dalila. I'm 15 and I'm from right here."

We go around the room and Simone is the last to stand and introduce herself.

"I'm Simone. I'm 17. And I'm from Okemos." She seems extremely nervous. Her voice shakes a bit and she never looks up from her feet.

Abigail stares at Simone before she stutters, "It's nice to meet all of you. Now I'll tell you a little about the class and what we're going to be doing today."

Abigail walks around the room and hands out a sheet of paper to everyone.

"This is an outline of the program. Don't worry you won't have homework or any tests. This is just to give you a heads up. You'll see that today is all about introduction. I want everyone to express who they are through their art in what they feel is their aesthetic. Hopefully by the end of this program you all will have a better understanding of the type of art you want to create and how you want to create it."

Abigail gestures to the back left corner of the room. "We have all the supplies you'll need but you're more than welcome to bring your own if you'd like next time."

The class gets up and they crowd around all of the art supplies. After a few minutes of rummaging everyone has retaken their seats. They look up at us with expectant eyes.

"Well don't be shy. Get started," I say.

I walk around and see so many different things. Portraits, landscapes, graphic shapes, cartoons, colors, charcoal. This group is so diverse in style, I can tell already. Excitement bubbles up inside of me. This will be fun.

Six o'clock is now here and it's time to wrap everything up. The class puts back the supplies they used. They each hand in their work.

"So, on Monday we'll look at what everybody did. There will be a critique from myself and your peers too." Abigail smiles at the class and begins to hand out the gift bags. "I hope you all enjoyed your first day with us."

As everyone disappears from the room, Simone still sits in her seat. Abigail had been giving her weird looks all class and Simone avoided eye contact. Her hand was stuck to her forehead, acting as a shield.

Abigail stops in front of Simone and looks as if she wants to say something. She looks at me and leaves the room instead. Simone finally looks up from the table. She looks worried.

"Hey Simone, what's up? You okay?" I take a seat next to her.

She nods but I don't believe her.

"You look like something is on your mind." I try to coax an answer out of her.

"Vanessa you can't come around anymore. And I won't be coming here again." Simone looks down at her twiddling fingers.

"What?" I giggle out. "Well why not? I thought we were girlfriends." I nudge her elbow.

Simone scoots away and looks at me with a fierce look in her eyes. "Please, promise me you won't talk to Neil anymore."

"Neil? You mean your Dad?"

"Yeah, whatever. Just promise. You have to stay away for your own good." She looks at the clock on the wall and jumps out of her seat. She starts to leave the room but looks back and says, "I'm serious Vanessa."

"But Simone, wait a minute!" I yell out to her but

she's already gone.

I stay seated at the table in a state of confusion. *What just happened here?* My head falls into my hands. I see camel colored ballet flats walking back in the room. I look up at Abigail. She comes and sits in Simone's seat.

"Abigail, you did really great today. I'm very impressed."

She smirks and thanks me. "Thanks but I have something to tell you."

"What's up?"

"You remember when you asked me about knowing a girl from high school named Simone? Well she was here today. The girl Simone in today's class is who I knew through my old roommate."

"Are you sure? She's only 17."

"Well she was supposedly 18 two years ago so I don't know what's going on but that's her."

I don't have any reason to doubt Abigail. She's always honest and very trustworthy. But it just doesn't make sense.

"And I probably should've mentioned this before but a while ago a man that came to see you here was very inappropriate with me. He was rude and kind of scary. She left with that same man just a minute ago. I think we should dismiss her from the class. I really have a bad feeling."

I've just received too much information at once. It's making my brain hurt. I don't even know what to think or feel.

"I think she just dropped out of the class anyway so I don't think we have to worry about that. I have to go now, but thanks for letting me know everything." I get up and walk out of the door leaving Abigail sitting alone.

When I get outside Neil is standing right at the front door. I almost bump into him and clutch my chest.

"My God, you scared me."

"Just wanting to say 'Hi.' Haven't heard from you."

I see Simone in his truck flailing her arms around and shaking her head in a 'No' motion.

"What you looking at?" Neil turns around and Simone leans back into her seat.

"Nothing. Just a bird."

He nods. "So? Where you been?"

"I haven't been anywhere. I haven't heard from you either Neil. I guess we've just been busy."

"Busy huh?" He takes his cap off and runs his hand through his oily hair. "Well let's get together soon."

As I look at Neil's face it clicks in my mind that he's recently shaved his face. It's been smooth the last few times I saw him which is not how I originally met him. My stomach begins to feel uneasy.

His smile makes me uncomfortable and I have the urge to run away. Something tells me if I turn him down to his face it won't end nicely. I've seen flashes of his anger and I don't want any part of it.

Nancy's information rings in the back of my mind.

Simone's warning is fresh. They both seem to tell me to decline Neil's invitation.

"Yeah let's do that. But I don't know which day yet. I'll have to call you and let you know."

I try to step around him but he blocks my way.

"Don't forget." His voice is low and demanding. He touches my chin and smiles a smile of mischief. His icy blue eyes go right through me before he turns on his heel back to his truck. They drive away with Simone's face glued to the window.

ooo

It's been almost a week since the first class at the museum. The junior and pre-teen classes are going great. Everyone showed up and Abigail has been doing such a fantastic job. Simone kept her promise and hasn't shown up to any more classes. I never called Neil to set up a date and in return I've received call after call from him. I have yet to answer one.

I've spent all my free time in my garden and catching up with Aundrea. She's supposed to stop by tonight for a movie night in. Until then I think I'll enjoy my hard work and relax out back with a good book.

I'm a sucker for good historical fiction. Philippa Gregory is one of my favorites. I've already read *"The Other Boleyn Girl"* but it never hurts to re-read a book you love. A glass of cold iced tea reinforces my coolness in the shade.

A loud car drives down the street and takes my attention away from the book. It parks across the street from Nancy's house. A bunch of teenagers pile out of the car. They lean on the car laughing and talking so loudly I can no longer concentrate.

While I listen to their blabber I realize I haven't seen Nancy at all since she came back home all dolled up. She usually is always so busy doing God knows what but her car hasn't moved from the driveway. Unless she's been out while I've been at work.

I guess I'll just see her tomorrow. She invited me over for her book club meeting. I have to admit that I haven't read whatever book of the month she's chosen. I don't even remember what it was. But she always has a catered lunch with endless champagne. I definitely don't want to miss out on that.

Ding.

'Vanessa please call me back. Why are you ignoring me?'

A text message from Neil. You would think being ignored for a week would make a person leave you alone. But I guess that doesn't work with him.

Ding.

'Can I come see you?'

I roll my eyes. *My goodness.* I bring my thumb to the keyboard and just as I start to respond Aundrea appears at my gate.

"I thought I'd find you here. I kept knocking but guess you couldn't hear from all the way back here."

"Drea, hey girl!" I click my phone off and stuff it into my pocket. I open the gate for her and we walk towards the patio. "Come on in. You want something to drink? I just made fresh tea."

"Is it a Long Island?"

We laugh simultaneously. "No. But I do have some vodka if you're feeling risky."

"Perfect. It's always happy hour."

Aundrea looks so nice and fresh today. Her hair is pulled back into a ponytail, so you can see all her features. Her skin is glowing. Her smile is bright and her lips have a pop of pink on them. She's wearing a really cute orange top that falls off her shoulders. The 5 inch open toed heels are the icing on the cake.

"Where are you coming from? You look so pretty." I take a shot of vodka and grimace. It sure knows how to burn your throat.

"Nowhere really. I've just been running around taking care of some errands."

"Well now you can relax. I have everyone's favorite movie snacks. Popcorn, frozen pizza, chips."

"Let's make a pizza. I haven't eaten all day."

We drink and talk while we wait on the pizza. By the time it's done we both have a nice buzz going on. The vodka has risen my body temperature so the air had to be turned on.

We sit like a couple of kids on the floor at my coffee table with our food and blankets. Aundrea insisted on a scary movie so we're going to watch '*The Conjuring.*' We're glued to the screen. I'm scared out of my mind but I can't let Aundrea know that. We're both jumping and screaming so she's probably figured it out already.

I look away from the screen because the music is building so I know something crazy is going to happen. I think I see a figure outside of my window. I blink really hard and then it's gone. There are weird noises outside of my house. I know this isn't an interactive movie. I'm starting to feel creeped out.

"Did you hear that?" I hold my blanket close to my body.

"Hear what?" Aundrea jumps at my voice.

"I think I heard footsteps."

"Footsteps? I didn't hear anything. The movie is just freaking you out." Aundrea dismisses me and returns her attention back to the haunted family on the tv screen.

My phone lights up and I take a look at it. A missed call from Neil. *This guy just doesn't give up.* It lights up again as I'm holding it. A voicemail.

"*Vanessa I know you've gotten my messages and calls. The games are over. You will talk to me one way or another.*"

My breath catches in my throat. *Was that a threat?* I feel the color drain from my face. I throw my phone from my hand like it zapped me and I was getting revenge. Aundrea hasn't noticed anything and I watch the rest of the movie with her like nothing has happened.

Aundrea gathers her shoes and we kiss cheeks before she strolls out into the dark night.

"Call me when get home!" I yell out to her back.

"Okay, bye!" Aundrea gets in her car and disappears into the night.

I lock the front door and run to my bedroom. I close the door and lock it behind me as well. My fluffy covers act as my fortress as I force my mind to relax and go to sleep.

ooo

I wake up under the covers. All around me all I see is white. I peek from under the covers and my eyelids feel like they weigh 100 pounds. It's well after noon. I haven't slept in this late since college. Aundrea and I had a good time minus my internal freak out.

I check the weather and it'll be in the low 70's. Sounds like a jeans and flowy top kind of day. I take my time getting ready. I spend an hour on my makeup and an extra 15 minutes on my hair. Nancy is very sophisticated and so are her friends, if not more than her. I want to look the part for her gathering today.

The kitchen is illuminated with the sun's light and it

finds its way into the living room. I love having big open windows. Everything is always nice and bright during the day and I get the moonlight at night. The space feels so open but welcoming and relaxing too. I take a seat at the kitchen's island that also acts as my part time bar. There's a glass bowl of fresh fruit waiting for me on top of the cream granite. I eat a banana to ease my hunger but leave room for Nancy's meal. I don't want to get there and not be hungry.

As I'm getting ready to leave I see red and blue lights flash through the windows alongside my front door. I rush outside to see what's going on. There are three police cars and an ambulance outside of Nancy's house. I run over but they won't let me past the walkway. One of Nancy's friends is crying hysterically near the bushes.

"Mary! What the hell is going on?" I yell out to her but she just continues to cry.

Uniforms come in and out of Nancy's house like a revolving door. The front door is open and I see a forensics guy taking photos all over the place. Yellow tape is now being put up as a barricade.

An officer walks by me and I grab his arm.

"Officer what happened? Is Nancy alright? We were supposed to meet for lunch."

In my heart I know she's not alright. If she were there wouldn't be this scene at her home. Mary wouldn't be hiding in plants crying her eyes out. But I have to ask.

"Are you a relative, Miss?"

"No I'm her neighbor. But-"

"I'm sorry Miss I'm not at liberty to discuss anything." He pulls away from my grasp and disappears inside the house.

I call out to Mary again. "Mary! Please! Tell me what is going on."

She finally looks up from her palms. Her eyes are bloodshot and puffy. Her tears have left streaks down her foundation covered face.

"She's dead Vanessa! She was murdered!" A detective comes over to her and brings her inside the house.

I'm stunned. Mary's words hit me right to the core. My eyes begin to water and I cover my mouth to try to cover my sobs. I look around and notice that everyone on the block has come out of their homes. People are hugging their door frames. They're on their front lawns. I see heads peeking behind curtains in windows.

I feel hands on my back pushing me along. A voice that seems miles away speaks to me.

"Ma'am this is a police investigation. You're going to have to leave the premises. I know you're concerned but I promise we'll do everything we can to figure out what happened."

I never look at his face. I don't even feel my feet moving. My front door just keeps getting closer and closer. When I make it up the steps my knees buckle and I slide down onto the porch. Next to my hand lies a single red rose.

A note is taped to the stem. *So someone was here last night.*

I have to be careful when I remove the note. There are thorns ready to draw blood. My hands tremble as I unfold the small piece of paper.

It reads, *'Maybe you'll thank me this time. Don't disappoint me.'* A tear drops and smears the letters.

I don't understand. What would Christian mean by thanking him this time? I thanked him last time. Unless they were never from Christian.

My stomach falls to my feet. I stumble inside and lock the door behind me. The foyer is spinning. My chest is heaving. My breathing is erratic. I don't know if I feel safe here anymore. I have to get out of here.

I'm like a tornado ripping and running through the house. I pack two bags full of clothes, shoes, makeup, anything I think I'll need. I check each window to make sure it's locked. I secure the patio door behind me before I run to the gate. I toss my bags in the backseat of my car and speed out of the driveway. My tires make a screeching noise as I pull off down the street. I float down to the stop sign and see a detective staring at me through my rearview mirror.

I don't even call Christian on my way to his place. I just show up at his doorstep banging on the door like a lunatic. I leave my car parked on the street with my bags still inside. Thank goodness he answers the door and lets me in.

"Christian what is this? Did you leave me this?" I shove the rose letter in his face.

"What? What are you doing here?" His face is scrunched together. He clearly hasn't left the house. He's wearing sweatpants and a wrinkled t-shirt, something he would never be seen in.

"I can't stay at my house. It's dangerous. Just tell me if you wrote this, please?"

Christian looks at me then reluctantly at the note.

"No I didn't leave you this, Vanessa. Now can you tell me what your deal is?"

"In a minute. I need help bringing in my bags." I grab his hand and pull him towards the front door.

"Your bags? What do you have *bags* for?"

"I just told you my place is dangerous right now, Christian. Didn't you hear me? I have to stay here for a while."

"A while? Can't you just go to Aundrea's?"

"You're kidding me, right?! You can't be serious. I need you right now." Tears swell up in my eyes and my voice shakes. I let go of his hand and stare at him in disbelief. Christian can really be an asshole sometimes.

"Baby, I'm sorry. Come here." He walks towards me and takes my hands in his. "I'm just taken off guard here. What the hell is going on?"

"I'll tell you after we bring everything in."

I end up only carrying my phone and purse. Christian takes care of the rest. His biceps bulge and flex, which would normally send sensations throughout my body. But not now.

My mind is in one million places right now.

Christian puts my bags on his black wooden bedroom floor. His place is super modern and has a loft feel to it. He's in the middle of downtown Ann Arbor with the best view. His condo sits on the 10th floor overlooking the city. The lights at night are breathtaking. Everything is either black, gray or white. Geometric shapes and glass are everywhere you look.

He joins me on his sleek black leather sectional couch. He doesn't speak, just looks at me with a questioning gaze.

"I know it wasn't you that left me a rose a few weeks ago. What I don't understand is why you would say that you did."

He waits a few moments before he speaks. Maybe deciding if he'll lie again or just be honest.

"You were excited about it. So, I just went along with it. Is this all really about a flower?"

My head falls into my hands and I let out a huge sigh.

"No, Christian. It's about the person that gave it to me." I think about Simone's warning, the threatening voicemail and my mind jumps to Nancy and I break down. "Nancy was murdered, Christian. I don't understand what's going on. I'm scared."

"Murdered? What? Who's Nancy?"

"My neighbor. We were supposed to get together today and when I got to her house there were police everywhere. There was an ambulance. She was killed right in her home."

His eyes are wide open. "Wow. That's terrible." His strong hand rubs my back in a circular motion. "But what does that have to do with your flower person?"

"I don't know. Don't get mad, but I went on a couple of dates with this guy-" He immediately removes his hand from my body and places it in his lap. "You were always so busy, and anyway I think he has issues or something. He always seems angry. His daughter is a nervous wreck and she told me not to come around anymore for my own good."

"So you met this guy's daughter?" I can tell he's getting upset.

"Just listen. Not too long before that Nancy was telling me some guy named Tom was lurking around my house and told her he was my gardener. Obviously he's not and I don't even know a Tom. She told me he had a shaved face and the guy has one too. Now all of a sudden she's dead. And look at the note from today. I mean, come on!"

"That's crazy Vanessa. You're just paranoid."

"I'm not. This all can't be just coincidental."

"Well, for one, maybe this daughter told you to stay away because she doesn't want you dating her dad. Where's her mother?"

"She's dead."

Christian gets quiet.

"Oh, and I almost forgot. The daughter is supposedly

17 and in high school but Abigail said she knows her from college two years ago. None of this shit makes sense. There's something not right with him. And he left me a message last night that kind of freaked me out." I lean back on to the couch, now facing the big floor length windows. Birds fly past and I follow them right back to Christian's face.

"Okay, well-" Christian shakes his head and rubs his temples. "If this is all somehow connected then I'm glad you came here. Maybe you shouldn't go to work tomorrow. I'll stay here with you."

"But my class. I can't leave Abigail alone."

"Are you concerned about your safety or not? You need to lay low until we know for sure if you're right."

I think it over for a moment.

"Yeah, you're right."

"Have you talked to the police about this guy?"

"No."

Christian gives me a straight face.

"Sorry, I wasn't exactly thinking about that. I was just thinking about getting somewhere safe."

We stare at each other for a while. I'm not sure what he's thinking but I'm glad he can be my safe haven.

ooo

I slept with my body glued to Christian's. Any way he turned, I turned. However he moved, I moved. I don't know if I'm putting this crazy story together in my mind or if it's actually true. But being with Christian last night made me feel safe.

Christian and I lay in the bed and watch movies on demand all morning. Towards noon I ask him to put the tv on the news. I want to know if they'll show any coverage on Nancy. Sure enough, they do.

"Yesterday morning a woman identified as Nancy Stein was found murdered in her home. She was discovered by a friend around 11:45. Police say the victim had already been dead for about a week before she was found. There was no sign of forced entry and police are still looking for suspects. More on this story as it develops."

The news reporter stands in front of Nancy's house. The screen momentarily leaves the reporter's big blue eyes, thin lips and platinum blonde hair to show a picture of Nancy. It's of her standing in her foyer full of joy, which is no longer a reality.

"This is so sad. Nancy was such a nice lady. And to think this happened right next door. I really can't believe this."

I'm talking more to myself than I am to Christian. He grabs my hand and gives it a good squeeze.

"I'll go make us some coffee."

As he leaves the room my phone begins to ring. It scares me half to death. The screen displays a phone number I don't recognize. I'm too nervous to answer so I let it go to voicemail. The caller leaves a message. I want to ignore it but the red notification is just staring at me and daring me to listen. My fingers tremble as I listen to the message.

Christian comes back into the room and sits down beside me.

"Who was that? You look like you've seen a ghost."

I hesitate.

"Don't tell me it was that guy again. I can't believe you got involved with somebody like this."

"No. It was the police. They want me to come down to the station."

CHAPTER EIGHTEEN

NEIL

"What did you do Simone?! This is your fault. I know it is!"

Anger takes over my body. My blood boils. Simone's smug face looks back at me. She's mocking me.

"What are you talking about? I didn't do anything."

"I knew I shouldn't have sent you to that class. I *knew* you were up to no good."

My feet nearly make a dent in the floor I'm pacing back and forth so much.

"The art class? Sir, I really don't know what you mean. I went to the class, you picked me up. What could I have done?"

The innocence in her voice sends bolts up my spine. If I concentrated hard enough I'm sure lasers would shoot right out of my eyes ending all her bullshit. She thinks I'm some idiot. She thinks I can't see right through her. Has she forgotten who's in charge here?

Next thing I know my hands are locked around her neck. She gasps for air and tears leap from her bulging eyes. I let go and watch her slide to the floor. Fear is written all over her face. It feels good.

"You sneaky son of a bitch! You turned her against me! How could you?!" Spit flies from my lips and drown her. I get on the floor, right in her face, daring her to deny it.

"Please! Neil don't kill me please." Simone reaches to grab my arm but I snatch it away from her.

"What do you mean don't kill you?" My voice is just above an aggressive whisper. "I love you Simone why the fuck would I kill you?"

Simone doesn't answer me. She covers her face and cries obnoxiously loud. I yank her hands away and smack her so hard her cheek turns red.

"I said why the fuck would I kill you Mo?"

"You said you would." She tries to shield her face with her hands and muffles her voice.

"You're a liar! You're just jealous that Vanessa is more beautiful than you. You don't want us to be together. Admit it."

"No. I don't want you to be together. But I'm not jealous. Vanessa's a nice lady and you're…"

"I'm what? I'M WHAT?!" My voice booms and bounces off of the walls and back into my ears nearly knocking me out.

Simone looks at me, finally. Her eyes are red and puffy. She sniffles before she yells out, "Crazy! Okay? Neil you're fucking crazy!"

I slap her again as hard as I can. Her head should be turning right off of her neck. I'm not crazy. She is. After all

I've done for her this is how she treats me. I've given her everything and I'm trying to give her a mother but she's ruining it for the both of us.

"I'm crazy? But I've given you a life with me. I'm trying to make it better, give you a family. Isn't that what you want? A family?"

"What family?! Look at what you do to me. I don't want you, Vanessa doesn't want you!"

"Don't you dare say that! Vanessa loves me, more than you ever have. Ungrateful little bitch." I yank her off the floor. She tries her hardest to get away from me but she can't. She's weak.

Simone falls to the floor. She kicks and screams as I drag her by her hair. The more she fights me the harder I pull. I slide her across the living room floor, through the kitchen and she thumps down the basement stairs. I toss her on the mattress that she loves so much.

"Don't you fucking move." I press my finger into her forehead and she turns away from me.

I leave the basement and lock the door behind me. I need reinforcement to get Simone to behave how she should. I walk out of my front door to get to my garage and a neighbor is staring at me.

"Can I help you?"

The idiot almost wets himself with the water hose. He fumbles with it and backs away from me. I'm not even near him.

"Uh, is everything okay over there? I heard noises."

"Ever heard of horror movies and surround sound? Mind your business."

I leave him standing there and go in my garage. It takes me a while to find what I came here for. But there it is.

I walk by the neighbor with my chain in hand. I feel his eyes on me but he doesn't say another word. I push open my front door, slamming it behind me. I go back into the kitchen and find my duct tape.

Simone is still on the mattress waiting for me. I tape her mouth shut. She doesn't even resist. I wrap the chain around her waist and attach it to a pipe close to the ground. She won't be giving me any more trouble now.

"This is what you deserve Simone. If you learned respect and how to appreciate things you wouldn't have to get punished. You'll have plenty of time to think about your behavior because you won't be leaving this basement ever again."

Her head hangs low. I expect to see her big green eyes look at me, pleading with me to let her go. Instead she rests her head on the wall. Her gaze never breaks away from the floor.

ooo

"Boy go get me another beer." Dad belches and tosses his empty bottle aside.

I check the refrigerator and see nothing but an old

onion and expired milk.

"There isn't any more beer."

Dad doesn't say a word.

*"Dad? Did you hear me? You don't have any more b-
"*

"Why didn't you tell me before we were running low?!" Dad storms in the kitchen. His eyes are wild and angry. "Well don't just stand there. Go get me some more!"

I don't have any money to get Dad a beer but I'd better not say it or he'll give me a good beating. Instead I wait until he goes back and sits down then grab some cash out of the jar he keeps in the cabinet above the forks and stuff.

He grunts and waves his arm shooing me out of the way when I walk across the room to the front door.

"I'll be right back Dad."

The sun blinds me as soon as I get on the porch. I haven't been outside in days. The liquor store is right up the street on the corner. I know the man Paul that runs the place. He always gives me pieces of candy when I come in.

The bell above the door dings as I walk in. There's a big fan in the corner and it nearly blows me right back out onto the street. I see a couple of the neighborhood kids fooling around near the register. I keep my head low and walk towards the back where all the beer is.

I lug the case of beer back to the front praying that the kids will leave before I make it up there. They don't leave.

"Hey there goes Poor Boy!" The leader, Danny, calls out. His friends follow.

"Hey Poor Boy."

"Poor Boy."

"What you doing Poor Boy? Getting your drunk of a father his medicine huh? How many does that make today?" Danny laughs at himself and his friends back him up.

"Leave me alone Danny."

"Oh I'm not bothering nobody. You need help carrying that big 'ole box back to your shack?"

"That's enough. You boys get on out of here and go home to your mamas." Paul kicks Danny and his friends out the store.

Paul slips me a peppermint with Dad's change.

The door dings and I'm back in the sun light. Danny and his friends are right outside the door waiting for me.

"Look at those shoes Poor Boy. They talk more than you do."

They all laugh and point. I ignore them and run home. I'm out of breath once I reach my doorstep. I get inside before Danny and his friends can catch up to me.

Dad is passed out in the couch when I get inside. The tv screams at his sleeping face. I put his beer in the fridge and lock myself in my room.

ooo

My body is soaked. If Simone wasn't locked in the

basement I would've sworn that she snuck in here and dumped a bucket of water on me. I need to stop having these dreams. Vanessa is the only way. She can relax me and my mind. If she would just talk to me I can find out what Simone said to her and I can fix it.

It's quiet. There's no smell of food cooking. I don't hear any dishes clattering in the kitchen. The one downside of Simone being punished is that so is my stomach. I inhale a bowl of oatmeal and a piece of toast with grape jelly. I bring Simone her now cold bowl of oatmeal and a banana. She's still sleeping. I rip the tape from her mouth and she wakes up instantly.

At first I try to feed her. I scoop oatmeal onto the spoon and guide it to her lips but she doesn't open her mouth. She stares at the food like it's some sort of poison. So I try the banana. She does the same thing. She keeps turning her head away from me.

"Fine. Don't eat. You aren't hurting me none."

I set the banana inside the bowl of oatmeal and leave them by her side.

"Try not to get into too much trouble today Mo." I pinch her cheek and head back upstairs.

I decide to skip out on work and focus on getting Vanessa back. I figure I'll swing by her job. She won't have a choice but to hear me out, we'll be in a public place. I doubt she'd want to make a scene. I told her she would talk to me one way or another and I meant it.

When I get to the museum I don't see Vanessa's car in its usual spot. There is another car there so maybe she just parked somewhere else today. There are parents walking in with kids and walking out without them. They must have one of those stupid classes.

On top of the desk at the entrance is a sign that says, *'Class in session. Please ring bell for assistance.'* Next to the sign is a gold bell that you hit with your hand, like the kind I've seen on movies in fancy hotels.

I ignore the sign and follow the little kids. None of the parents seem to notice that I don't have any of my own. They walk them to what I guess is the classroom and turn back around to leave. I don't turn back around.

I end up in a well-lit room that has circle tables and colorful pictures on the walls. Instead of seeing Vanessa in front of the room I see Abigail and she still looks like shit. I stand right beside her. She doesn't notice me at first but when she does she jumps right out of her ugly sweater.

A little boy with his front teeth missing pulls on Abigail's sweater.

"Who's that Miss Abby? Is he helping us today?" He points at me.

I bend down to the boy's level and answer his question before Glasses has a chance to.

"Yes I am. I'm Tom. What's your name?"

The boy opens his mouth to tell me but Abigail shoos him away.

"Go have a seat. Class is about to start."

The nameless boy pokes out his lip and finds his seat next to a chubby girl with sparkly shit in her hair.

"I don't know what you're doing here but you need to leave. Now." Glasses sounds serious but how can I take her serious when she can't even look me in the eye?

"I'm not going any fucking where until you tell me where Vanessa is. I know she's around here somewhere."

"She's not here. So just go."

She waves her hand at the door. She gives a weak smile to the class. When she scoots away from me and I take a step forward. I'm so close she can feel my breath.

"Where is she?" I talk through gritted teeth. I sound like I haven't had anything to drink in weeks.

She inches around her table and makes her way towards the door.

"Miss Abby where are you going?" A kid calls out to her.

"I'll be right back guys. Just give me a second I have to talk our helper really quick."

I follow her out of the room.

"Look I don't know what kind of sick stuff you've got going on but Vanessa isn't here. You need to leave before I call the cops. Maybe they'd be interested in Simone. I know her, you know?"

"What the fuck did you just say?" My eyes narrow. "You stupid little bitch!" As soon as I raise my fist to pummel her ugly face some kid's mom comes rushing back in the museum.

"Sorry, I forgot to leave Landon's medicine." The mom takes a closer look at us as she rushes over. She sees my rage and Abigail's fear. "Is everything okay here?" She looks from me to Abigail for an answer.

"We're fine. Just go take care of your kid." I try to sound as calm as possible.

"Are you sure?" She looks at Abigail.

"Yeah. Everything's fine. I'll be in there in a second." She smiles and smooths down her skirt.

The mom hesitates but leaves us. I wait until she's out of earshot to talk.

"You're dead *Miss Abby*."

ooo

I pull up to an empty driveway. Vanessa's lights are out. I don't understand. I refuse to leave without any answers. Too bad Old Bitch isn't next door for me to get answers out of.

No one is outside so I decide to put matters into my own hands. I walk up her driveway and hop the fence. She has big rocks outlining her walkway around the backyard. I take one of the rocks and smash a glass pane out of the patio door. I stick my hand through the jagged square and unlock the door. The door swings open and welcomes me inside.

I finally get to see every inch of where Vanessa lives.

I don't have to imagine the pieces that don't fit in the picture, that are blocked by walls and doors. The kitchen is white with granite countertops. All the appliances are stainless steel. The knobs are crystal. She has cream colored bar stools with silver studs holding the cushions together.

The kitchen leads to the living room to the left. Big fluffy couches and blankets. A huge flat screen tv sits inside a wooden entertainment center. I feel like I'm at some exclusive beach house in California.

The entertainment center has shelves that are full of pictures, movies and books. There are two pictures of Vanessa with some guy. She seems way too happy next to him. He has light brown skin, brown eyes, dimples and perfect teeth. The complete opposite of me. I forgot all about her saying she was seeing somebody when I asked her out that first time. This must be the prick. And wherever he is must be where she is. Without even thinking I smash the pictures on the floor. I stomp on them for good measure.

I need to find something in here that will tell me where he is. Or at least who he is. I destroy the kitchen and living room and find nothing. Her closets are full of useless bullshit. Just as I am about to give up I search through her dresser. Inside her underwear drawer is a note. *'Wish you could've came with me. So I'm sending a little bit of Miami to you. Can't wait to see you again. -Christian.'* At the bottom of the stationery in gold printed letters is the name Christian Conner next to Skylit Industries. *Bingo.* I grab a handful of

Vanessa's panties and stuff them in my pocket before I leave out the back door. I'm already inside so I'm able to unlock the gate and walk right out to my truck.

The ride home is peaceful. I rub Vanessa's panties in between my fingers and knuckles the entire way. They're soft and smooth. The lace scratches my skin, sending bolts through my arms into my cock. I so badly want to use my other hand to rub myself. But I don't have time to pull over. I have to get home to do some digging on this Christian dick.

I don't have a computer at home so I have to use my phone to search around the Internet. Christian Conner must be a popular name. There are a million of them on Google. I decide to search Skylit Industries instead. It will be easier for me to narrow things down.

Skylit Industries is some architecture company. Their headquarters is in New York but I guess they have a few branches scattered throughout the country. I assume he works at the Ann Arbor location. On the front page it's a list of all the recent shit they've done. Pictures bragging about how great they are. At the very bottom is a contact link. Only a phone number and address to their headquarters.

I call the number and a lady that sounds like she just got screwed answers the phone.

"Skylit Industries, New York."

I wait for her to tell me her name but the line stays quiet.

"I'm looking for Christian Conner. We did business a

few months back and I can't seem to locate his number."

"And what branch does Mr. Conner work at sir?"

"The Ann Arbor office."

"Okay I'll transfer your call to his office."

"Wait, can't you just give me his number?"

"Sorry sir I'm not at liberty to give out personal information of our employees. I can give you the Ann Arbor number and they can direct you to his line. But I also could just transfer you."

This bitch is lucky she's not in front of me.

"Just give me the number."

"Okay. Let me know when you're ready for it."

I clench my jaw. "I'm ready."

"734-555-5678. Is there anything else I can d-?"

I hang up. I immediately dial the phone number and it rings in my ear.

"Skylit Industries, Ann Arbor. This is Diane. How may I direct your call?"

"Hi Diane. I have a meeting there tomorrow morning and I just need the address."

"No problem sir. Can I get your name to make sure we've already confirmed your appointment?"

What is with these broads not just giving me what I want?

"I've already confirmed *Diane.* Can I just get the address *please?*" I'm really starting to lose my patience.

She gives me the address and my smile almost breaks

my face. Looks like I'll be playing hooky again tomorrow and taking a trip to Ann Arbor.

ooo

Today couldn't come fast enough. I wake up full of energy and I'm ready to go. I almost leave without feeding Simone. I actually don't want to give her anything. But I don't know how long I'll be gone so I give her the usual, oatmeal and a banana. I leave a bag of chips too just in case.

The drive is over an hour long but it feels more like 20 minutes. I end up in front of a gray building with tall glass windows everywhere. It's not too tall, about six stories high, but it is wide. *'Skylit Industries'* is above the front door in big bold yellow letters. I drive around to the side of the building to the visitors' lot. My pickup definitely doesn't fit in with all these BMWs and Mercedes.

There's a small gym in the back of the building. I can see a man on a treadmill through the huge window while I walk around to the front. *Why the fuck would they need a gym in an architect place?* The long silver handles are ice cold under my hands and the door weighs 100 pounds. When I get in the door I even see *'Skylit Industries'* under my fucking feet.

A blonde lady in a white suit sits behind a tall desk on the right wall. She's looking down at a computer and her fingers look like she's typing but I don't hear any keyboard clicks. She looks up at me and her eyes are greener than the color green.

She doesn't give me a funny look. She looks at me like a normal man coming into a fancy building. I made sure I looked like I could really be here for a meeting. Fresh shave, a little gel in my hair and I'm wearing the one pair of navy slacks I own with a crisp white shirt.

"Good morning sir. How may I help you today?" She smiles and her teeth are big and straight.

"Yes, I have a meeting with Christian Conner at 9:30." I drum my fingers on the desk.

She types away and stares at her computer screen confused after a million mouse clicks.

"I'm sorry. I don't see any appointments for Mr. Conner until this afternoon. What's your name? Maybe you've mixed up your days."

"Sean Bradley."

More mouse clicks.

"I don't see a Sean Bradley in this month's schedule at all. Are you sure you had an appointment?"

"Yes I'm sure! I've driven a long way to make this meeting today. Are you telling me it was for nothing? This is ridiculous!" I fake anger and she buys it.

"I'm sorry Mr. Bradley. I'm not sure what happened. I'll give Mr. Conner a call to try to figure this out. You can have a seat in the lounge straight back." She points to her right.

I walk down the hall and it opens up into a great big

sitting area. You can see a fountain through the glass wall surrounded by a garden. There are plants next to the couches and the tables have magazines about buildings on them. I take a closer look and it's just books of Skylit buildings. There are hallways on each side of the lounge leading to more rooms and an elevator. Instead of sitting down I walk down one of the hallways.

There are names beside each door. Lawrence Brown, Tracy Song, Jon Lessett. Not interested. I turn around and go down the other hall. The first name I see is Christian Conner. The door handle is just like the one on the front door. I try to pull the door open put it doesn't budge. I push it, nothing. *Fuck.* Of course it's locked. The glass beside the door is the foggy kind so I can't see inside.

I hear shoes tapping on the floor. The taps get louder after each second. They're coming towards me.

"Mr. Bradley?" The lady calls out to me.

I don't want her to see me snooping around so I run down to the elevator. I hit the button over and over until the doors finally slide open. I pick the third floor and press on the button to close the door.

"Hello?" The lady calls out again right before the elevator shuts and takes me upstairs.

Once I get upstairs I don't stay long. I walk around long enough for the lady to get back to her desk. After a few minutes I go back downstairs. I don't need her telling me that Christian has no idea who Sean Bradley is. I already know he doesn't. I need to get out of here and just wait it out for him outside. But I can't find another exit.

I hope her back is turned when I pass by to leave but it's not.

"Mr. Bradley. I was looking for you in the lounge, but you weren't there." Her voice sounds like she's accusing me of something.

"I was looking for the bathroom. The coffee I had earlier went right through me."

"Well I got ahold of Mr. Conner and-."

I cut her off. "You know what, I checked my phone while back there. Seems as though there was a mix up." I keep walking towards the door as I'm talking. "Thanks for checking and everything. I should be going."

"Mr. Bradley!" Blondie yells but I'm already out the door.

It's a little after 10 am. Blondie said Christian would be here in the afternoon. That could take forever. He could be here at 12, 3, 4 o'clock. But I don't have a choice but to wait. I pull out of the parking lot and circle the block. When I come back around I park across the street at some over the top furniture store. Now I wait.

My stomach is completely empty. I can't risk leaving and missing Christian. I chew on my tongue and swallow my spit instead.

It's coming up on 1:30 and I see a white Range Rover park across the street at Skylit. They use the other side of the building where it's assigned parking spaces. It's taking this moron forever to get out of the car but when he does I recognize him instantly. The sun beams off of his brown skin. He makes a face and I can see his dimple from here. It pisses me off. This is the piece of shit my Vanessa has been hanging around.

He stays in the building for a few hours. I see people coming and going and he's still inside. I'm starting to sweat through my shirt. It's damp and sticks to my skin. I cracked the windows but the sun is beating down on me from the windshield. This guy better hurry before I die out here.

Christian finally walks out the front door. He looks around himself before he goes back to his car. I start my truck and get ready to follow him. Follow him straight to Vanessa.

CHAPTER NINETEEN

VANESSA

"You're back! That was fast. I made us dinner."

Christian walks in the door and immediately unbuttons his shirt. I smile at his bare chest. He's gorgeous.

"Yeah, I didn't have much to take care of today. Just a meeting and a few phone calls." He takes a seat at his glass top table.

"So what happened with the guy that thought he had an appointment? Did you sort that out?"

"Not really. He was gone when I got there. Stephanie said she didn't get to tell him I was coming in. She said he left in a hurry."

"That's weird."

"Especially since she told me he was very upset about me not being there. Oh well, must not have been that important."

I pour us both a glass of wine. I take a gulp and Christian stuffs his face with bread.

"So, do you have to go in the office tomorrow?" I really want him to come with me to the police station.

"No but I'm going to New York tomorrow morning."

"What? New York? I thought you were going to go to

the police with me."

"Nessa look, I never said I was going. I said if I could. The meeting got moved up to tomorrow. Our project is starting soon. I can't not go." He cuts his salmon and shoves it in his mouth.

I leave the conversation at that. I guess I'm just going to have to tough it out and take care of business by myself. I would ask Aundrea but I don't want to bother her with my mess.

Christian breaks the silence.

"Have you gotten any calls or texts from your flower friend? What's his name?"

I roll my eyes at his comment.

"It's Neil and no I haven't, thank God."

"Well maybe after you do whatever you have to with the police you'll feel comfortable and can go back home."

"Trying to get rid of me already?"

"Never." Christian gets up and kisses my forehead. "You can stay until I get back from New York in a few days. Everything should be blown over by then."

He tries to hold my hand but I pull away.

"Yeah, let's hope so."

○○○

Christian wakes me up. He's making all kind of noise. I told him he should've gotten his luggage together last night but he decides to do it now at 6 am. I try to cover my face with a pillow but it's too late, I'm up.

"Do you want me to take you to the airport?" I yawn and stretch my limbs in opposite directions.

"No, you go back to sleep. I'll drive myself." He zips his bag and comes around the bed to give me a kiss. "I'll let you know when I land."

I watch him leave the room and the front door slams shut not too long after.

I don't want to wake Abigail at this hour so I send her a text.

'Sorry Abigail but I won't be in again today. Some last minute stuff came up and it's pretty important. I'll absolutely be there tomorrow. Call me if you need anything.'

I drag myself out of bed and turn the shower on. I wait until it's nice and hot and steamy before I get in. It's been a long couple of days and I need some me time. The water beads beat down onto my skin and it's so relaxing. I wash myself three times then I take my hair down from its bun. The water soaks my hair and cascades down my face. I stand under the stream for a few minutes and just breathe.

Mary's sobs suddenly flood my brain. They were loud and terrifying. I can't imagine what it's like to find my best friend murdered. I picture Aundrea and I can't even complete the thought. I hear Mary's words all over again. *'She's dead! She was murdered!'* My tears mix in with the water. I can't the difference as they rolls down my cheeks and pass over my lips.

I get dressed and slick my hair back into a ponytail. I put a small amount of mascara on and a little lip gloss. I think I could be taken seriously by a cop looking like this.

I make a cup of coffee to accompany me on the drive back to Okemos. The sun blinds me on my way to my car. I haven't been outside since I got here. The parking lot is jam packed. I guess it's not working hours for people around here.

The coffee hasn't helped me much. I'm still so very tired. I finally make it to the precinct and I just want to take a nap in my car. Unfortunately I have things to do.

When I get inside I wait for Detective Rowley, the man that left me a voicemail. He comes out in a gray suit and checkered tie. His hair is brown and thinning but he has a full beard. He leads me to the back into the interrogation room and I have to admit I'm a bit freaked out.

We sit opposite of each other. My legs shake from under the table. Detective Rowley looks at me with a bored expression and his fingers in his beard.

"Would you like anything? Coffee? Water?" Rowley leans into the table and clasps his hands together.

"No. I'm fine, thank you." I look around the room. It's small and drab.

"So, Vanessa Ramirez, right?" He looks at me expectantly. I nod. "How do you know Nancy Stein?"

"Well she's, was my neighbor."

"Did you guys speak? Hang out together? How was the relationship?"

"Yes we spoke. We spoke all the time. I would come over for her book club meetings every month. The day she was found was the day of this month's meeting."

"I see. So the book club meeting is why you were trying to come into her house?"

"Yes and because I saw Mary crying. I didn't know what was going on." I swallow hard.

"Do you remember what you were doing on April 28th around 7:30, 8 o'clock in the evening?" Rowley leans back in his chair and folds his arms.

"The 28th?" I stop and think for a moment. I go back in my mind by the week to try to remember what I did on that specific day. "I think that's the day that I ran a few errands after work."

Rowley interrupts me. "Where did you go?"

"I went to Home Depot, Meijer, and then I went home for the night. I ate and watched some tv."

"Were you home alone?"

"Yes."

"When was the last time you saw Nancy?"

"Um, that day actually. When I got in my driveway she was telling me about some guy that she noticed in my backyard before and that she thought she saw him again. Actually, I want to tell you about this man. I think he has something to do with this."

He completely ignores my last statement. "What did Nancy do after you talked to her?"

Is he even listening to me?

"She went in her house."

"So you were the last person to talk to her before she was murdered?" Rowley's voice sounds very accusatory.

"Excuse me? What are you trying to say?" My voice rises a little.

"You sure you didn't leave your house and make a visit to Nancy?"

"What?! No I did not. Are you accusing me of doing this?! This is crazy! What reason would I have to kill Nancy? She was my friend." My voice cracks.

"Exactly what I want to know. Why would you leave the scene in a hurry with luggage the way you did? Seems pretty suspicious to me."

A tear falls from my cheek. "That's because I got scared. You got the wrong person. I swear."

"So who would want to kill a helpless old lady like Nancy Stein?"

"I have no idea. But it wasn't me. This guy Neil something. I don't know his last name. But you need to be looking into him. He's leaving me creepy notes and messages. I think he's the guy Nancy saw in my backyard."

I show Detective Rowley the note Neil left with the rose. I show him the text messages and let him hear my voicemail. I let him know what Abigail told me about Simone and Simone's warning to me. I even tell him about Neil's outburst at Malin's. I have Detective Rowley's full attention. He lets me go and assures me they will take a closer look into Neil.

When I leave the precinct I go back to Christian's. After a while I get bored and decide I'll stop by the museum to see how Abigail is doing. It's Thursday so there are no classes today, she should be having a pretty laid back day.

Abigail looks exhausted when I spot her. She's not at the front desk. I find her sitting next to one of the statues and leaning against its leg. Her hair is in a braid that looks a few days old. I can see the bags under her eyes behind her glasses.

"Abigail?"

She jumps a foot into the air.

"Are you okay? Why are you back here?" I try to talk softly. I don't want to startle her any more.

"I thought you weren't coming today." She wipes her eyes.

"I wasn't. But I handled the emergency. I wanted to stop in and see how things have been going. Everything is alright, right?"

She doesn't say anything. She takes a deep breath and gets up. I follow her back to the front. She sits down behind the desk and shakes her head.

"The classes have been fine. The kids are great. I'm just...your friend came here. He threatened me Vanessa." She looks at me then. Her eyes rimmed red.

"Oh my God. What happened?" I touch her arm and

she's trembling.

"He told me I was dead. He was mad because I wouldn't tell him anything about where you were. I told him I was going to call the cops if he didn't leave."

"When was this? Has he been back?"

"A few days ago. He hasn't been here since then but he's crazy Vanessa. I knew it the first time I saw him. He's going to kill me."

I can't believe Neil got to her too. This guy is insane.

"No, don't worry. I've gone to the police about him. They're going to take care of him. Okay?"

"She just a nods her head.

"You know what? You don't have to stay. You can go home. Take a few days off. Go stay with some family or friends or something so you won't be alone."

Abigail stands and gives me a hug.

"Thank you." Her voice is just above a whisper.

Abigail puts her phone in her back pocket and walks out the front door with her head down. I don't think it's safe for me to be here either until Neil is taken care of. I need to stop back home for some clothes but I'm too scared to even go back. I decide to go to the mall instead and grab a few things.

I go to Twelve Oaks Mall. It's out of the way but it has all the stores I like. I stop at BeBe first. I'm going through the racks and I have a weird feeling like someone is watching me. I look around and it's just me, a few customers and the people that work here. It's pretty small so it's not like someone has anywhere to hide.

I can never buy clothes without trying them on so I take a few dresses to the fitting room. The fitting rooms here don't have doors. There are big oversized curtains and my curtain keeps moving. Feet keep walking past and they aren't women's shoes. The pit of my stomach feels funny.

I gather the dresses I want and snatch my curtain open. There's no one there. I creep out of the room and there's no one in the hall either. On my way to the register I see a man leaving the store. He's wearing jeans, boots and a cap. Just like Neil. My breath completely leaves my body.

"Ma'am? Are you all set?"

I jump at the sound of the sales woman's voice.

"Oh, yes. Sorry." I give her a weak smile and she rings up my purchase. When's she's done I hurry out of the store and decide it's time for me to go.

I'm paranoid the whole way through the mall. I keep looking over my shoulders but I don't see Neil at all. Nordstrom's door is getting closer is closer and I need to get out.

The sun is setting. I can barely see where I'm walking in the parking lot. My shoes click clack and cars roll by. Finally I'm at my car and I hop right in. I sit for a minute and just catch my breath. I need to get back to Ann Arbor now.

The sun gets lower and lower and basically blinds me. My sunglasses aren't really doing their job. I have to pull my visor down and drive under the speed limit until the sun completely goes to bed.

About 30 minutes in the sky is black. My windows are down and the wind whips my ponytail this way and that. Miguel sings through my speakers. My nerves have finally calmed down.

As I get closer to my exit I switch from the left lane to the right. A car behind me does the same. *No big deal.* Off the ramp I drive a few miles and signal to turn left. The car behind me does the same. *There is an apartment complex on the corner maybe they're going there.* I pass the complex and so does the car. Christian's condo is only a few miles away. I need to get there. Instead of signaling this time I make a hard right and the car behind me keeps straight. *Thank goodness.* I let out my breath that I didn't even realize I was holding.

Usually there would be a swarm of students roaming from bar to bar at this time. But it's summer break and the downtown area is a ghost town on week days now. I breeze through and Christian's place is right ahead.

I'm about to turn into the parking lot when I'm blinded by someone's headlights. They're turned all the way up and they're headed right towards me. I put my car in reverse and try to back into any open space. The car speeds up and turns towards my driver door. I look down to put my car back in drive. I panic and I my fingers don't do what I want them to. I look out the window with tear filled eyes and brace for whatever is coming my way.

CHAPTER TWENTY

NEIL

Vanessa is unconscious. My truck is smashed so deep into her car that they look like one big truck with 8 wheels. Smoke comes up from under her hood. Her head is on her steering wheel. I run over to the passenger side and pull her from the car. She's still breathing.

I carry her like my bride over the threshold to my truck and sit her inside. I go back to her car and grab her purse out. I don't need anyone snooping around when they see her car here. We're the only ones out on the street and I need to hurry before someone looks out their window and comes down to see what all the noise is about.

When I back away from her car I do it fast just in case something was to get stuck. I don't care about the damage to my car right now. I'm just happy it's still drivable. I don't speed on my way back home. I can't chance drawing any attention to myself. I take my time and savor my alone time with Vanessa. I look over at her and there's blood on her hairline. It looks like it's drying up. Her head knocks up against the window. She's still out.

I rub her thigh. I squeeze it and move my fingers in circles. I just want to rip her pants off and feel her skin. I look at her tits that are begging to be let out of her shirt. My hand moves to them and my hand shakes from excitement. I feel myself get hard underneath my jeans. I close my eyes just for a second and I veer off the road. The bumps along the shoulder bring my attention back to the highway.

I try to think about anything besides Vanessa. Anything that will get me home without running into a ditch. I turn on the radio and put it on a rock station. I hate rock music but at least it won't get me excited. It'll just make me get home quicker so I can turn the shit off.

When we make it to my house Vanessa is somehow still unconscious. I'm not complaining. I'll get her settled in her room and when she wakes up she'll have a good welcoming. She's going to love it here.

I pull all the way into the driveway so no one will see that my front bumper is all fucked up tomorrow morning. I think about having to carry Vanessa around the house to the front door, through the living room and kitchen, then down the basement stairs. Now I'm wishing my back door wasn't nailed shut, this would be a lot easier. But thanks to Simone I have to take the long way.

I carry her like a baby through the front door. I set her on the couch so I can close and lock the door. I expect Simone to be sleep when I get downstairs, but she's not. I'm outside of Vanessa's room door when Simone goes crazy.

"What are you doing?! Is that Vanessa? What is she doing here? What did you do to her?!" Simone screams. She tries to get up but she's chained down, she can't move.

Her screaming takes me off guard and I make a mistake and hit Vanessa's head up against the door frame. Now Vanessa is awake. She looks around and her eyes land on Simone. She turns back to me and when she meets my eyes hers almost pop out of her head. She starts flopping around like a fish out of water.

"HELP! HELP! Somebody please!" Vanessa yells and screams but too bad no one can hear her from down here.

I throw her to the ground and pin my knee to her chest. My hand covers her nose and mouth.

"Shut the fuck up! Nobody's coming for you." I press my hand closer and closer to her face so that she's suffocating. "I don't want to hurt you Vanessa, but I will."

"Stop! Please don't kill her Neil!" Simone won't be quiet. I see red. The sound of her voice makes me cringe.

"Do you want it to be you?" My eyes burn a hole right through her body. She shuts her trap and stares at the floor. She keeps sniffling and it's pissing me off.

Vanessa's face is still covered. She bites the palm of my hand. When her teeth separate from my skin I slap her just hard enough to get her to understand I'm not fucking around.

"You're going to sleep in your new room tonight and you're going to like it." I open the door and everything is just how I left it. "I didn't have time to set a bed up for you. I didn't know you would be here so soon, so you'll just have to sleep at your desk."

I expect her to fight me on the way into her room but she doesn't. She looks around and just stands in the middle of the room for a while. She eventually pulls her chair from under the desk and sits down. Her heads falls into her hands.

I hover over her chair but she doesn't look up. I give her a big hug from behind and kiss her ear. "Good night Vanessa."

She pulls away from me. "Don't touch me. Just get away from me." She's crying.

Unconsciously I ball my fists. I feel my temperature rising and I stop myself before I knock her head off her shoulders. It takes all the willpower I have to just walk away. I leave both of them downstairs and lock the door behind me.

ooo

Last night was the best sleep I've had in so long. I didn't have any dreams. I didn't wake up wondering where Vanessa was. I already knew. We're under the same roof and it makes me feel things in my stomach.

I throw my clothes on then I go downstairs to let Simone out to use the bathroom. I almost think that her and Vanessa will be out talking or something but Vanessa's still in her room. *Good.* Simone looks like a piece of shit. Her clothes are dirty. Her breath stinks. And her hair needs to be combed.

I unchain her from the wall and hold her hand the

whole way up the stairs to the bathroom. She walks all wobbly and looks like she still wants to be sleep.

"Alright clean yourself up. Vanessa is here and I need you to look nice."

She gives me a *'are you fucking kidding me'* look. I push her on the toilet seat. "Just do what I fucking say. And hurry up because you're cooking us breakfast before I go."

I stand outside the bathroom door while she showers. When she comes out her skin is dripping and so is her hair. She brushes her teeth with her body still wrapped up in a towel. I walk her to her room and pick out her clothes. A white shirt with the shoulders cut out and light blue jeans.

Simone is making french toast and bacon. It smells so good. I haven't had real food in a while. I eat a couple of pieces of bacon before she's done cooking. Normally Simone would get an attitude about me eating before everything is done but she's acting like I'm not even here. She hasn't said a word.

She sets the table while I go downstairs to get Vanessa. Vanessa is on the floor next to her room door. Her back is up against the wall and her arms are wrapped around her legs. Her head rests on top of her knees.

I give her shoulder a good shake. "Vanessa, wake up. I made us breakfast." She doesn't move.

I walk around to the wall that her head is facing. I get down on the floor next to her. She's not sleeping. Her eyes are wide open.

"Didn't you hear me? Breakfast is ready. Let's go. I don't have all day."

"I'm not hungry." She doesn't even look at me.

"Well you better find an appetite. Let's go." I lift her off the floor and guide her with my hand on her back up the stairs.

Simone is waiting for us at the table. She's already started eating.

"You don't wait for everybody before you start eating? You know better than that Mo."

She looks up at me. "Sorry." Her mouth is full of bread and dripping with syrup.

"Sorry, huh? You act like you haven't eaten in days."

I pull a chair out for Vanessa, in between me and Simone. "Here you go. You want orange juice? Milk?" She doesn't answer. "Orange juice it is."

Vanessa stares at her plate while Simone cleans hers and I devour mine. She hasn't eaten a bite. She slams her hands down on the table and looks at me the way Simone always does.

"What the fuck is this? WHAT THE HELL AM I DOING HERE?!" Her body shakes.

"You just need time to adjust. You'll feel better later. Simone will help you. You can keep each other company while I'm at work." I take the last gulp of my orange juice. "You sure you don't want to eat? Because this is it until I get back."

"You're insane," Vanessa says.

"Suit yourself." I clear the table.

Vanessa stands from the table. "I won't be here when you get back."

"Oh, I think you will."

"No I-"

I rush over to her and pin her against the wall by her neck. "You will do whatever I want you to." I hit her head against the wall. "This is your life now Vanessa. Get used to it." I let go of her neck and grab her arm instead. "But since you want to act out I have something special for you."

I force her back into the basement and chain her up in Simone's spot. The chain is long enough for both of them so I sit Simone next to Vanessa and they're both bound.

I squeeze Simone's cheeks. I lean in to kiss Vanessa but she turns her face away from me.

"You girls don't get into too much trouble." I check my phone and I'm running late for work. "Gotta go." I get up to leave and I almost laugh at the looks on their faces.

I speed the whole way to work and even run a few lights. I get there one minute before I'd be late. My supervisor, Kevin, walks over to me before I can grab the keys for my garbage truck.

"Neil, where have you been?"

"I'm not late. I got here right on time. I know I'm usually early but I overslept. See ya." I grab the keys and start walking towards the door.

"Neil-"

I turn around with one foot still in the building and the other one out of the door.

"You haven't showed up for work for two days and we haven't heard from you."

"I had some type of stomach virus. I'm all good now though."

"Well, I'm glad to hear that but unfortunately you no longer work for us. I'm going to need for you to give me your keys." Kevin sticks his arm out and waits for me to drop the keys in his hand.

"WHAT?! I no longer what?" I feel like I was just thrown in a fire pit. My hands ball up around the keys and they stab my skin.

"This is what happens when you no call, no show. Especially two days in a row." Kevin has a smug look on his ugly red face. He looks like he's been sitting under the sun for weeks. "I wish you the best of luck Neil, now the keys." He's still holding out his sausage fingers. He smiles at me then.

I throw the keys right at his face. They miss by an inch. They hit the wall and fall down to the floor. Kevin jumps and looks at me with his mouth open.

"Fuck you and your *best of luck*."

I stomp back to my truck. I slam the door behind me and the car shakes. I punch the steering wheel so hard that the horn blares. A few birds fly away out of the trees. I drive to find the nearest bar. It's early but I don't care. My hand stings as I grip the steering wheel and bloods drips down the steering wheel to my jeans.

All the way across town I pull up in front of a rundown place called "Lady Cat." The building is made of peach colored wood. There's a tall sign with a girl kicking her leg up. I'm sure it lights up at night. I park my truck and make my way to the door. They're closed. I put my face up to the window and see someone inside behind the bar. I bang on the door until the guy comes to the door.

He yells through the door. "We're closed. Come back in a few hours."

He starts to walk away but then I bang on the door even harder.

"Just let me in. You won't even know I'm here."

"Buddy, we're closed."

"C'mon. My wife is leaving me. I just lost my job. I just need a drink, that's all."

The guy stands at the door for a few seconds before he says, "Alright. Come on in." He opens the door for me and flop down at the bar. There's pink fur and cheetah print everywhere in this dump. There's a small stage in the middle of the room with a short pole. There's a few booths on the wall facing the stage. Looks like I'll be spending my day here. I put my feet on the bar stool next to me, order whiskey and wait for the entertainment.

CHAPTER TWENTY-ONE

SIMONE

I'm sitting here with Vanessa and I can't believe it. I told her to stay away but she didn't. Now who knows what Neil has planned for her, for us. She's been crying all morning and talking to herself like, *'Why is this happening to me? What did I do? I have to find a way out of here.'* What she doesn't know is that there is no way out. She's Neil's now and that's forever.

I look over at her and she has her head up against the wall. She moves her head back and forth like she's telling someone "no."

"You know, it's not so bad if you follow the rules. At least you won't have to go to work anymore."

Vanessa looks at me like I'm speaking another language. One she can't understand.

"What?! Aren't you the one that told me to stay away from Neil? If it's 'not so bad' why would you tell me that? I mean, look at us! We're chained up in a basement Simone! We have to get out of this."

"We can't get out of this. Do you have experience breaking metal chains?" I give her the same look she gave me a minute ago.

"No. I don't. But we can come up with some kind of plan to get out of here when he lets us upstairs like this morning. Don't you want to get away? I know he's not your Dad, Simone. What about your real parents? Don't you want to get back to them? I'm sure they've been looking for you."

My face falls. How does she know he's not really my Dad? Should I tell her the truth? Even if I do tell her it won't make a difference. I'm stuck here forever. I don't have anyone to go to and even if I did Neil would never ever let me go without a fight. Too much has happened.

"What do you mean he's not my Dad? What would make you say that?"

"A little birdie named Abigail told me you guys' history. It doesn't make sense for Neil to be your Dad. And plus, you don't act like he is either." Vanessa waits with an expectant look on her face. Her eyebrows are raised and her eyes are wide. She thinks she's Oprah or something.

I roll my eyes. "I should've known she'd open her big mouth. Fine. He's not my Dad, but it doesn't matter anyway."

"Why doesn't it?"

"Because my Dad is dead. My Mom is dead. This is it."

I don't know how but Vanessa's eyes get even bigger.

"Dead? What happened?" She touches my hand.

"I don't really want to talk about it. Just know that

this is my life and it's just what it is." I shrug my shoulders.

"How long have you been here, Simone?"

She barely finishes her question before I blurt out, "Two years."

Vanessa shakes her head. She has pity in her eyes as if she isn't tied up with me.

"Well that's two years too long. We're going to get out of this. You've got me now. Trust me, this won't last much longer."

Trust her? All I've done is trust people. Trust that everything would work out. Look where that got me.

Vanessa squeezes my hand gently. She smiles and wipes a tear from my face. I look into her eyes and see something I haven't seen in a while; kindness and care. *Oh, what the hell, what's one more person?*

I decide to tell Vanessa everything.

CHAPTER TWENTY-TWO
SIMONE
11Years

Mama and Daddy are on their way to take Audrina to the airport. I decided to not go. Mama and Daddy like to run millions of errands whenever they get in a car. I'm at the neighbor lady's, Miss Deirdre's, house. I always come here when they have somewhere to go. I keep telling them I'm old enough to stay home alone but they won't listen.

Miss Deirdre made popcorn for us. The extra buttery kind, the best kind. We're watching some law show she likes. It's pretty boring but it's better than the news.

"Do people get killed all the time in big cities in real life like on here?"

She pushes her fluffy hair out of her face and turns to me.

"Unfortunately, yes. Crazy stuff happens all over though. You have to be really careful. It's not like how it was when I was younger. You didn't hear about all this stuff."

We watch a few hours of her show before we notice the time. The sun is starting to go down. The sky is a pretty pink and orange color.

"How much longer are my Mom and Dad going to

be?"

"You tired of me already?" Miss Deirdre playfully pinches my arm.

I laugh. "No. I was just wondering."

"I'll call your Mom and see where they are." Deirdre's chunky fingers pry her cell phone out of her back pocket.

I get up and look in the refrigerator for something to drink. Miss Deirdre always has all the good snacks and drinks. There are like four different juices and pops to choose from. I pick a can of Mountain Dew.

I go back into the tv room and Miss Deirdre shrugs her shoulders at me.

"Neither one of them are answering the phone."

They always answer their phones. "Let me try." I hold my hand out for her cell phone.

"I've already called them twice each. They'll see the missed calls."

"Then send a text. Say, '*Just calling to see where you are. Simone insists you call back.*' Then they'll know they need to hurry up."

Miss Deirdre sends the text. We wait and watch more tv. The time is slipping by and still no call or text back from my parents. It's now dark outside. *What on Earth are they doing?*

I'm lying down on the couch half asleep when there's a knock at the door. I jump up knowing it's Mama and

Daddy. *It's about time.* I'm so ready to go.

Miss Deirdre looks out the window. She sees me putting my shoes on and tells me to "hold on a second." She answers the door and I can hear her say, "Can I help you?"

I peek around the wall and Miss Deirdre is covering her mouth. She turns her head towards me and there are tears swelling up in her eyes.

I walk up to her and grab her hand.

"What's wrong Miss Deirdre? What's going on?"

She squeezes my hand so hard that I think my fingers are going to fall off. I pull my hand out of her grasp and hold it to my chest with my other hand. She grabs my shoulders and gives me a really big hug.

"Simone, sweetie." Her voice cracks and she wipes her face with the back of her hand. "You're going to have to leave with these nice people here."

"Why? Where's my Mom?" I look from her to the lady standing in the doorway. There's a policeman with her. The lady smiles at me but it doesn't look happy.

"Your Mom and Dad were in an accident."

"What? Are they at the hospital?" I wait for her to answer but she doesn't. "Let's go see them." I pull away from Miss Deirdre and she stands.

"They didn't make it Simone. I'm so sorry." Miss Deirdre cries and shakes her head.

I must've misheard her.

"What do you mean they didn't make it?" I start to

scream. "What are you talking about?! Where are my Mom and Dad?!" I go to the lady at the door and shake her arms. "Go get them! Bring them back to me now!"

"Simone, please! They're only here to help." Miss Deirdre pulls me away from the lady.

"Simone," the unknown lady speaks to me. "I'm Monica Lane and this is Officer Brady. I know this is hard to process but you're going to be in good hands. Now we can't stay long so we'll give you a few minutes to stop home next door and get a few of your things."

"I'm going home but not with you. I'm not going anywhere until my Mama gets back!"

"Your Mom isn't coming back. I really am sorry but we have to get going."

"Miss Deirdre I don't want to go with them. I want to wait for my Mom and Dad." I sob through my words and snot flows out of my nostrils.

"I know sweetheart. Please just do what they say. You have to."

Miss Deirdre gives me a hug that could squeeze my soul right out. I wish it did.

I leave with Mystery Monica. She's pale with red curls in a ponytail that barely touches her collar. She's wearing a gray suit and white shirt. They're both too big for her. I probably weigh more than her and I'm just a kid.

We walk next door to my house and I unlock the front door. Mama gave me a key a while ago for emergencies. This is the last time I'll get to use it. Monica and Officer Brady stay downstairs while I go to my room and decide what to take with me. I stand in the middle of my room lost and confused. *How could they not be here right now? How is this even happening?*

I cry the whole time I pack my suitcase. I stuff as many clothes as I can inside of it. I make sure to grab Sophie, my lucky snow globe and a picture of me, Mama and Daddy outside in front of my treehouse. Audrina took it for us. I can't find a picture of me and Audrina so my necklace will just have to be enough.

When I get back downstairs Monica is walking around our living room looking at and touching everything. Brady is sitting on the couch looking as if this is the most boring night of his life. It's the worst night of mine. I look at the front door expecting Mama and Daddy to walk through it and tell me this is all some big mistake. There was a mix up. But it doesn't happen.

I don't speak I just wait for one of the strangers in my house to notice that I'm here. I have one giant suitcase and a book bag. This is usually my look when we go on our annual winter Duluth trip. Monica spots me first.

"Looks like you're ready to go." Monica walks toward the door and opens it for us. She lets me walk through first.

"You got it from here?" Brady asks Monica. She tells him everything is fine. He gets in a different car than us.

"Where is he going?" I watch him drive away.

"He has other things to take care of tonight. Looks like it's just me and you." She tries to sound cheery.

Monica helps me put my things in the car. I let the trunk slam and I climb in the back seat. I fall into the cushions and sit as close to the door as possible. My fingers grip the armrest harder and harder with each bump in the road.

"What happened to them? I know you said there was an accident. But what happened?"

Monica stumbles over her words at first like she doesn't want to tell me.

"They were on a back road and a deer came out of nowhere, jumped right in front of their car. They hit the deer and lost control. The car spun out and hit a tree." She clears her throat and loosens her already loose shirt around her neck.

I just cry with my head in my hands. I imagine Mama's pretty face covered in blood. Glass shattered on Daddy's face. Them crushed in our car and they couldn't get out. It's not fair. My crying must be getting on Monica's nerves because she changes the subject.

She tells me I'm going to stay with a "really nice family" that has a couple of kids of their own. They live in a nice neighborhood and I'd have my own room. She goes on and on about how great they are. The Grants.

"My Mom has a sister. How come I can't go with

her?" I sniffle and wipe my nose on the back of my sleeve.

Monica looks in her rearview mirror. She tries to look at me but I'm glued to the door, making me invisible.

"Well, she wasn't available. Are you guys close?"

"No. I only met her when I was a baby so I don't remember her. I've seen all kinds of pictures of her though. Maybe we can try her again later."

I touch my best friends necklace and lean my head on the window. Monica looks in the mirror again with a sad look on her face. I know my face looks worse. Silent tears roll down my cheeks the whole way to The Grants' house.

We pull up to a big brick house with white shutters and a pale yellow door. Lights shine from the ground, making the house visible from a block away. I can see that the grass is a healthy green even in the dark. The same kind at my house.

A lady with a big white smile answers the door. Her hair is big and blonde. She has on huge diamond earrings with the matching necklace. Her nails are French tipped and she smells like vanilla. She's even wearing high heels.

"Oh, welcome!" The lady pulls me in quick for a hug. "I'm Stephanie and you must be Simone. You're gorgeous!" She lightly slaps my shoulder. "The kids are sleep and my husband isn't home yet so you guys can meet tomorrow. Come in, come in. I'll give you a little tour of the house."

I don't really pay attention to anything she says after that. I follow her around her house. She points at things and smiles. Everything is shiny. Everything looks expensive. After her tour Monica leaves and says she'll be back soon to check on me. I don't even know Monica but seeing her leave makes me sad. Now I'm left with Stephanie and her teeth.

"Rough night huh?" Stephanie bends down to look me in my eyes.

I don't respond.

"Well I'll show you up to your room. You can get ready for bed."

I follow her up the stairs while I lug all my stuff by myself. My suitcase makes a clunking noise on each step.

"Try to be quiet dear. You'll wake the kids. They have school in the morning" Stephanie is already at the top of the stairs. She leans on the banister and waits for me to join her.

"Am I going to school too?" I'm out of breath coming up the stairs.

"Not yet. We're going to get you settled in here. You'll go next week."

There's a door immediately to the left of the stairs. I look to my right and the hallway is long and wide. This is the only door on this side. I go inside and it's a bedroom. A very small bedroom.

Everything is white. The bed. The sheets. The walls. The carpet.

I turn around and see that Stephanie has already left. I climb into the bed with my clothes still on. It's just me and Sophie. I squeeze her tight and try my best to go to sleep but every time I close my eyes I see Mama and Daddy crushed under metal.

I decide to look at the stars and talk to them. There's a small window above the headboard. I sit up and turn around to see the dark sky. The stars twinkle and dance; well the ones that aren't covered by trees. I notice two that are really close together. They almost make one big star. I imagine they have arms and are holding each other close.

"I miss you so much already. I wish you didn't leave me. I'm at some stranger's house and I just want to go home. The lady here seems nice but she's not you Mama. She doesn't look like you, smell like you, dress like you. What am I supposed to do without you and Daddy?"

My tears soak the front of my t-shirt. I rest my head on the wall and cry. I talk to Mama and Daddy until my words turn to snores and my heavy eyelids close for the night.

ooo

The next morning the house is very noisy. There are doors slamming and water running. When I wake up, I'm still sitting crisscross and my head is still resting on the wall. I turn my face and nearly fall out of the bed.

There's a boy sitting right next to my bed staring at me. He smiles when he sees that he scared me. He has perfectly styled blonde hair. His eyes are hazel and slanted. He has little specks of freckles that are so light that they're barely noticeable.

"Kids! Come get breakfast before you go!" I hear Stephanie's voice yelling up the stairs.

The boy gets up slowly and walks out of my room without a word.

I don't know if Stephanie's invitation included me so I just sit and wait until I hear people leaving the house. I don't smell any food anyway. When Mama made breakfast the smell of food is what woke you up. You wouldn't have a choice but to go downstairs to settle your rumbling tummy.

Stephanie knocks at the open door. "You didn't hear me call for breakfast?"

Stephanie is wearing white dress pants and a silky baby blue shirt. Her hair is pinned to one side in curls. She's wearing a face full of makeup and her eyelashes look like wings. I look at the clock and it's only 8 am.

"I didn't know you meant me too." I pick at my finger nails.

"Well I said 'kids' didn't I? You're a kid aren't you? I wanted you to meet Max and Madison."

I shrug my shoulders.

"Don't just sit there all day. Get dressed." Stephanie walks out of the room.

I run after her. "Are we going somewhere?"

She turns around on the stairs. "No, but no one's allowed to sit around all day in pajamas." She looks me up and down. "Or yesterday's clothes."

I go back into my new room to look for something to wear. I decide on faded blue jeans and a light purple t-shirt. If I'm not going anywhere there's no point in getting dressed up.

Stephanie never showed me where the bathroom was so I have to go find it. There's doors all along the walls and I open each one. A closet. A girl's room. A boy's room. I see double doors at the end of the hall but that's probably Stephanie's room. To the left of Stephanie's room is another staircase. To the right is the bathroom. Finally.

The floor is cold and a shiny marble. The shower is big and by itself. There's no tub. The shower doors are glass and spotless. I don't see a drop of water on the shower floor or in the sink. The towels are perfect. The toilet paper hasn't even been unraveled. It doesn't look like anyone uses this bathroom.

I go back out to the closet and grab a towel and washcloth. They're nice and fluffy.

The water gets hot immediately. The steam floats around the room and attacks the mirror. I step in the shower and let myself get pummeled. The more the water runs the more my tear ducts try to betray me. I sniffle and water gets up my nose making me cough like crazy.

I let myself cry. I let my tears mix in with the water. I let out my sadness, confusion and pain while I'm here by myself so I won't do it in front of Stephanie and her family. They're doing something nice for me and I don't want them feeling bad.

I get out the shower and my hair drips down my back. I find conditioner under the sink and rub some all over my hair. After I dry myself off I pat my hair just enough to make it stop dripping all over the place. There's no comb anywhere in here that I can find so I'll just have to leave my hair big and curly and free. How I've always wanted to wear it.

I throw my clothes on and head downstairs to find Stephanie. I check the kitchen first but I don't see her. There's a plate with a blueberry waffle sitting on the island. I go over to take a bite and it's so hard I could break my tooth on it. I find the trash can behind a door that looks like it's a part of the wall. It's at the end of the kitchen next to a hallway. I throw the waffle out and I hear Stephanie's voice.

I follow it down the hallway and it leads me to a door that's slightly cracked. I peek in and see the corner of a desk and a wall of books.

"She's doing amazing already. She loves the kids. They adore her….Uh huh. Not yet. We were going to put her in school with Max and Madison. I know it's almost the end of the year but I have connections with the board and I can get her in...They are? Well how is that happening? Oh, okay. Yes we'll bring her."

I hear her chair move and I run away from the door back into the kitchen. I can't get caught eavesdropping. I don't know who she was talking to but whoever it was, I know she was talking to them about me.

Stephanie walks into the kitchen. She looks at me and

smiles. She pulls a bottle of wine from the refrigerator and pours a huge glass. It's 10 am. Mama never drank wine this early.

"Ms. Stephanie?"

She turns with the glass down her throat.

"*Mrs.* Stephanie."

"Sorry, *Mrs.* Stephanie. Is there going to be a funeral for my Mom and Dad? Will I be able to go?"

"Oh I don't think so sweetie."

"Why not?"

"There isn't anyone to give them a funeral. From my understanding there isn't any other family that's why you're here with me."

"But what about Janice, my Mom's sister? Or Ms. Heather and Mr. Jack?"

She pours another glass of wine.

"I don't know who any of those people are." She smiles and puts her hand on my back. She lightly pushes me forward so that I will walk with her. "Let's go to the playroom. You can watch some tv."

We go down the hallway with the office Stephanie was just in. At the end of the hall the path opens up on both sides. To my left I see a staircase, probably the second one I saw upstairs. To my right is another bathroom and what she calls the playroom.

The playroom is the only room I've seen that has some color to it. They're dull colors but at least it's not all white. There's a big couch on the back wall to the right and an entertainment center with a big screen tv and video games on the wall to the left. Straight ahead is a small table in front of a huge floor length window.

I sit on the couch and Stephanie turns the tv on. She hands me the remote and turns to leave the room.

"You're not going to stay and watch tv too?"

There's that smile again.

"Oh no dear. This isn't...my environment. I'll be upstairs if you need me."

And again I'm left alone.

ooo

Stephanie comes in the playroom with a boy and girl following behind her. I'm guessing Max and Madison. They have on school uniforms that are plaid and ugly. They throw their book bags on the floor and look at me through squinted eyes. Max looks amused and Madison looks disgusted.

Madison has light freckles just like her brother. She has bone straight blonde hair that's pulled away from her face by a soft yellow ribbon. Her lips are full and her eyes are wide, not like her brothers. She's wearing a smaller version of her Mom's diamond earrings. She even has her nails French tipped like her too.

I straighten up on the couch and fidget with my clothes. Them looking at me is making me nervous.

"Kids, this is Simone, your new sister. Simone this is

Max and Madison, they're twins."

"She's not my sister," Madison says. She folds her arms and rolls her eyes.

Stephanie turns to Madison and says to her in a lowered voice that everybody can still hear, "I know sweetie. But we have to call her something."

Stephanie looks back to me and smiles that big smile.

"Whatever." Madison rolls her eyes and sits down at the table.

"Okay, well you kids make nice and I'm going to get back to my reading. Do your homework before your father gets home."

Stephanie's heels click clack on the marble floor. They get quieter the further away she walks.

"Reading is really code for pills." Max finally moves out of the doorway and sits next to me.

"Max!" Madison slams her hand on the table.

"Oh relax." He waves her off. "So Simone, how old are you?"

"I'm 11. How old are you guys?"

"13," They say in unison.

We all just sit and stare. I squirm.

"So, why you here?"

"She's obviously just another project for Mom." Madison rolls her eyes again. That must be her thing, like her Mom smiling.

"Actually my parents died. I had to come here

because I didn't have anywhere else to go."

"So, you're an orphan?" Max smirks. "Cool."

"That is pretty cool," says Madison. "What if we were orphans?"

They both laugh.

"What's funny about being an orphan?" I feel my eyes welling up but I fight back the tears.

"Oh, nothing." Max pats my knee. "We're so sorry about your loss." He still has a smirk on his face.

Madison laughs, "Max you're so mean."

"I am not." He gets up and retrieves his and Madison's book bags.

He sets both of their folders in front of them. They kick their shoes off under the table at the same time.

"Oh and we don't like the tv on while we do our homework so you might want to turn that off." Madison nods her head towards the tv.

"Sorry." I turn the tv off.

"Actually you can just leave all together until we're done," she says. "Thanks." She smiles.

Once I leave the room I hear them laughing together. Laughing at me.

I go down the hallway to the extra staircase to see where it leads. When I get to the top of the stairs I realize I was right. I'm right outside of Stephanie's door. I don't know how she hears me but she does.

"Simone? Is that you?" She calls from behind her

door.

"Yes."

"Can you come in please?"

The doorknob is cold beneath my hand. It clicks as I turn it and the door swings open.

Stephanie's room looks like a palace. Her bed is bigger than any bed I've ever seen. There's a couch at the foot of it. To the far end of the room on the right is an opened door that leads to her walk in closet. The light is on and I can see shoes on top of shoes.

Stephanie's voice snaps me out of my awe. She's lost in the middle of her bed.

"I need you to clean up a bit before Scott, my husband, gets home. I want you to make a good impression."

"What do you mean? Clean what up?"

"Yourself. You need to do something with your hair. Put something nice on too."

"I don't know what to do with my hair. I don't have a comb or a brush or anything."

"Get Madison to help you once she's done with her homework. Okay?"

"Yeah, okay I guess."

"You can go now. Close the door behind you."

I leave and go back into my room. I don't have anywhere else to go in this house. I don't have anyone to talk to. I sit in the floor and pick at the floor until my fingernails become a part of the carpet. I guess this is a good time to unpack.

After I put all my clothes in the dresser I look for somewhere to put my snow globe. I decide to place it in the window sill over my bed. It can always be there when I need it and Mama and Daddy will be able to see it through my window and know I'm okay. I shake it for good luck and imagine I'm in the globe catching the snowflakes with Daddy. I'm going to miss our snowball fights.

I decide to change my clothes so I won't drift off into a daydream coma. I don't think I have to get too fancy so I choose black jeans and a glitter gray top. I change my purple socks to black socks. When I look at myself I think I look great. I don't see anything wrong with my hair but I better do what Stephanie says. I don't want to get in trouble on my first day here.

I go back down to the playroom but both Madison and Max are gone. They're not in the kitchen or living room. They must've gone upstairs without me hearing them. I knock on both of their doors but I don't get an answer from either. As soon as I start to walk away Madison peeks her face out of her door.

"What do you want?"

She looks like a floating head.

"Your Mom said for you to help me fix my hair. She wants me to look nice to meet your Dad I guess."

She squints her eyes and purses her lips as if she thinks I'm lying.

"She did." I notice my voice is whiny so I clear my throat. "Go ask her yourself."

Madison rolls her eyes and opens her door wider. She waves for me to come in. She holds the door with one hand while the other one holds her hip. I feel her eyes on me when I walk past her.

Madison's room looks like something out of an interior design magazine. White is the main color. No surprise. But she has pops of gold and silver. She even has her own bathroom. I want to sit down but I'm scared to touch anything.

"What am I supposed to do with this?" Madison points to my head. "I only know how to do my own hair."

She's changed out of her school clothes. She's wearing a white sheer blouse with a white tank underneath. The collar is rounded and fluttery like a butterfly. Her pants are white with soft gold shimmer. She looks like she works in an office.

"I don't know. I really just need a comb and a brush. I know how to do a ponytail."

Madison goes into her bathroom. I hear her rummaging around under the sink. She comes back with a pink comb and a black brush.

"This is what my friends use when they come over if they forgot their own. But you can keep them."

Maybe Madison is nice after all.

"I'm sure they wouldn't want to use them again after

you have."

Maybe not.

"Do you have any grease or gel or something?"

"What? No. I have some hairspray."

"No thanks. I'll just use water. Thanks for the comb."
I turn towards the door to go to the hallway bathroom.

"Wait," Madison calls after me. "On second thought,
I can help you. We can do a cool new style and not a boring
ponytail."

I hesitate.

"Come on Simone." Madison rolls her eyes again.

"Okay, sure."

We go into Madison's bathroom, which is the same
size as my room. She has a vanity set up and I sit down. Her
fingers pick at my hair and I see her face scrunched up in the
mirror.

"I don't know anyone with curly hair."

"How could you not know anybody with curly hair?"

"I just don't."

Madison attempts to comb my hair but my dry curls
are now really tangled. My scalp is on fire.

"It's easier to comb when it's wet!" I yell at her and
hold my head.

Madison looks confused but moves out of the way so
I can get to the tub. I'm on my knees wetting my hair and I
feel a towel hit my back. I squeeze excess water from my hair
and wrap it up in a towel until I sit back down. Once I get

back to the vanity I rub my hair a bit then sit down.

"Put a little conditioner in it," I tell her.

The conditioner is cold on my scalp. Madison rubs it around then starts to comb my hair.

"You have really bad split ends," she says.

"Split ends?"

"Yeah. It can break your hair really bad. You should let me cut your ends a little."

I get butterflies in my stomach.

"Um, no. I think that's okay."

"It'll only be an inch of hair. You won't miss it. Trust me."

I've never gotten my hair cut before, even an inch. But I don't want my hair to break off. Madison has really nice hair, so maybe she's right.

"Okay, just an inch."

Madison already has the scissors in her hand ready to go. I close my eyes. She gathers my hair into her hand and I hear the sound of the scissor blades touching each other as she cuts.

"There. Look how pretty it is now."

I open my eyes and I'm horrified. My hair that was to the middle of my back is now sweeping against my shoulders. It's uneven and jagged.

I scream.

"Madison! What did you do?! All my hair is gone!" I look on the floor and see a pile of my red curls sitting there.

I look at her face and she's smiling.

"You did this on purpose! Why would you do this?" I stomp my foot and tears flow from my eyes once again.

She just laughs.

I lunge at Madison but she's quicker than me. She pushes me to the floor and kicks me. She kneels down to my face and holds the scissors near my cheek.

"Are you crazy? Try that again and I'll do worse than cutting your stupid hair. Got it?"

I push her off of me.

"Leave me alone Madison."

She leans against the wall and folds her arms. The scissors are still in her hand. I run out of the bathroom and head straight to Stephanie's door. I don't even bother to knock, I just burst right in. All I see is blonde hair sticking out of the covers.

"Stephanie! Mrs. Stephanie! Look what Madison did. She cut off all my hair!"

She frowns her face and her eyeballs peek open. She takes a deep breath and sits up against her pillows.

"What happened?" She doesn't look interested.

"I asked Madison to help me with my hair like you said but she cut it all off! Look!" I point to my head. I'm still crying.

Madison comes into the room.

"Mommy she's crazy. She told me to cut it. Why else would I do that?"

"I did not!"

"Yes you did. Mommy I'm not lying. She doesn't like it and wants to blame it on me."

"Simone you can't come in here screaming and trying to get Madison in trouble for something you asked her to do. You should've thought about it longer before you decided to chop your hair off. Now look at you. It looks worse than before."

I touch my hair and my lip quivers.

"I swear I didn't Mrs. Stephanie."

"Enough. Go play or something. Don't bother me with this stuff."

Stephanie lays back down. I guess we're dismissed. I look at Madison and she smiles at me. She walks out of the room and goes into her own. I hear a lock click after she shuts the door.

I can't even go back in my room. All I will do is sit there and cry and my hair. About Mama and Daddy. So I go back down to the playroom. When I walk in Max is sitting on the couch with his feet stretched out on the foot stool. He looks at me for a second and turns his attention back to the tv. He doesn't even notice my hair.

I take a seat on the far end of the couch away from Max. We sit in silence as he watches some action movie that blares through the speakers. My stomach starts to rumble. He must hear it.

"Don't worry my Dad will be home any minute. He

always brings takeout so you'll eat soon."

Ten minutes later Mr. Grant comes home. I hear the front door slam shut.

"Steph, I'm home," He yells up the stairs. "Kids I brought pizza."

I follow Max into the kitchen. Mr. Grant is unloading a couple of liters of pop into the fridge.

Mr. Grant is tall and slim. He has brown hair and brown eyes. His face is clean shaven and his jawline is square. He's wearing a powder blue shirt with dark pants. His tie is shiny and looks expensive.

"Hey Dad."

"Hey son. You been behaving yourself?"

"Yeah, of course."

"You finish your homework?"

Max nods his head.

"What about your sister?"

"Yeah she's done. She's in her room."

Mr. Grant looks around Max and his eyes land on me.

"And you must be the new kid. Welcome home." He reaches his hand out for me to shake. I grab his hand and his grip shatters my fingers.

"Interesting hair."

My stomach falls.

"You getting along good here?"

Madison comes strolling in the kitchen and looks me in my eye. She waits for my answer.

"Yes, just fine. I love it here."

We all go into the dining room with our pizza and pop. I sit down and eat dinner with my new family in my new home.

CHAPTER TWENTY-THREE
SIMONE
11 Years

It's been a few months since I've been with the Grants. My once hopefulness is gone. Max and Madison hate me. They've even convinced all the kids at school to hate me too. Stephanie is always out of it and Scott is never here. Most of the time I just lock myself in my room so I can't be bothered. It doesn't always work.

Madison's friends are sleeping over tonight and I couldn't be less excited. According to Stephanie they're both our friends and it's both of our sleepover. That couldn't be further from the truth. I'm not looking forward to tonight at all.

Stephanie turned the playroom into a spa for the night. The table is full of nail polish and makeup. Glitter is all over the place and I'm going to be the one that has to clean it up. I thought a taco bar would be cool but Madison shot that idea down. It wasn't "classy" enough.

Stephanie hired a chef for the night, who's already here. We're going to have Italian food. From the appetizers, to dinner and the dessert. He has little printed out menus for us that says we're going to have cheesy tomato bruschetta, chicken parmigiana and cannolis. I don't know what any of it is but it sounds delicious.

My empty stomach would love to eat right now but I have to wait until Madison's friends are here and are nice and pampered. I skipped out on breakfast which was just Stephanie's pancakes. Her pancakes are the worst. They're either gooey or burnt. Madison and Max obviously don't know any better because they eat up anything she cooks.

It's around 4pm when Madison's friends start to show up. We're on summer break so they're all acting like they haven't seen each other in years. Ava shows up first. She's wearing long pigtails and shorts that look like she ripped them from a pair of pants herself.

"Hi Simone," Ava says.

"Don't say 'hi' to her. Come on." Madison pulls Ava up the stairs. "We'll put your stuff in my room."

"Is anybody else here?"

"Not yet. Tess and Zoe are on their way though."

Their voices fade into silence once they're in Madison's room and the door closes. Max comes strolling out of nowhere and stops in front of me. He has a bag of M&M's and pops the peanut candy into his mouth as he stares at me.

"What do you want Max?"

"Why aren't you upstairs with your *girlfriends*?" He flutters his fingers when he says 'girlfriends.' "I'm sure Ava missed you."

"I'm not in the mood." I turn away from Max and

head towards the fake spa.

Max annoyingly follows me.

"What mood would that need to be?" He sits knee to knee with me.

"One where I felt like being bothered and I don't."

"I won't have to bother you. Maddy and her friends will have that covered. Have fun."

Max smiles at me before he walks out of the room. A few moments later there's a beeping noise, meaning someone either went out or came in the house. A basketball dribbles outside and I know Max must've went out to the driveway.

The doorbell rings and I rush to the front door so I can beat Madison to it. Maybe her friends will be nice to me when she isn't around. I open the door and both Tess and Zoe are standing there with big smiles and even bigger overnight bags. Their smiles disappear when they see me in the entryway instead of Madison. They're moms drive off without a second look.

"Great. You're still around?" Zoe says.

"Why wouldn't I be?"

Neither of the girls answer my question. They push past me into the house.

"Where's Madison?" Zoe frowns her face at me.

"Girls! How are you?"

We all turn around and see Stephanie floating down the stairs. I can smell her perfume from here. She has on dark jeans, a white turtleneck and a pale pink blazer. Looking at her you would think it was the middle of October and not August.

"Go and put your things in either Madison or Simone's room. Hurry back down so we can eat bruschetta and do makeovers." Stephanie seems really excited.

"Now Simone remember, we don't want any problems out of you tonight. This is supposed to be fun for you girls so don't ruin it."

I just nod my head and go along with what she says. I'm not the troublemaker in this house but she refuses to believe it.

The chef places a long plate of bruschetta on the dining room table. There's a small plate in front of each chair. One for each of us girls. Stephanie has taken out her fancy glasses for us to drink out of. Each is filled with bottled water. I would rather have juice. After a few minutes of me and Stephanie sitting in awkward silence, Madison and her friends come downstairs and join us.

Bruschetta is clearly just a fancy name from cheese toast. It's really good though. I have three pieces before Stephanie gives me the 'you're eating too much' face. She would think one slice is pushing it. She barely ever eats. I only see her with wine and salads. She probably told the chef to make her a salad instead of the chicken we're going to have.

When we're done with the bread we all go into the playroom. Madison stops her Mom from crossing through the doorway. She puts her hand up to her Mom's chest.

"It's okay Mom. We can do our own makeovers. Just call us when the entree is ready."

Madison, Ava, Tess and Zoe all sit at the table and start picking out their nail polish colors. They don't even give Stephanie a second look. Stephanie blinks hard and walks out of the room with her head down but her big permanent smile is still on her face.

"I think you hurt her feelings Madison," I say.

"Mind your business Simone. You're lucky you get to be involved."

Her friends all giggle behind their hands. I keep my mouth shut and sit in between Ava and Zoe. I just don't want to be next to Madison. I pick out an orange-ish pink color for my nails. Tess picks purple. Zoe has yellow. Ava likes the baby blue and Madison picks out red.

"I'll do yours for you Simone," Ava says and smiles at me.

"I thought you were going to do mine." Madison pulls on Ava's arm a little.

"I can do both. It's an odd number of people Maddy."

Ava rolls her eyes and gives me a dirty look.

"Just do mine first then."

Madison doesn't wait for Ava's answer. She places her polish next to Ava and puts her hands on the table in front of her.

"Do hers Ava. I can do my own anyway."

I don't join in on their conversation. They're talking about going back to school and what boys are hot and hoping that there will be new hot boys. All they ever talk about is clothes and boys. Even if I were to try to say anything Madison would call me a kid and tell me to shut up.

I polish my nails in silence. I'm very careful to not get any on my fingers. I put the quick dry top coat on and they look amazing. Shiny, smooth and perfect.

Ava looks at my hands and she's obviously shocked.

"Wow! Those look really good. Like from a salon. How do you know how to do that?"

"I don't know. I just do. I used to draw and paint a lot before I was here so maybe that's how."

"Really? That's pretty cool. I want you to paint mine."

Ava finishes up Madison's nails and turns to me. Madison's face is red like fire. Her face is all frowned up and she's pissed.

"Hey Maddy I'll start on your makeup. Come on." Tess must see Madison's anger too and wants to calm her down.

Madison always gets mad if I say anything to any of her friends. But she gets really mad about Ava. They're like best friends. Madison is embarrassed of me and she wants everybody to hate me as much as she does. I don't know what I've ever done to her. I've only tried to be a good sister or whatever I'm supposed to be to her but it just makes her angrier.

I don't want to be close with Madison or Max anymore because they're so mean to me. But I don't want to have to be by myself all the time. It gets lonely. When Mama and Daddy died everything else went with them. I'm at a new school and I have no friends there. I haven't talked to Audrina since she went back home. I don't even know if she knows what's happened. What hurt is it going to do if I'm friendly to Madison's friends?

After I finish Ava's nails I leave them to tend to their makeup. I look for Stephanie and find her sitting at the dining room table with a bottle of wine that's almost empty. She doesn't hear me come into the room.

"Mrs. Stephanie?"

She jumps out of her skin.

"Simone, you scared me. What do you need?"

"Is it okay if I eat now? The girls are doing makeup now and I don't know how long they will be. I'm pretty hungry."

"Go ahead. You can make your own plate. I sent the chef home. Everything is wrapped up on the counter."

Stephanie points in the direction of the kitchen and turns her attention back to her wine glass.

I make my plate and pour myself a glass of juice. I'm sick and tired of water. I go back into the dining room and sit next to Stephanie.

"Coming back to keep you company." I dig into my plate and it's the best thing I've ever tasted. "Did you eat already?"

"Yes dear. You forgot we had bruschetta?"

"That's all you're going to have? This chicken is really good. You should try some."

"No. I've had my share for today."

"What time is Mr. Grant coming home?"

"I don't know." She gets up from the table in a rush. "Hurry up and eat so you girls can start your movies."

Stephanie leaves the dining room. She goes up the stairs and a few moments later I hear her room doors shut.

When I'm done eating the other girls start to make their plates. I tell them I'll wait for them to start the movie. I don't think they care either way. I watch tv in the playroom until they finish.

They all come back into the playroom with small plates and cannolis on top of them. Ava brings a plate in for me. We all sit on the floor cross legged facing the tv. Madison goes through her movie selection in the entertainment center and puts in a DVD.

Madison picked "Mean Girls." I've never seen it before. Tess, Zoe and Ava all get excited when they see what we're watching. As the movie plays the girls are glued to the screen. They recite some of the lines on cue. If I would've watched this movie a few months ago I would've thought that Regina was the meanest girl on the planet but she has nothing on Madison.

The movie ends and I'm left downstairs to clean up

everybody's mess. I put the dishes in the dishwasher and put the leftover food in the refrigerator. I make sure all the lights are out before I go upstairs.

Madison and her friends are in her room. I hear them talking and laughing. I know Stephanie wanted us all to have a sleepover together but I think I'll just go to my room.

I turn my light on and my chest immediately tightens up. My lucky snow globe is shattered in a million pieces on the floor. There's a huge wet spot underneath the glass. The little girl is broken in half and reaching up towards the ceiling. When I get closer to the mess I notice that Sophie is hurt too. She's cut down the middle with stuffing all over my bed.

I cry silent tears. These were the last two things I had to remember my life before this. I felt safe with Sophie. I could imagine I was sleeping at home and I would wake up to Mama. Without my snow globe all my luck is gone. They're dead and I know Madison did this.

I know a confrontation won't solve anything. I also know trying to tell Stephanie what she did would be even less successful. I have to be smart like Madison. I have to think like her. I'll get her back.

A few hours into my sleep my bladder wakes me up. I try to ignore it but it's about to burst. I use the moonlight coming through the window to help guide me to the door. I step into the hallway and before I make it to the bathroom I hear noises coming from Madison's room. I hear whispers and giggling. I walk up to her room and the door is slightly cracked. Thankfully the hallway is pitch black so no one can see me. I look inside and I can't believe what I see.

Madison is sitting on Ava's lap on top of her messed up sheets. They're kissing with tongue and touching each other. I cover my mouth before any sound can escape from it. Zoe and Tess are knocked out on the floor on their makeshift beds. I wonder if they know about Ava and Madison. This is why Madison is so territorial about Ava. She's her *girlfriend*.

I can't go to the bathroom up here now. They'll hear the toilet flush and know that I probably saw them. I sneak downstairs. I'm lucky that there's carpet on the steps so no one can hear a thing. I use the bathroom next to the playroom and go back to my room. I finally have something on Madison.

ooo

It's been a few days since Madison's sleepover. Everything's the way it normally is. Mr. Grant is gone. Stephanie is drunk somewhere. Madison is being rude and Max is egging her on.

Stephanie says she's tired of hearing our voices so she sends us outside to get some fresh air. She tells us to go ride bikes because she doesn't want to hear us acting like animals outside either.

I trail behind Madison and Max who ride side by side. We ride to an ice cream place a few blocks away. Whatever we order is up to Madison. She's in charge of money because according to Stephanie she's the responsible one.

They each order a banana split. I walk up to the counter to make my order.

"Are you all together?" The girl behind the counter asks me.

"Yes. Can I have-"

"No we're not. She's not getting anything," Madison says to the girl.

"Yes I am Madison. Cut it out. Can I have one chocolate scoop in a cup?"

The girl moves towards the chocolate ice cream but Madison screams at her.

"You better not make her any ice cream. I'm the one with the money so I'm calling the shots. She's not getting anything. Got it?"

The girl looks back and forth between me and Madison. She opens her mouth to say something but almost immediately closes it right back. She listens to Madison. Madison and Max walk to a small table and begin to eat their ice cream. The girl looks to me and whispers, "Sorry."

"Madison what is your problem? Why can't I have any ice cream? I didn't even do anything."

"Did you not hear me? I'm in charge. So sit down and shut up."

Max laughs.

"What's so funny Max?" You think this is funny?"

"Yeah, actually. Look at you." He stuffs his mouth and laughs some more.

"It's not. It's not fair!"

They ignore me. They finish their sundaes and talk to each other. I'm just like a ghost. I might as well not even be here.

I'm fuming the entire way home. Madison and Max ride much faster than me and make it home before I do. They're standing on their front lawn waiting for me.

"Hey Simone, how was your chocolate scoop?" Max yells out and Madison bursts into laughter.

"Laugh all you want Madison. You just wait."

"What are you gonna tell on me?" She laughs some more. "We all know that doesn't work."

I pull into the driveway and sit on the bike with my feet planted on the concrete.

"About the ice cream? No. But let's see how Stephanie feels about you and Ava."

"What about me and Ava?" Her voice gets low.

Max looks at us confused.

"You know what. She's more than just your friend Madison. I know everything."

"You little bitch."

Madison runs through the grass towards me. I try to hurry and ride off on the bike but my foot gets stuck in between the pedal. Madison shoves me hard and I fall with the bike coming with me. I land on my ankle and I hear a loud crack. I scream out in pain and I can't move. I struggle to get the bike off of me but it won't budge.

"Shit," Madison mumbles under her breath.

"Help me please. I can't move." I cry out to either of them.

They both run inside the house leaving me by myself in the middle of the driveway.

CHAPTER TWENTY-FOUR
SIMONE

Vanessa hangs onto my every word. She interrupts me every so often to ask questions. I wish she wouldn't then I could finish quicker. I don't like to remember the Grant family. They were terrible to me. I prayed all the time that my Aunt Janice would come save me but she never did.

"I was with the Grants for a year. After my ankle was broken people started poking around. I eventually got sent to a group home after Stephanie had to go to rehab."

"Do you know what happened to Madison and Max?"

"They stayed with their Dad. Other than that I've never seen or talked to them again."

I go on to tell her about my time at different group homes. I never went to stay with another foster family and I hated it. That's all I wanted was a family. I tell her how I thought I found a sister in Amber but I was wrong again. Losing Amber and Calvin was really hard on me and it's ultimately what led me to Neil. He seemed nice. Weird, but nice. He acted like he understood my pain. He made me feel better. He took me in when I really had run out of options. He was my knight in shining armor turned into my greatest mistake and my greatest nightmare.

Vanessa's mouth is to the floor. She looks like she's in pain. She shakes her head and closes her eyes.

"You've been through so much and you're so young. I couldn't imagine. I'm so sorry all those terrible things happened to you. You didn't deserve any of it. And you don't deserve this." She points to the ground and I know she means Neil and everything that comes with him.

"So what are we going to do when Neil gets back?"

"Just leave everything up to me. He won't have a choice but to let us go."

Vanessa hugs me. Her touch melts my body. It feels real. It feels strange. I haven't had a real hug since Calvin. My Calvin.

ooo

I've been spending a lot of time with Calvin ever since I spent the night after The Red Room. It's only been a week but the more time I spend with him the more comfortable I feel around him. Amber all of a sudden doesn't like him anymore. She tells me to ditch him and that he's a loser. I'm starting to think she's jealous.

She and Corey have been having issues because he can't seem to remember they're "exclusive." I tried to tell her when I saw him and Jessica together. But she never listens to me because she's older and knows more. She "forgets" they're exclusive sometimes too. She does her own thing so I don't understand.

Calvin and I are going to go out today for a midday date. I want to look nice so I ask Amber to help me out.

"Amber please? I want to look good."

"You already look good." Amber applies lip gloss to her lips.

"You know what I mean."

"Okay I'll help but you can't borrow any of my stuff today."

"Why not?"

"Because I don't want you to."

Amber picks out a tight, stretchy skirt with a colorful print. She tells me to wear a plain v-neck t-shirt with it. I pair the outfit with sparkly sandals. I wear my curls half up, half down. Amber does my makeup. She does a light natural look. I look really pretty.

"He should be here soon so I'll go downstairs to wait," I say to Amber.

"Sure. See you later." Amber's attention is on her phone.

I sneakily grab one of Amber's necklaces off her dresser before I walk out the door. It'll add the last touch I need. I fasten it around my neck. The gold chain feels cold on my skin. The blue stone rests on my chest and catches the light.

I wait outside of South Westmore for what seems like forever. Calvin still isn't here. I go back inside to check the time and he's over an hour late. I sit on a bench across from the elevators. I just look at people come and go.

Luckily one of those people happen to be Abigail.

"Abby," I run up to her. "Can I use your phone for one second?"

"Simone I'm going to be late for class."

"Just for a second, I swear. It's an emergency."

Abigail reluctantly hands over her phone. I've remembered Calvin's number by heart and click the numbers on her touchscreen phone. His line rings and rings with no answer. I try again and I get the same outcome. I guess he forgot about me.

I give Abigail her phone back and she rushes out of the door. I decide to go hang out in The Den for now. I don't want to go back to Amber's room so she can laugh at Calvin standing me up. I sit in a booth alone and watch tv.

The news is on and they're talking about some accident. Behind the reporter is a car all banged and burnt up. It must've caught on fire. It looks just like the car Calvin has. The lady says the person who was driving was a student here at this school and my stomach falls to the floor.

Calvin's picture flashes across the screen and my heart shatters into one million pieces. I run out of The Den and get in the elevator up to Amber's room. I bang on her door.

"Who the fuck is banging on my door like they're the police?" Amber opens the door and she's wearing a frown.

"Amber! Oh my God! Calvin is dying!"

"What? He's what?"

"I just saw it on the news. I've been waiting for him and I thought he stood me up but he didn't." Tears roll down my face and my chest feels tight.

"How do you know? What happened?" Amber comes to sit next to me on her bed. She grabs my hand.

"I don't know. Some accident. His car caught on fire. It was on the news. We have to go to the hospital to see if he's okay."

Amber looks from my face to my neck. She rips her hand away from me.

"Is that my necklace Simone?"

"Huh? What?"

"You heard me. You stole my necklace?!"

"I didn't steal anything. I was just borrowing it. But forget your necklace. Did you hear what I just said?"

"Take it off right now."

I unclip her necklace and place it in her waiting hands. She smiles when the gold touches her skin.

"Well look at the bright side Si-Si, at least you weren't stood up."

ooo

I'm not sure what time it is but I assume it's around 5 o'clock because I hear noises upstairs. Neil is home. I look over at Vanessa and she's fallen asleep.

"Vanessa," I whisper her name. "Get up, Neil is

back."

She doesn't wake up.

"Vanessa!" I say her name through my teeth and give her a tap.

She jumps up and looks around. She looks confused as if she doesn't remember where she is. Her eyes land on me and her expression softens. She wipes her eyes and nods her head in a 'yes' motion.

Neil loudly comes down the stairs. He looks drunk which isn't a good sign.

"How are my two girls? Did you have fun today? Were you talking shit about me all day?"

"We're hungry," I say.

"Excuse me?" Neil's eyes are bloodshot red.

"Hi sir. We've missed you but we're really hungry."

He smiles.

"That's better."

"No, no, no," Vanessa chimes in. "We're not doing this. We didn't miss you but you're going to miss us because you're going to let us the hell out of here."

"And why would I do that?"

"Because if you don't you'll get caught. Pretty soon someone's going to come looking for me and guess what? They'll come straight here."

Neil looks amused.

"No one's going to be looking for you sweetheart. You're mine now."

"I've been to the police, Neil. It's over. Let us go."

"You haven't been to any police. Stop lying before I make you." Neil gets in Vanessa's face.

"I have. They know about everything, including Nancy." Vanessa smiles and Neil smacks it right off of her face.

"You little cunt." He punches her. "Fucking bitch."

Vanessa kicks and screams. She looks to me for help but I don't know what to do. *This was her grand plan? I could've told her it wouldn't work.*

"Neil, stop it! Leave her alone."

Neil raises his fist to me. I instinctively flinch but he never hits me. I open my eyes and see that he's unlocking the chain around Vanessa's waist. He throws her aside and she hits the wall with a smack. He comes to me and unlocks me too.

"What are you doing?" I start to panic.

"Get the fuck up," Neil says to Vanessa.

She doesn't move.

"I said get up!" He grabs her by the arm and yanks her to her feet.

Neil pulls both of us upstairs. We wiggle and squirm but he's too strong. He leads us to the front door.

"If one of you make any fucking sound I swear I will kill you."

We both know that he means it.

Neil opens the door and forces us out of the house. He

pushes us up against his car and tells us to get in. My feet tell me to run and not look back but my fear paralyzes me. I look down the street at all the open space. My view is blocked by Neil's huge body.

"I said get in." Neil pushes me into the car.

I look to my left and Vanessa is already inside. She's crying.

Neil hops in. He connects his phone to his car charger and speeds out of the driveway. I don't know where he plans on taking us but I know that wherever it is will be the last place we ever see.

CHAPTER TWENTY-FIVE

VANESSA

We've been on the road for a few hours. There are signs telling me that we're in Indiana. I occasionally take a glance at Simone and her face stays glued to the window. Neil's eyes never leave the road. No one has said a word and it's driving me crazy.

"Neil where are we going? You can't do this."

"Vanessa just be quiet. You've done enough," Simone says.

I see her face for the first time since we've been in the car. She has the same look on her face that she had when she warned me to stay away from her and Neil at the art class.

I see the pain behind her big green eyes. They glisten from tears that have yet to fall. She's still beautiful in all her hurt. Her curls fall around her face chaotically but perfect at the same time. Her lips involuntarily quiver. A broken girl, Simone is. A hurt girl. A scared girl. But a beautiful girl.

I imagine Simone as a little girl. The look of love and admiration in her eyes when she looks at her Mom. Her cheeks getting rosy when she's around her Dad. Having the world and having it ripped away.

I can't let her down. I feel responsible for her now. She's been abused and abandoned for years. I want to see a smile on her face. I want genuine joy to burst from her body. I want uncontrollable laughter to escape from her mouth. I want Simone to finally live.

Her eyes beg me to just shut up and cooperate. I break her stare and look at Neil. He's mumbling under his breath. His knuckles are white. His body lightly shakes as he drives but not because of the car.

Against Simone's wishes I speak again.

"Neil, can you stop please? I really have to go to the bathroom."

"No. Hold it."

"I can't hold it! I'm damn near ready to pee all over your seats."

Neil runs his hands through his hair. He clenches his jaw. He blinks really hard. His eyes are closed so long that I get scared that he'll crash or veer off the road.

"Neil please. I really have to go."

"Fine! Just shut the fuck up."

We pull off on an exit in the middle of nowhere. The sun is starting to go down and the area looks creepy even with a pink and orange backdrop.

We pull up to a store that has Christmas lights. Christmas lights in May. There's one other car in the parking lot. An old white Taurus.

As soon as the car stops I open the door. My foot isn't

even on the ground before Neil swoops down on me and squeezes my arm.

"No funny business, you hear me?" Neil whispers in my ear and his tongue touches my lobe right before I pull away.

"Get off of me!" I try to pull away but he just squeezes harder.

"I don't think you get it Vanessa." He pins me against his truck. "The more you fight the harder you make things for yourself. Now quit being a little bitch and find some brains." His finger pokes me in the side of my head.

I stare into his eyes. I can't penetrate the icy blue surface.

"Got it."

He lets me go and walks on my heels. He turns around when he notices Simone is still sitting inside the truck. He pulls me over to her door with him. Simone is paralyzed in her seat. She looks like she's seen a ghost. Neil knocks on the window.

"Hello? Earth to Mo. Get your ass out here. I'm not leaving you alone."

She doesn't move. Neil yanks the door open and pulls her out. Simone looks up at Neil terrified.

"I can't go in there."

I can tell Neil is losing his shit, even more than usual.

"And why is that?" Neil talks through clenched teeth.

"I just can't."

Neil gives Simone the most evil look I've ever seen on a person's face. His hand wraps even tighter around my arm. His free hand balls up into a fist. I feel like I'm losing circulation in my arm. I squirm under his touch but it doesn't matter. Simone gets the point and starts to walk towards the store's front door.

Neil lets go of me when we get inside. He instantly changes. He's smiling. The color has come back to his face and he's no longer shaking. He looks normal.

There's a young girl behind the counter. She's reading a magazine. A big pink bubble hides her lips. She sucks it back into her mouth and pops her gum.

"Excuse me, can I use your bathroom?"

"The bathroom is only for paying customers." She doesn't even look up from her magazine.

"It's just that we've been on the road for hours now and it's kind of an emergency. Please?"

"As soon as you buy something."

"Okay we will." I turn to Simone who's staring at the girl. "Pick something out. Anything."

Simone looks like a deer in headlights.

"We're not buying anything. You're just going to have to hold your piss or go outside. I don't really care."

We all look at Neil. He looks uncomfortable with all eyes on him. Simone still looks like a deer and the girl looks disgusted. The girl points to her left, my right.

"The bathroom is over there in the back."

"Thank you. Come on Neil."

"What?"

"Come with me. Don't you have to go too?"

Now the girl's eyes are on me.

"Simone go ahead and pick something. The nice girl will *help* with anything you need." I put extra emphasis on the word 'help,' hoping she will get the point.

"Neil?" I start moving toward the bathroom.

Neil squints his eyes at me. He shifts his weight and stuffs his hands in his pockets. He looks over at Simone who still hasn't moved. The girl is looking at us like a circus act.

"No, you go ahead. I'm gonna stay here with Mo. Now hurry up."

I hesitate. But if I don't go I'm scared to find out what would happen next. I head to the bathroom. I lean on the wall in frustration. I wish there was some way for me to leave a message in here for the girl to find.

I stand there defeated. There's nothing here but toilet paper and soap. There's no notebook or marker that will magically appear for me.

Finally my brain clicks. I can use the liquid soap to write with. I hit the pump like crazy letting mountains of soap pile up in my palm. I smear the soap across the mirror above the sink. I spell out 'Please help. Call police.' I go over the letters a few times to make sure they're visible and readable.

There's a knock on the door and I jump out of my

skin.

"Vanessa enough of your shit. Let's go."

"I'm coming." My voice shakes.

I look back to the mirror and I feel my heart squeeze in my chest. I almost want to wash the message off. What if Neil comes in here. I'm terrified. My body starts to shake and I don't know what to do.

He knocks again.

"Now!"

I take a chance and leave the soap on the mirror. When I walk out I stay really close to the door and close it behind me. Neil tries to peek inside but I'm too quick. He moves like he wants to go in.

"Something is wrong with the toilet. It has all kind of shit in there and it won't flush. The girl should probably take a look before anyone else goes in there."

I grab Neil's hand and pull him behind me as I walk back toward the front of the store. I don't want to give him any chance to doubt me and go in the bathroom. When we get to the front we find Simone still in a trance. The girl is back into her magazine.

"Miss? You might want to check on the toilet in there. It's a mess."

She looks up as we reach the front door. I give her an earnest look. She's so preoccupied with herself that I hope she can read it and understand. It's important that she reads the liquid soap as quickly as possible. Our lives depend on it.

Neil and I are halfway out the door before he grabs Simone's arm and drags her out with us. We all climb in Neil's truck. I see the girl still looking at us through the window. *Please just go to the bathroom.* She must hear my thoughts because she finally gets up and goes to the back of the store.

We pull out of the parking lot and get back on the highway. Simone is turned around and she's looking out the back window.

"Simone what did you get?"

I have to tap her before she realizes that I've spoken to her.

"A snow globe."

Simone pulls a round ball out of the paper bag in her hands. It fits in her palm perfectly. In the middle of the globe is a woman, a man and a little girl. They're each holding a snowball. She shakes it up and flakes circulate all over. I look at her face and she's smiling with tears in her eyes.

ooo

We make it to Illinois when Neil pulls into a rest stop. He shuts the car off and leans his chair all the way back crushing my legs. I scoot out of the way and I'm now knee to knee with Simone. Neil takes off his hat and puts it over his eyes and folds his arms.

"How long are we going to be here?" My stomach rumbles.

"Stop asking questions. We'll be here until I decide to leave.

"But we're hungry."

"And so am I. Get over it."

"But-"

Simone nudges me. She shakes her head and mouths, "Stop it, please."

I start to speak but decide against it. I leave her to her snow globe and Neil to his sleep. His snoring vibrates throughout the car. It's obnoxious but it doesn't seem to rattle Simone at all.

I try to get comfortable but it's nearly impossible with the small space and all the pain my body still feels from the accident. The accident this mad man caused. I look at my face in the rear view mirror and I look terrible. There are bags under my bloodshot eyes. My mascara has left rings around my eyes. I look like a zombie. Like I haven't slept in ages.

I think about Christian. He should be back home by now. I think about what must've been going through his mind when he walked in and saw that I wasn't there. Did he find my car wrecked in front of his building or had it already been towed away? Did he call my phone? The police?

And Aundrea. I talk to her all the time. She has to have called me. I know she must be worried since I can't return any calls. I never told her about the serious issues with Neil though, she may not even think I'm in any danger.

It's time to take matters into my own hands, again.

I inch my way to the door, making sure not to bump into Neil's chair. When I reach for the lock he rolls over and his hats falls from his face. I freeze and hold my breath. I wait until he settles and his snore starts back up before I move again. I carefully pull up the lock and slowly pull the door handle. Fresh air hits my face and I jump out of the truck. I turn around and see how horrified Simone's face is.

"Come on. Hurry, let's go." I whisper to her.

"Are you crazy?! Get back in here before he wakes up and sees you."

"No, Simone. This is our chance. Please get out."

She doesn't budge.

I run over to her side of the car and yank the door open. I try to pull her out of the car.

"Vanessa please stop. He's going to kill us!"

She starts to cry and she fights me off of her. I stumble and she slams her door shut. The noise wakes up Neil. He straightens up and turns around. He sees Simone crying and me outside of the car. He jumps out and runs toward me.

"What the fuck are you doing? You think you're funny huh? You think you're smart?"

He pins me up against the truck. His hands hold me in the air by my neck. He yells at me but I can't even make out what he's saying. I'm too busy scratching at his hands and struggling for air.

Simone bangs on the window from behind me.

"Neil stop! She wasn't doing anything I swear! Just stop please!"

He bangs my head on the window. The color in my sight starts to get hazy. Darkness begins to block my vision. I feel my heart slowing down. Suddenly I fall to the ground. I gulp down all the air my lungs can take at once. I cough uncontrollably.

I can finally see again and I see that Neil has moved on from me and is now stomping Simone into the ground. I want to get up and help but my body doesn't let me. My legs wobble and my lungs feel like raisins.

Neil picks Simone up from the ground. He carries her over his shoulder. He pushes me out of the way with his leg and opens the car door. He tosses her inside like an old bag of laundry. He grabs me by my hair and drags me across the concrete. I can't even scream. I'm thrown in right next to Simone. Her body is scrunched in a ball and she hugs her snow globe close to her chest. I scoot next to her and lean on her arm. I expect her to push me off or yell at me but she doesn't. She puts her arm around me and pulls me closer.

We sit together and stare ahead as Neil begins to drive again.

CHAPTER TWENTY-SIX
SIMONE

It's really dark out and Neil is running out of gas. I can tell he's really tired too. He didn't get much sleep back at the rest stop because Vanessa has been acting crazy. I'm all for messing with Neil but this is different. This is a Neil I never want to see or be around. I know what he's capable of and it scares me to death.

I feel like I've been hit with a truck. Neil might've fractured or broken something. His heavy boots felt like boulders crashing down on me. Every bump in the road sends shooting pains from my head down to my toes. Vanessa extra weight on me isn't helping but I don't have the heart to tell her to move. I know she's been trying to help, even though she hasn't, and I don't want to be mean. I know Neil, she doesn't.

The ride is silent. I look out of the window and just stare at the few stars I can see behind trees and lights. This drive is making me very unsteady. I've been on these same roads so many times before going on the annual Duluth trip with my parents. We're on the exact same route. I haven't been in this direction since I was 10 years old. When we were at the Christmas shop I thought I was in a dream. It seemed like I had gone back in time. I felt like a little girl again. I half expected to see Daddy standing at the counter with hot chocolates. But he wasn't there. I wasn't in a dream. I was in the real world, a world that's a nightmare.

My brain shuts down and my eyes give up on me. The blur of nature outside turns into complete darkness. My cheek is pressed up against the cold glass window. I feel my body go limp and I fall asleep.

I'm woken up by falling out of the car. I catch myself before my face hits the concrete. Neil is standing over me still holding the door. Vanessa is half hanging out of the car. I look around and we're in the parking lot of a Best Western.

"Vanessa you're going to go in there and get a room on the third floor." Neil reaches in his pocket. He peels back a couple of bills. "Here."

"I doubt they're going to take this. You need a credit card to book hotels."

Neil punches the car.

"Just do what I say for once!"

She jumps and scurries inside of the hotel. After a moment she comes back out and puts her hand out to Neil.

"They don't accept cash." She has a smug look on her face.

Neil reluctantly hands her his card. He doesn't like to be wrong.

"How is she going to use your card? She's not you."

Neil rolls his eyes at me.

"This ain't the Four Seasons."

A few minutes pass and Vanessa is standing in front of us again with two room keys. Neil takes both of them. We walk inside the hotel, which looks more like a motel to me, and the man at the counter stares at us until the elevator doors close. The third floor comes quick. The doors open and there's a mirror on the wall right in front of us. I look just as bad as I feel. I get close to the mirror and stare into my eyes. They look dead.

Neil yanks me away from my reflection and marches down the hallway. We're all the way in the back in room 329. There's two queen sized beds, a small refrigerator and a flat screen tv on top of a desk.

"I'm going to take a shower if it's okay."

Vanessa is talking to Neil and he waves his hand at her.

She closes the bathroom door and the water comes to life immediately.

Neil grabs the comforter and pillows from one of the beds and makes a pallet right in front of the door. He lies down without even taking off his hat or boots.

"You comfortable?"

Neil pulls his hat down over his eyes in response.

The bed is calling my name. It's begging me to come keep it company. I touch the sheets and they're smooth and cold. The covers are tucked so tightly under the mattress that I have to yank them out. My arms scream at the effort.

I kick my shoes to the floor. I peel my socks off of my aching feet. I move my fingers in a circular motion against my skin making my toes tingle. I feel like I've lost 10 pounds just from removing my shoes.

I wish I had clean soft pajamas. My jeans are going to be stiff and terribly uncomfortable to sleep in. I'm not stripping down so I'll just have to get over it. I scoot under the covers and pull them up to my nose. I grip the sheets as if someone will come up and try to steal them away from me. The cool bed soothes my pain a little and the pillows feel like a piece of heaven. As soon as I feel my body drifting into sleep Vanessa opens the bathroom door and wakes me right back up.

I peek my eyes open. Vanessa has put her clothes back on. Her hair is damp and it sticks to her shirt. She tiptoes over Neil's body and limps her way over to the bed I'm in. The closer she gets the more I can see bruises on her neck. I didn't notice them before.

"Do you mind if I get in with you?"

I shrug my shoulders.

She slides underneath the comforter. Instead of her scooting in she stays at the edge of the bed. She might as well lie on the floor.

"Why is Neil by the door," she whispers.

"Because he doesn't want us, you, to leave. Why do you think we're on the third floor?"

"What do you think he has planned? Where do you

think we're going?"

"I don't know Vanessa. Maybe we're moving to Idaho where we'll be the only people for hundreds of miles and he can do what he wants with us. One big happy family."

Vanessa looks away from me.

"Sorry for causing more problems. I'm just trying to get us out of this mess. I promised you that I would."

"Well cut it out. You're going to get us both killed. You're lucky that I saved you earlier."

"What are you talking about? When?"

"At the store. If it wasn't for me punching Neil he would've choked you to death for sure."

Vanessa blinks hard and furrows her eyebrows.

"I didn't even realize you did that. Look Simone-."

"Let's just go to sleep please. I'm sure we'll have a busy day tomorrow."

Before Vanessa has a chance to go against what I've said I roll over and burrow deeper into the covers. I stick my arm out to turn the lamp off on the nightstand. I pull my arm back in and hug the pillow. I look into blank space and count imaginary clouds until I fall asleep.

ooo

I'm surrounded by roses, sunflowers, daisies, baby's breath, lilies, bleeding hearts, orchids and every other flower you could think of. I don't know how all of these flowers are together but it's definitely the most interesting garden I've ever seen. It's the most beautiful garden I've ever seen.

I'm lying on the ground. The grass blades tickle my skin and the dirt is so soft it crumbles under my touch. Lucky fluff floats around overhead. Butterflies, bees and birds fly together as friends in the clear blue sky.

I follow the path of a hummingbird and it leads me to a big Grandmother Willow tree like in Pocahontas, only the branches grow lavender flowers and not leaves. Leaning against the strong bark of the tree is Mama. Her hair is long and flowing in the wind. Her smile shines like the sun. She's clothed in a white dress and her skin is luminous.

Mama reaches her hand out to me. I look around to see if anyone else is witnessing what I am. We're the only two here. Her arm is still outstretched and she calls for me. My eyes stay focused on her perfect face as I walk towards her. She pulls me into a big hug. Her arms are strong but delicate at the same time. I melt inside her embrace. I want to cry but I can't. It's like the atmosphere won't allow any tears to escape.

We sit in the grass and smile for what seems like hours. She has food with her in a small basket. I don't know where she pulls two homemade lemonades from but they're delicious.

"Are we in heaven Mama?"

She smiles.

"No silly. We're right here." Mama points to my heart. "And that's where I'll always be, Daddy too."

"I thought I lost you guys forever."

"We'll never leave you Mo."

I scoot really close to Mama and nuzzle up on her shoulder. She rubs my hair and looks into my eyes.

"You're just as beautiful as always." She frowns. "But I don't think you know just how beautiful. Not just your outer beauty, but your inner beauty. You've forgotten it. You gave up. I know your father and I left the physical world when you were pretty young but this isn't how we raised you. I'm disappointed."

I never want to disappoint my parents. They're the best things that ever happened to me. They gave me joy. They gave my life meaning. But they're not with me so life is different now.

"You don't have to give up on life because we're not physically in it."

Is she reading my mind?

"I know there's an amazing girl in there. But you have to know it too. I don't want you to hurt anymore Simone. I want you to find the strength to live again. Because your life is worth living. Don't forget that. It's time to bloom."

Suddenly it feels like we're in an earthquake. I look at Mama and she doesn't seem affected. I look around and nothing is moving but I'm shaking violently. It's becomes so unbearable that I start to feel like I'm being pulled apart. I try to hold onto Mama but I can't. She disappears and so do I.

My eyes open and somehow I've ended up on the
floor. My legs are sprawled out and my head is basically
inside of the opening at the bottom of the nightstand.

I hear screams. At first they sound far away but they
grow increasingly louder. I turn to my right and the bed is
shaking. I pull myself up and Neil is on top of Vanessa. His
pants are at his ankles and so are hers. He's raping her right in
front of me. I'm frozen to the floor.

He puts his hand over her mouth to shut her up. She
uses my move and bites his skin. He pulls his hand back and
mutters "*bitch.*" He slaps her hard. His handprint is left on
her cheek.

The phone starts to ring. I don't know if I should
answer it. The sound blares in my ear. It stops. Immediately
after it starts to ring again. Over and over and over. Neil gets
up and unplugs the phone. He picks it up and hurls it across
the room. I jump and scoot against the wall. I wish I could
become a part of it and be done with this.

Neil gets dressed and sits down to put his boots back
on. Vanessa is still half dressed and shaking, entangled in the
sheets. Her screams have stopped but her crying hasn't.

"Shut the fuck up and get dressed. It's time to go."

She doesn't move.

"Are you deaf now?! Move it!"

Vanessa jumps at his loud voice and struggles with

her pants. I see her fingers tremble from here. She can't even get the zipper to work. Neil pushes her hands aside and does it for her.

"You're useless," he says to her before he grabs her arm making her stand.

He turns to me.

"You too Mo."

I've never wanted to be invisible more than right now. I don't want any of what Vanessa just got so I listen. I walk over to them and my legs feel like they weigh 100 pounds. I'm scared to look at Vanessa. I don't want to see the look on her face. But she looks right at me and I've never seen a sadder look in my life. Not even from myself.

We walk out of the room in a single file line. An employee of the hotel is coming down the hallway as we're leaving. They look pretty upset.

"Excuse me, sir?"

Neil ignores the man and pushes past him. We follow.

"I'm talking to you!"

He's ignored again.

We get to the elevator and Neil punches the button so hard I thought that it might shatter. The man is now standing right with us.

"I don't know what was going on in your room but I don't like whatever I believe is going on." He looks at me and Vanessa with pity.

"Other guests have called with complaints of loud

noises and screams coming from your room. We have called the police and they should be here any minute."

This guy thinks he has authority but he doesn't know who he's talking to. Neil grabs him by the collar. The man instantly shrinks to about two inches. Neil looks like he's about to hit him but he pauses. He looks at us and throws the man to the floor.

The elevator doors open and Neil pushes us inside. The man is still on the floor as the doors close and he's left behind. When we get in the lobby Neil begins to push us along. He seems to be in a panic. Vanessa and I try to move as fast as we can but we're both still in pain.

We all get inside of the truck and Neil pulls off so fast his tires burn rubber. I've never seen it done in real life. Neil is sweating and is as red as the devil's butt. He actually seems scared. None of us say a word.

Neil hops back onto the highway. He weaves in and out of traffic like someone is chasing us. Everything is a colorful blur looking out of the window.

We drive about a half an hour before Neil stops at a gas station. My stomach is touching my back so I get out to grab some snacks. Vanessa doesn't move to get out.

"Come on Vanessa. I know you've gotta be hungry." I talk softly to her.

I wait but she doesn't budge.

"Okay I'll pick something for you."

When I get inside Neil is shopping around for food

too. He looks at me and gets pissed.

"Why the fuck would you leave her out there by herself?"

"She's not going anywhere Neil. You've made sure of that."

He looks like he wants to curse me out more but doesn't. Instead he hands me $100 and says to pay for the gas and food. He says he's going to the bathroom.

I pick out chips, pop, candy, honey buns, peanut butter crackers and even some pizza that's spinning around in a heater box. I have to go back and forth to the counter to set things down because it's too much to carry at once. There's a girl already in line and she keeps looking at me. She's making me nervous.

"Do I know you?"

"I'm sorry you just look so familiar. You look just like a girl I used to know named Simone."

"My name is Simone." I sound like I'm asking her a question.

"Oh my God it's you! It's me, Brittany! Audrina's cousin." She smiling from ear to ear.

I can't believe my eyes or my ears. Brittany? I haven't seen her since I was 10 years old. She rushes over to me and squeezes me so tight that my lungs almost collapse.

"I can't believe it's you. It's been so long." I don't know what to say.

"Too long. We've missed you."

"Yeah?"

"Of course. So sorry about your parents too."

My stomach falls.

"We all would've reached out but no one knew how to find you."

"That's okay." I don't like talking about Mama and Daddy's death. "So what are you doing out here?"

"I'm on my way to Duluth. I go to school out here and I'm on break."

"College?"

"Yeah. What about you? What have you been up to? Wait until I tell Drina."

As she's talking my attention is grabbed by the tv behind the counter. It's on a news station and they're reporting about Neil. She follows my gaze and we both listen to what they say.

"Police are looking for murder and kidnapping suspect Neil Weiss." His picture is shown on the screen and my jaw hits the floor. *"His last known whereabouts were at an Illinois Best Western with two females. He is said to be driving a black Ford pick-up truck. Please contact police if you have seen him or have any information."*

I look at the bathroom door that Neil still hasn't come out of. My heart starts to race and my palms become sweaty. Brittany starts talking to me again but I can't even hear her.

Neil emerges from the bathroom and I could just die right here. He comes up to me and he isn't happy.

"You still haven't paid for this shit? I can't leave you to do anything."

Time has stopped. Brittany stares at him and so does the girl behind the counter. They both look shocked and terrified. They both look outside and see his black truck. I turn to Brittany and mouth *'Please, no'* and shake my head. Now her jaw is the one on the floor.

The employee takes Neil's money. Her fingers shake and she forces a smile as he leaves.

"OH MY GOD! Is that the guy from the news? We have to call the police."

"Brittany please-"

"Did he kidnap you? Simone you have to leave with me."

"I can't." I start to cry.

"What do you mean you can't?" She looks like she wants to hit me.

"You don't understand. He'll kill me. I have to leave with him."

She stays quiet for a second. She looks outside and looks at him as he pumps the gas. She taps her foot on the ground and pinches the bridge of her nose.

Neil sticks his head back inside the gas station and yells at me.

"What the hell are you doing in here? Let's go!"

He leaves.

I look at Brittany and I wonder if she can see the fear

oozing from my body.

"Okay look. Take my phone." She digs around in her purse and extends it out to me. "Keep this with you at all times. Don't let him see it, okay?"

"I can't."

"Simone, do it." She puts the phone in my hand. "Turn the ringer off. You're going to call for help. Do you understand?"

I want to refuse. I want to run away. But then I see Mama. I see her in the garden and I think about what she told me. She wants me to be strong. She wants me to bloom. I look out at the truck and I can see Vanessa through the window. She looks defeated.

It takes everything in me to take Brittany's phone but I do it. I do it for Vanessa. I do it for Mama and most importantly I do it for me. I give Brittany one more glance and run out of the gas station. I can feel her eyes on my back.

"What were you doing in there Mo?"

"Uh nothing." I stutter. "They just really liked my hair and were asking questions about it."

"Questions about your hair?"

"Yeah." I can't look him in the eye.

"I don't know why. Your hair looks like shit."

Neil screeches off again. I turn around and see Brittany standing outside of the gas station. She looks at our truck until she's a speck in the background that fades away. Her phone feels like a brick in my pocket. Having it makes me nervous but excited at the same time. My adrenaline is through the roof. I have to stop myself from smiling, Neil will get suspicious.

I want to tell Vanessa that we'll be okay. That I'm going to save us. But I look at her and she looks like a puppy that's lost its owner. She still hasn't even looked at anyone. She just stares out the window. Her body is curled up and she hugs her knees. She hasn't even stretched. She's like a sad statue. I think we've traded places.

Hours pass and we're still driving. We're in Wisconsin now. I don't know where Neil plans on taking us but in the back of my mind I hope it's Duluth. If we end up in Minnesota my life would come full circle. It would be a huge sign of something good. I'd be back in a place where I have so many memories, good ones. I can't go there and make bad ones.

I get so bored in the car that I start daydreaming. I imagine that it's January and I'm getting ready to go skiing. Mama's there, Daddy, Audrina, Brittany, Ashley, Ms. Heather, Mr. Jack and even Grandma and Papa are there too. We're in a big cabin with our coats and boots on. Our thick gloves hold cups of hot chocolate. The marshmallows aren't even melting.

I'm not sure what we're talking about but we're all smiling and laughing. The fireplace in the background crackles and sends comforting heat waves toward us. When our cups are empty we all get up and go outside. The snow falls slowly. The flakes land on my nose and melt into heart shaped water droplets. The ground crunches under our feet and it's such a satisfying feeling. Nothing is more beautiful than being on top of a mountain on a cold winter day.

We each go down the slope in perfect form. We look like an Olympic team. We go back up and come down again, over and over. When everyone is tired and out of breath I have to think of something else to keep us all here. I scoop snow into my hands and pat it into the perfect circle, the perfect snowball.

I throw it at Daddy for old time sake. He looks shocked. He looks around to see where it came from and then he spots me. I shrug my shoulders and laugh. The battle has begun.

Audrina, Brittany, Ashley and I are on one team while Daddy, Mama, Ms. Heather and Mr. Jack are on the other. Grandma and Papa just watch and cheer everyone on. This is the best time I've had in years.

We grab all our gear when the sun starts to set. We put everything back inside of the cabin. Everyone goes to their rooms to change into footsie pajamas. All of us gather around the fireplace with our snacks to get ready for scary stories. We stay up all night telling stories and watching movies. I watch as everyone finally falls asleep right where they sit.

My daydream fades away as my mind registers what I'm actually seeing outside. We're now in Minnesota. I can't believe it but the signs tell me it's true. A huge smile breaks my face. I almost scream from excitement but then I look around and realize that no one else is happy.

I'm not sure what city we're in when Neil gets off of the highway. He drives on deserted back roads. Every so often a house pops out of nowhere and then there's miles of empty land. We go deeper and deeper into the woods until we're driving up hills. There are so many twists and turns just like a maze. There is no way I would be able to find my way out.

Neil comes to a stop in front of a small cabin. The wood is dark and old. The door is green with a black handle. Besides the trees surrounding us there isn't anything else to see. I don't know how Neil knew this place was here but I'm not going to ask.

Neil gets out of the truck and opens Vanessa's door. She was leaning on it so he has to catch her before she falls face first into the ground. He grumbles something under his breath about her being a "stupid bitch" and drags her to the front door of the cabin. She isn't even trying to fight him off.

There isn't even a lock to get in. He opens the door easily and they go inside. I wait until i can longer see them in the doorway before I get out of the car. I hop out and sticks break under my feet. My shoes sink into the wet ground. I've never been to Minnesota at this time of year before. It looks and feels much different than being here in the winter. Everything is sad and drab instead of sparkling with icicles and snow.

Even though it's spring the air still has a little nip to it. The wind whips my hair back and forth. My shirt slightly flaps against my stomach. I hug myself and rub my arms to fight off the chill. Neil hasn't come back looking for me so I decide to explore.

I walk around the cabin and I complete the trip in a few seconds. It really is that small. The cabin has a chimney so at least I know we'll be able to sit next to a fire to stay warm. Behind the house are tons of wood blocks that I assume are for the fireplace. *I wonder who cut them and just left them here.* There aren't any other entryways besides the front door. I only see four windows for the entire cabin and they're skinny slivers of glass. They're maybe big enough for a five year old to squeeze through but that's it.

I start to walk off at the back of the cabin. There are trees on top of trees. The leaves are wet and soggy. The branches all look weak. There isn't anything out here to see. I don't even see any squirrels, birds, nothing. We're alone.

I go back to the cabin and find Neil leaning against his truck. He's talking to himself. He hears my footsteps and looks at me with hate in his eyes.

"Don't ever run off like that again Simone. You stay where I can see you."

"I didn't run off anywhere. I was just looking around."

"SHUTUP!" He balls his fists and slams them in the

air. "I'm tired of these little mind games you and your mother keep playing with me."

"Me and my what?"

"You heard me. I'm the Dad around here I make the rules! So whatever the fuck you bitches think you're doing is done!"

His nostrils flare and spit flies from his mouth. His chest heaves up and down violently. This psycho really thinks he's my Dad and that Vanessa is his wife. I don't even want to go near him.

"Go in the house Mo."

I just stare at him with my arms still folded. He walks toward me and I take a few steps back. He moves faster and I know he's going to hit me. I take off running. I know there's nowhere to go but I don't know what else to do. My body can't take another hit.

I'm in a full sprint and my eyes begin to water as the wind smacks me in the face. I look back and see that he's right behind me. He's breathing like a wolf chasing his prey. I lose my footing and fall to the ground. I tumble down the hill and I can't stop myself from falling. I feel like I fall faster and faster after each roll.

Next thing I know I'm in a body of water. I've landed on a family of rocks in a creek that cuts through the woods. I try to get up but I can't move. My entire body feels like I'm on fire and the water isn't helping. I try to push myself up with my feet but as soon as I put pressure on my legs I scream. It feels like one million razor sharp knives are stabbing me in all directions.

I moan and cry as I stay stuck in this creek. I stop moving and trying to get up because I'm only causing myself more pain. I cry and my tears burn my eyes. A crunching sound grows louder which I know means that Neil is close. I flop my arms down in frustration and I feel Brittany's phone in my pocket. I remove the phone as fast as I can and shove it down my shirt and into my bra.

I hear Neil's laughter.

"Look at you." He crouches down next to me.

"Don't touch me, please. Just leave me here."

"You always do this shit to yourself Simone. You know I've never met anyone so stupid. Stupid, stupid bitch."

Neil grabs me under my arms and lifts me up. My entire backside is soaked. My hair drips into my shirt down my skin. Neil puts me over his shoulder and turns away from the creek. There's nothing I can do about it but cry. I'm his little rag doll.

My legs flail with each step he takes and the pain is excruciating. I scream and holler but my voice falls on deaf ears. Neil makes it back to the cabin and he kicks the door open. My head is bent all the way down so I can't really see how everything on the inside looks. I see his feet make a left turn and we enter a bedroom. He drops me to the floor with a loud thud. Neil walks out and I hear the front door close behind his feet.

The stabbing feeling hasn't gone away. I have to push myself up against the wall using only the strength in my arms, which aren't that strong. When I finally feel the wall touch my back I stop torturing myself. My arms shake and they feel like they have their own heartbeat. Just something as simple as breathing is a task.

My eyesight is blocked by tiny dots in my pupils. Like the kind you get when you stare at the sun too long. The dots emit rainbow circles. I blink extra hard and rub my eyeballs until they feel like they'll pop right out of the socket. It doesn't help that much. But it helps just enough for me to make out feet hanging off the bed in front of me. They're small and twisted together. Vanessa's in here with me.

"Hey Vanessa," I whisper. "Come here."

She doesn't move.

"I know you're awake."

Still no movement.

I leave her alone for a while hoping she would come out of her bubble and talk to me. I'm not sure how much time has passed but it seems like forever. The silence is killing me.

"I'm getting us out of here...I have a phone."

Vanessa sits up then. She looks skeptical but I have her attention.

"Don't kid around Simone."

"I'm not."

I pry Brittany's phone out of my shirt and show it to Vanessa. Her eyes light up like a kid meeting Santa.

"Where'd you get that?!"

"Shhhh!" I put my fingers to my lips. "Be quiet."

We both get silent. Vanessa leans over and looks out of the doorway for any sign of Neil. She turns back to me with expectant eyes. I wave her over and she finally scoots off of the bed. She tiptoes her way across the floor and sits against the wall right next to me.

"So...let's see."

CHAPTER TWENTY-SEVEN
SIMONE

I start to hand Vanessa the phone but she takes a harder look at me and the phone falls in her lap. She grabs my hand gently. Her face wears a frown.

"What happened to you?" She puts the back of her hand to my forehead.

"Nothing. It's not important right now."

I'm sweating profusely. I inhale small bits of air so my breathing sounds very choppy. I can't see my face but I'm pretty sure there's no color in it. I can just feel it. I look down at my aching legs and the left one is sitting at a slight angle. Vanessa's hand leaves my forehead and goes to my leg. I scream like a mad woman. Her touch sends flames throughout my body.

Vanessa jumps back and mutters the word, "shit." She grabs the phone out of her lap and navigates to the call keypad. She dials 911. She holds the phone to her ear but she isn't saying anything. She hangs up and calls back. She's still quiet as she bites her bottom lip.

"What's the problem?" I don't think I can take the pain much longer.

"It's not ringing. There's no signal in here!"

I take a big gulp of my own spit.

"Try going by the window."

She crawls over to the window and sits underneath it. She calls and hangs up when it doesn't connect. She tries one more time.

"Hi! Oh my goodness! I don't know where I am but we need the police and an ambulance. My friend and I have been kidnapped and I think she has a broken leg….Hello? Can you hear me?"

Vanessa pulls the phone away from her ear and looks at the screen. She bangs her head on the wall.

"No, no, no!"

The call must've failed again.

"What are you doing?"

The sound of Neil's voice makes both of us jump. He stands ominously in the doorway.

"What? No-Nothing."

Neil starts to walk toward Vanessa very slowly. He has a tall bottle of beer in his hand. Vanessa crouches even further into the floor.

"Who were you talking to?" Neil's voice is eerily calm.

"Simone."

"Didn't sound like that to me. Stand up."

Vanessa doesn't budge. Her scared eyes search the bedroom for a hero. But there isn't one.

"I said stand up!" His voice rises a little.

She complies but keeps her hands behind her back. She tries to look him in the eye but his stare is too strong for her. Her eyes quickly go to the floor.

"Turn around," he says.

Vanessa turns and simultaneously brings her arms to the front of her body, keeping them hidden from Neil.

"Let me see your hands."

"What?"

"Show me your hands. Now." Neil grabs the back of her neck.

Vanessa hesitates but eventually she slowly brings her hands in his view. I can see her arms shake from across the room.

"What the fuck is this?" Neil points to the phone. "Where the fuck did you get this?"

You could hear a pin drop.

"Cat got your tongue, huh?"

Neil finishes off his beer. He looks like he's about to slam it against Vanessa's head. She cringes and braces for impact. Instead of the glass hitting her it comes crashing to the floor. Glass shatters everywhere. Some even makes its way over to me.

Neil takes the phone from her and throws it across the room with all his strength. It hits the wall to so hard that it breaks and falls into pieces. Neil beats Vanessa until his fists turn blue. It's worse than I ever got, or seen. And there's nothing I can do.

I block out Vanessa's screams and cries for help. Her voice turns into white noise. I stare blankly at the broken phone. Our chances of ever getting out of here just crashed against the bedroom wall. We're going to die here. Me sitting against this wall immobile. Vanessa in a pool of her own blood.

Neil tires himself out and finally stops pounding Vanessa's head in. He kicks her for good measure before he walks away. He looks at me but it seems like he's looking right through me as if I'm not even here.

He steps on top of my left leg instead of walking around or over me. He uses me as a bridge. I feel my bones crushing even more. I hear them crack. A sound escapes from my mouth like no other sound I've ever heard before. I almost don't recognize my own voice. The pain is excruciating. I swat at his foot to alleviate the pain but I'm no match. He's taking pleasure in my pain and laughs in my face. I'm on the verge of blacking out.

Neil's feet finally find their way to the floor and he goes over to the phone and stomps on it to break it further. When he's satisfied he leaves us in the room again. I hear him flop down on something loud and springy in the other room, probably an old couch. His breathing eventually turn into snores.

I can't believe I'm in a hidden cabin with a broken leg and a maniac that has probably killed someone right in front of me. Vanessa hasn't moved from her spot. I can't see her face from here. The bed blocks everything but her feet.

I honestly never thought things would ever get this bad. I thought moving in with Neil would be a step in the right direction for me. I could get out of the streets for good. In hindsight it was the worst decision of my life. Neil has gotten crazier by the day. People are dead and by the looks of things it won't be long before I am too.

I kind of blamed Vanessa for his new found rage but it's really not her fault. She doesn't know when to quit but she shouldn't have to. She didn't ask for any of this. Neil sucked her in and wouldn't let go. Now look at her. Look at both of us.

After sitting so long my butt starts to get numb. I wiggle around to put some feeling back into it but it just aggravates my bladder. It's full and ready to burst. I try my hardest to lift myself with my arms and with the help of the wall but I can't do it. I unbutton my pants to take some of the pressure off but that only helps for a few minutes.

"Neil! Please come help me."

He doesn't come. He continues to snore.

"Neil!! I have to pee really bad! Neil!"

I know he has to hear me but he just keeps snoring.

I dig deep and find the strength to drag myself. I pull myself out of the bedroom and into the living room. With each slide across the floor my leg feels worse. It feels like it will detach from my body at any moment.

Halfway across the room I'm out of energy. I lean

back on my elbows and let my head hang back. I won't make it to the bathroom. I don't even know where it is. I yell out for Neil one more time but he's obviously in a really deep sleep.

After what feels like hours of just lying in the middle of the floor my bladder wins and I piss myself. A 17 year old girl just peed on herself. No one can see me but I cry from embarrassment. I cry because I'm angry.

I stay in this spot all night. The sun is gone and I'm left in the darkness wishing I would just die. Before I can even cry again for the millionth time Neil wakes up. He looks at me like he doesn't know why I'm here.

"How did you get in here?" He still sounds asleep.

"I pulled myself in here. I kept calling you but you wouldn't answer."

He walks over to me and bends down as if to pick me up.

"What is this? Why is the floor wet?" He rubs his hands on his jeans.

I'm too embarrassed to answer him.

He grabs me under my knees and armpits and holds me like a baby. He looks at the ground and then lifts me over his shoulder to look at my backside.

"Did you fucking piss yourself Simone?!" He throws me to the ground.

There's a big boom. At first I think it's because he's thrown me to the wooden floor but then I hear it again. Neil does too. He turns toward the front door. He walks very slowly and puts his ear to the door. As soon as he does the door flies off the hinges and sends Neil falling to the ground.

An army of people rush inside. All I can see are flashlights. They're blinding me. Their feet stomp inside and they're screaming.

"Neil Weiss come out!"

"Vanessa are you here?"

Someone spots Neil on the floor and yanks him up. Neil fights back and they get in a scuffle on the floor. Another person joins them and uses a taser on Neil. His body flip flops around like a fish out of water.

The men run around the house. It's so much happening and I don't know what's going on. One of the men almost trip over me. He bends down to my eye level. His flashlight shines on me and blocks his face.

"I've got somebody," he yells out.

"Can you move?"

I shake my head 'no.'

"Just sit tight. Everything will be okay."

A few people go into the bedroom. A few moments later Vanessa is being carried out.

"We have Ramirez."

I turn my attention back to the guy that was fighting Neil. He has him pinned to the floor but Neil is like an animal, he isn't giving up. He rips the taser away from his body and gains control over the man on top of him. The taser man pulls out a gun and aims it right at Neil. Neil is quick and uses the fighter as a shield. He has him by the neck and he's stuck in front of him. The man spits and coughs and kicks his feet to get away but it doesn't work, Neil just squeezes tighter.

The gun stays aimed in their direction and the man doesn't seem like he knows what to do. He speaks into a walkie talkie on his shoulder but I can't even hear what he's said. My mind can't register what is happening around me. This can't be real.

I try to stand and my leg stops me before I can even start. The pain brings me back to reality. This is no dream and I need to get out of here.

For the first time I notice the flashing lights outside. There are even sirens blaring through the woods. The person holding Vanessa takes her outside. Someone comes in and slides me on a stretcher. I can't even speak. My mouth is touching the floor.

As I'm put in an ambulance I see more men rush inside the cabin. I try to look around the EMT to see what's going on but she's purposefully blocking my view. She shines things in my mouth and eyes and asks me a million questions I don't give the answers to. I finally look at her and she's round with big red cheeks. Her hair is pulled back into a braid. Her glasses are bigger than my face.

"Where's Vanessa," I blurt out

"She's in a different ambulance."

"Is she okay?"

Before the lady answers me two loud gunshots ring out around us. Everything goes silent and my breathing stops. I'm sure my heart has stopped too. I stare at the open door of the cabin but it's too dark to see anything. A few moments later there are more gunshots.

"What's happening? What's going on?!"

The EMT ignores me and jumps out of the ambulance closing the door behind her. If I could move I would jump out right behind her. But I can't. Instead I try my hardest to hear what's going on outside but it's too much commotion to really know.

It seems like forever but the EMT lady gets back inside and her face is whiter than a ghost. As soon as the door closes we start moving. I want to ask her what she saw but I don't think she would tell me anyway. She makes me lie down and we ride listening to the sounds of the siren.

ooo

I'm in a hospital bed. Everything around me is bright and white. It reminds me of my room at the Grants'. If I wasn't so loopy from the pain medication I would probably be filled with anxiety. It takes all the energy I have to keep my eyes open. They feel like 20 pound bags.

The room smells like old people and it's making my stomach turn. A judge yells at some guy on the TV. I look around and I'm all alone. There's no nurse, roommate or even flowers.

My left leg is covered in a thick, stiff cast that I hate. My knee has been itching for ages and I can't get to it. I poke my nurse button and a very cheery lady comes into my room. She has red hair and freckles just like me. Her hair is pulled back into a wavy ponytail with a sparkly pin at the side of her head. Her fingers are long and skinny with white nail polish.

I tell her how uncomfortable I am. The nurse smiles at me and her teeth are hidden by braces. She fluffs the pillows behind my back and uses a long, skinny stick thing to reach down into my cast. As she scratches my knee I close my eyes in satisfaction. I tell her I'm hungry and she tells me she'll be back with some food. She leaves the knee scratcher behind and I tuck it into the side of the bed so I can keep it for myself.

As I wait for her to come back my mind goes back a few days. I had to go into surgery when I was brought into the ER and when I woke up I was staring into the face of a police officer. He was big with salt and pepper hair.

"So you must be Simone."

I nod my head 'yes.'

"How are you feeling?"

"I'm fine," I say trying to fight against my hoarse voice.

He gives me a smile.

"What's your last name?"

"Hanson."

"How old are you Miss Hanson?"

I start to say 17 but something makes me asks what today's date is.

"Today is May 12th."

"I'm 18." Today is my birthday.

"How long has it been since you've been with Neil?"

"For two years."

The officer looks at me with pity in his eyes. The same look I seem to get from everybody.

"Well I'm sure your family will be very happy to have you back." He smiles at me again.

I don't bother to tell him that I don't have any family. I don't want to see that look on his face again.

"How did you find us?"

"Well your friend Brittany helped us out a lot. We tracked the cell phone she gave you."

"But the call dropped when Vanessa tried to call the police."

"She had a 'track my iPhone' app on there. Led us right to you."

The nurse gets back and interrupts my daydream. She places a tray of slop in front of me. There's a slimy meat mixed into a yellow mushy stew, a peach fruit cup and a banana. I push the stew to the side and eat the fruit. Even the fruit is mushy. I force myself to finish it and try not to vomit.

After a while I get bored in the small hospital room. I swing my legs to the side of the bed and grab ahold of the crutches that lean on the wall next to me. Once I'm up I tie my gown extra tight so it won't fly open as I limp around. I leave my room and travel down the long hallway until I get to Vanessa's room. Luckily we're on the same floor.

I get inside and she's sleeping. The top of her head is bandaged. She has stitches in her eyebrow and lips. Both of her eyes are rimmed deep purple. I don't have x-ray vision but she's also bandaged around her torso under her gown, she told me yesterday. She looks pretty bad but better than when she was first wheeled in.

Normally I doubt the hospital would let me still be admitted here but they're doing me a big favor. I can stay as long as Vanessa is here. She told them she was my aunt. I think they knew we were lying but let it slide because of everything we've been through.

The police have been in and out since we've been here. They wanted to know all the ins and outs of Neil and how he tortured us. Vanessa was more emotional than me. I had more time to get numb to Neil. I never asked what happened to him back at the cabin. I haven't watched the news either. I decided I didn't want to know.

I pull up a chair and set it beside Vanessa's bed. I position it so I'm able to prop my leg up on the very end of the tiny mattress. The same judge is yelling on her TV. I reach down by my foot and grab the remote. I flick through the channels until I land on a something that is talking about animals. It's a documentary on arctic life.

I watch a woolly bear caterpillar freeze every winter

and emerge in the spring like it's brand new. It eats and eats and eats until it can make a cocoon to become a moth. It takes years on top of years. Who knew something could freeze itself from the inside out year after year and still live?

I feel like the woolly bear. My world has been cold and empty for a long time with bursts of happiness. The happiness never lasted because my situations were never good ones, even though I always thought they were in the beginning. The woolly bear is finally free from its frozen life when it becomes a moth. But unlike the woolly bear I hope my happiness and freedom lasts much longer than the short day they get with their new wings.

I look at Vanessa's sleeping face and deep down I have a good feeling. She's a nice lady with a big heart. She may think I saved us but she helped save me. With her I intend to heal my heart and fly and prosper with my new wings. Mama would be proud.

EPILOGUE
SIMONE

I waddle like a fat duck through the snow. I'm wearing long johns underneath a thick pair of jeans. Snow pants top it off. Underneath my coat is a long sleeved turtleneck and a royal blue hoodie. I cover my nose and mouth with my new fleece scarf, which is also blue. It's so bright you could see it from a mile away. I would just look like a big blob with a blue face. The cold air stings my eyes and they water relentlessly. I blink away the tears and look at the long way down.

"Ready?"

Audrina looks at me. I can tell she's smiling even underneath her bright pink scarf. I smile back.

"Ready!"

We sit on our sleds simultaneously and slide down the slope. We weave in and out, coming closer and going farther from each other. I look up at the sky and it's a pretty clear blue. Audrina reaches her arm out to me and I grab ahold of her hand. We go down the rest of the hill together.

The sleds begin to slow down and we come to a halt. We fall into the snow and we laugh hysterically. We help each other up and stand on our feet.

"Here they come," Audrina says.

We gather snow as quickly as we can and roll them into sturdy balls. We each hide behind a tree and wait for them to reach the bottom. They're laughing the whole way down. I spot Ashley first and launch my snowball at her head. Perfect aim. Audrina's comes flying out and hits Brittany in the arm. Ashley and Brittany scream and look for which direction they came from. Audrina and I snicker and duck lower behind the trees.

"There they are," I hear Brittany yell out.

Brittany and Ashley get off of their sleds and run right towards us. It becomes a full out chase. We all split up and I run like my life depends on it. I hear someone close behind me but I don't turn around to see who it is. The only sounds are our heavy breathing and the snow crunching.

I cut sharply to the right, going back up the hill, when I run smack dab into Ashley's chest. I immediately hit the ground. She sits on top of me and pushes me deeper into the snow, laughing the whole time. Then comes Brittany and Audrina. They've all jumped on me. Our huddle turns into a big hug on the ground. I wiggle my way out first and lie down on my back. They all follow suit. Our heads touch each other's and our feet are all spread apart. We're a human snowflake.

A few birds fly from branch to branch of the trees above our heads. Snow falls and sprinkles our faces. We look like ice queens with frozen eyebrows and red noses. None of us speak. We enjoy the music of nature.

Audrina's hand finds mine and we hold on to each other tight enough so that no one could ever pull us apart again. I reach out for Brittany and she squeezes my hand too. We stay like this for what seems like hours. The air is so cold and still I feel like we're frozen in time. I could stay like this forever with Audrina, Brittany and Ashley for the rest of my life and be satisfied.

After so long Ms. Heather, Mr. Jack and Vanessa find us. They tell us to come inside for some warm air and hot chocolate. They're scared we're going to turn into ice sculptures if we stay out any longer. Walking up the hill isn't as easy as sliding down it, not even close. I watch my breath escape my mouth with each step. My teeth chatter and I try not to bite my tongue. I shove my hands deep inside of my coat pockets and look down at my boots as I get closer and closer to the cabin.

We get inside and a pretty but angry fire is roaring inside of the fireplace. Pillows are already assembled in a circle beside it. Reminds me of Daddy. I smile at the thought of him. If I think hard enough I can actually see him in front of me. Him exactly as he was, like he never left.

"We made dinner, girls. Let's eat before anyone gets too comfortable," Ms. Heather says to all of us.

"I helped too." Mr. Jack has a sly look on his face.

Ms. Heather throws a towel at him and laughs. He ducks before it can hit him.

"You did not! Don't believe him."

We each take a seat at the long wooden table. The food looks delicious. Turkey, macaroni, cornbread, cranberry sauce and collard greens bless our plates and taste buds. The final and most spectacular touch is the peach cobbler for dessert. Vanessa made it and she sure knows how to cook some fruit. It feels like Thanksgiving instead of welcoming in a new year. But I'm not complaining, I have a lot to be thankful for.

I wish I could get seconds but there's no way I'd be able to eat anymore. My stomach is so full that I have to unbutton my jeans to breathe.

The fire calls our names and we gather around on our pillows. There's a bowl of marshmallows in the middle of the floor and Mr. Jack devours them. I think we're going to start the scary stories but something else happens.

"Simone we are so very happy that you're back. We wish we could have been around for you during your hard times but we couldn't find you. Your parents were family to us and we feel horrible for letting you get away."

Ms. Heather starts to tear up. She wipes her face and clears her throat.

"We have something for you."

She reaches behind her back and unveils a small box. Inside is a diamond bracelet with matching diamond hoop earrings. They glisten and sparkle as the light hits them. Engraved on the inside of the hoop is, *'Family forever. We love you.'* We pull each other into a big hug. I don't want to let go.

Everyone around us is getting emotional. Tears, hugs and smiles.

"Well let's get to the stories now. The hot chocolate is getting cold."

Just like Ashley to ruin a moment. I've missed her.

"Vanessa why don't you go first. We want to see what you got," I say to her.

"Me?" She points to her chest.

"I don't see any other Vanessa's around here."

Everyone laughs.

"Okay. I'll try."

Vanessa starts to tell us about a group of friends that went on a skiing trip but unfortunately their cabin was haunted. She gets so excited the more she talks. She wiggles her fingers around and drags her voice out in ghost form. We're all on the edge of our seats wanting to find out what happens next.

I look around and despite everybody being spooked out by the story Vanessa is telling I feel the happiness in the room. I feel the love. The Grants, Amber and Neil are all things of the past. I never have to feel any of the things I did when I was with them. I get to be here in my favorite place with my best friends, my aunt and uncle and my big sister.

Just as I start to feel sad about Mama and Daddy not being here I feel a light from within. I close my eyes and there is Mama. Sitting in her beautiful garden surrounded by bleeding hearts. Her hair blows in the wind. *'I knew you could do it Mo. I knew you were strong.'* I feel her arms wrap around me. Her embrace warms me from the inside out.

"I love you Mama," I whisper to her.

We hug tighter until I open my eyes and she's gone. Everyone's clapping for Vanessa's great story and she's beaming with joy. She looks at me for approval. I give her the biggest smile I have and clap for her too.

"Good job Nessa. Now it's my turn."